G-3

The Guardian of Earth Series

RIGEL CARSON

G-3

Contact information: maggietoussaint@darientel.net
Cover art by *Maggie Toussaint*

Muddle House Publishing
1146 Tolomato Drive SE
Darien, GA 31305
Visit us at www.muddlehousepublishing.com

Publishing History
First Print Edition, Muddle House Publishing, 2016
Print ISBN: 9780996770620

Published in the United States of America

Praise for The Guardian of Earth Series

This was a thoroughly engaging and fast moving novel. I read it the span of twenty-four hours, finding it hard to put down. Carson has a flair for plotting and is particularly skilled at mixing in elements of science and technology. There's a dire warning in her message, both political and environmental, and that's what makes this novel so relevant to our times. I highly recommend this book!—Joseph Souza, author, 5 stars

G-1 is a page-turning ecological thriller that could become chillingly real.—Nancy Cohen, author of Bad Hair Day Mysteries, 5 stars

I found G-1 fascinating. There are quite a few interesting characters in this book, but my favorite was Forman, the brilliant robot.—Polly Iyer, author of Indiscretion, 5 stars

One of the best near-future books period. I'm a sucker for near-future books. I've read a lot of them, but I've never read one quite like this. It grabbed me from the beginning with an intriguing mystery and it was written perfectly to keep the pages turning. I was rushing to the ending because I couldn't put the book down. —Jake Lingwall, author of Freelancer, 5 stars

Challenges facing the earth in 2065 hit home in this tense ecological thriller, with water supply the primary currency in a power game that jeopardizes an already threatened planet. Maggie Toussaint's depth of knowledge shines through in astute and compelling science. Well placed humor flares throughout the narrative. G-1 marks the start of an intriguing and relevant sci fi series.—Jennifer Skutelsky, 5 stars

This story contains a little bit of everything, even humor and light-heartedness. If you've read any of her other books, you'll find the same kind of quick wit, scientific truth along with some new inventions, and enough dialogue to keep the story moving...fast. Trust me...even if you're not a science-fiction fan, you'll still enjoy this unique story.—Rising Star Reviews, 5 stars.

Dedication

This book is dedicated to dystopian fiction fans everywhere.
You rock!

Acknowledgements

This book would not be possible without the generous help of others. My critique partner, Polly Iyer, is so helpful when things get out of whack. Gordon Aalborg did a bang-up job as my editor. Craig Toussaint did a beta read for this and my other projects, for those many kindnesses I'm thankful. Also, the gang at Booklover's Bench is always ready to lend a hand with blurbs. Thanks Terry Odell, Nancy J. Cohen, Terry Ambrose, Karla Brandenburg, Tina Whittle, and Karla Darcy for your keen eyes, wordsmithing, and marketing savvy. Thanks also to Traci Loya. She graciously allowed me to use her name as a character, a prize she won at the G-2 book launch on Facebook at Band of Dystopian Authors and Fans.

Chapter 1
Earth, December 2065

Zeke Landry scanned the constellations. Any minute now, the meteor storm would begin, and the night sky would sparkle and shimmer like Independence Day. Despite being alone with his wife on Lighthouse Beach, a sense of foreboding lingered in his gut. So much about his mission on Earth hinged on lies.

The gentle pounding of the surf drew his attention to the horizon. Starlight gleamed on the dark ocean as waves crested, advanced, and retreated from the shore. Familiar sights and sounds, all comforting and necessary to his weary soul.

"I don't see anything," Jessie said, massaging her neck and setting the binoculars aside. "If it doesn't start soon, I'm so out of here. You sure this is the right date?"

"I'm positive." Zeke's gaze darted from the sky to his wife's still-flat belly with awe. He was going to be a dad. "I've been tracking the vids from the space cams. Hang in there a few more minutes. This is a once in a lifetime event. You'll want to tell our son you saw the Great Meteor Storm, or the GMS, as the media calls it."

She pulled away from him and shot him a questioning glance. "How can you be so certain our child's a boy? What if we have a girl?"

Zeke disliked the distance she'd put between them. He closed the gap and nuzzled her blonde hair, its wildflower scent reassuring and invigorating. "Boys are the norm in my family."

Jessie poked him with her elbow. "I have a say in this, too. My mom and grandmom had sisters – no boys allowed on our family tree."

Secrets welled in Zeke's throat. Nothing about being an alien embedded in Earth's culture was easy. He didn't want to lie to Jessie, but he couldn't tell her the whole truth either. As a Taman, he'd begun fulfilling his destiny when he assumed the Guardian of Earth role from his late father a few months ago and fought off an alien invasion. Now, with Jessie's pregnancy, he'd successfully spawned the next

1

generation of Tamans.

He'd recently learned Earth was one of the last frontiers of the universe, and other civilizations were keenly interested in its fate. All that remained for him to do was to be the onsite caretaker for the planet, and to hand it off to his son in good shape. Zeke had a personal stake in Earth's future. It was his home.

Zeke grinned and touched the diamond-studded band he'd placed on her ring finger. "Believe what you like, only I hope you're not disappointed when my son arrives."

"Our child is welcome, whatever her gender," Jessie teased back.

The lighthouse loomed tall behind them, and underneath, hidden from all but Zeke, a secret chamber with a transmission chair for his routine reports to the Tamans regarding the technological achievements of Earth's citizens. Somehow the chair facilitated a clear communication channel through time and space. Learning that Tamans continued to exist after death, and that he had access to his ancestors around the universe, had been the first surprise.

His alien ancestry had been surprise number two. Not once in his childhood, teens, or even adulthood had he thought he was anything other than an island boy with some smarts. He'd been outright shocked a few months ago when he'd been thrust into global intrigue and international subterfuge. Until then, he thought he was a geeky misfit. But his off-the-chart intelligence and unique talents had proved him fit for the task of repelling invaders. With the planet's population safe from a galactic threat, he looked forward to less dangerous times, to loving his wife and raising his son.

A flicker in the sky caught Zeke's eye. He pointed up to Orion's belt. "Look."

"Gracious. That little thing is the meteor storm? From the media coverage, I thought the sky would blaze with fiery streaks."

"We'll only see the leading edge tonight. Meteors will continue to rain down on us for several days. Look. There's two more."

Jessie grunted as several streaks briefly flashed in the sky. "I feel like I should ooh and aah as if I'm watching fireworks. But they flash, streak, and disappear almost before I glimpse them, reminding me of those old-fashioned field of vision tests at the eye doctor. Why didn't scientists come up with a better name than GMS? It sounds lame. Other meteor showers have names like Leonids, Persids, and

2

Geminids."

"Unlike those relatively localized meteor showers, this event doesn't originate in one sector of the sky. Neither are they tailings of comets in our quadrant of space. These meteors hail from deep space. Our scientists can't wait to analyze them. They're watching for large meteors and tracking them, hoping they don't burn to a crisp on entry to our atmosphere. GMS is as good a name as any until we learn more about them."

"Sounds like PMS instead of GMS – too much gabbing and little to show for it. We've heard nothing but hype for weeks about this event. These puny meteors aren't much to look at if you ask me." She shot Zeke a sidelong glance filled with heat. "But it occurs to me we're alone on this beach. We could find another, more pleasurable, way to pass our time, husband."

His hand traced the swell of her feminine curves. "You don't have to ask me twice."

Jessie laughed and then her mouth gaped. Her head angled back, and her expression morphed to one of awe. "Look at that. Wow."

A large fireball blazed across the sky. Zeke followed the meteor's path to the horizon, wishing he was close enough to hear the splashdown. Science had always been his first love, but since meeting Jessie, his focus had broadened. He'd embraced the physical aspect of marriage with pleasure. At times like this, thoughts of making love to his wife clouded his intellect in the most carnal way.

She glanced over his head. "There's another one. Ooh and look over there. A really big one. What happens if they run into each other?"

A loud boom rent the sky, pulling Zeke back into the moment. "I've never heard a sonic boom from a meteor before. Too bad that big one landed in the ocean. I'd like to examine the rock. To answer your question, collisions are unlikely in ordinary meteor showers due to their single point of origin, but anything is possible with this meteor storm."

As the sky lit up with blazing cone trails, Zeke's intuitive focus expanded. The dolphins offshore were calling, he realized belatedly. He couldn't abandon Jessie to swim with the pod because this was his time with her. Married couples had date nights, according to Jessie, and he'd convinced her that stargazing on the beach constituted a date.

He'd have to return to the beach after Jessie went to sleep for the night.

Zeke inhaled the salt air, felt the sand crunch under their blanket as he shifted Jessie onto his lap. When he tipped her face up to meet his, he found moisture. Alarmed, he worried he'd missed something important. Being a husband wasn't as easy as he'd thought. "Jessie?"

She dashed at the tears. "Sorry. I just…"

"What? You can tell me. Did I do something wrong?"

"You're fine. We're fine. I'm… This is embarrassing. I spent most of my life taking care of Bea and managing the details of her singing career. My heart hurts because she's still stuck in that rehab facility. I wish she could see this sparkling sky. I wish she could live on Tama Island with us. Christmas is coming. Family should gather for the holidays."

Jessie's superstar sister had messed up her life with sex, drugs, and rock 'n roll, though the drugs had been of an alien nature. The government facility where she was being treated was both a prison and a medical facility. Thanks to Zeke's research on the chemicals Bea had absorbed, he'd saved her from madness and certain death. Others with similar exposure who had delayed treatment didn't survive.

"She's recovering," Zeke said. "That's important."

"I can't help it. I wish she were here. With us. She would love watching these meteors. She'd get the itch to write a song, and the tune would be a smash hit. I miss her."

"Would you like to visit her again? I can take some time off to accompany you."

"No. Bea freaked the last time I went there. I hated to see her so distraught and to see them pumping her with more drugs to keep her calm. Will she ever be normal again?"

Zeke tried to calculate the odds. Failed. Forman might be able to give her a statistical probability, but his robotic assistant wasn't objective when it came to Queen Bea, his former crush. Zeke had the same lack of objectivity with Jessie. He wanted Bea to be right again, but it was out of his hands.

"I don't know." His hollow reply sounded inadequate. "I wish I had a better answer for you."

She caressed his face. "I'm not a very good wife, sitting here in this romantic setting and feeling sorry for my sister. Truthfully, I'm at loose ends. The house is fixed up. You've got your work. All I've got is time on my hands."

He placed his hand protectively over her belly. "And a baby on the way."

"Yes, but the baby isn't due for seven more months. Is there something I can do in the lab to help you and Forman?"

Zeke loved his wife, but he couldn't focus as keenly on scientific matters when she was around. Having a male robotic assistant suited him perfectly. "We'll figure something out. You're a beautiful, intelligent woman. I'm lucky to have you in my life." He wiped the tears from her cheek. "Do you regret getting married without Bea there as your maid of honor?"

"A little. She's facing the consequences of her rash actions, but I'm being penalized as well. I'll call in the morning to check on her, and if she's having a good day, I'll speak to her."

Jessie shot him a tremulous smile. "Meanwhile, I have a husband to romance."

"I like the sound of that."

Chapter 2

Four hours later, with Jessie sound asleep in their bed and Zeke rested from a few hours of shut-eye, he jogged to the beach, shed his clothes, and waded into the midnight-black surf. He dove through the breakers, enjoying the cool wash of water against his heated skin. Several meteors streaked across the dark sky. He opened his mind to telepathic communication, summoning the dolphins.

A nudge to his side came almost immediately. Little Boz. And Nicola, Klickie, and Tunis. The dolphin pod dove and splashed Zeke for a moment, rejoicing in the contact, then Zeke settled into a back float, his hands on the heads of Nicola and Tunis. His thoughts linked with theirs, but instead of vectoring out to connect to the Tamans as he'd come to expect, the dolphins commandeered the link.

The water, Nicola said. *It's bad.*

Her mindlink words startled him. *Bad? How?*

She showed him a picture of sediment-filled water. The image looked like storm run-off water that was opaque.

I don't understand, he shot back.

Dirty. The water feels wrong.

Something was wrong with the water? His interest heightened, and he ventured deeper into the mindlink. *I will analyze the water. Anything else?*

The ocean feels bad, she repeated.

Does it hurt? Does your skin burn?

No burn. Hard to swim. Thicker.

The specific gravity of water didn't change. But the dolphins were reporting a problem. *I'll look into the matter.*

Boz butted into Zeke's hand. *I'm tired.*

What did dolphins do when they tired? *How can I help?* Zeke asked.

Fix the ocean, Boz said. *You are the Waterman.*

While Zeke's scientific expertise was in hydrology, he had also studied oceanography while getting his doctorate. However, Boz's new moniker pleased him. He'd never had a nickname before he became the Guardian of Earth. The Waterman. He liked it. *I'll do what I can. Do you require medicine?*

No! All the dolphins echoed in his head at once. *No medicine. No Browning Charles.*

Dr. Charles had captured Boz once before in the name of science and nearly drowned him. Zeke wouldn't hear of his dolphins being anyone's research subjects ever again. *There are other, nicer people than Browning Charles who can help dolphins.*

The water, the dolphins reiterated. *Fix the water, not the dolphins. Until then, we stay near freshwater sources where the water is better.*

Message received, Zeke said. The link quieted, so Zeke moved into the vacated space and quested out. His thoughts arrowed through the galaxy to Tween, the place where the spirits of his people resided.

His late father entered the transmission first.

Son, everything all right?

Yes. The dolphins summoned me. They're disturbed by the ocean. They say it's too thick.

Odd. Anything unusual happening?

Yesterday Baggy said he couldn't catch a bottom feeder to save his soul.

Was he serious, or just shooting the breeze?

Sure sounded serious to me. I've heard other rumblings about missing catfish and toadfish. But there have been no reported sightings of sharks or gators, which would have eaten them, and there hasn't been a deluge of recreational fishermen in the area. Perhaps it's a normal population dip.

Not like you to speculate. Have you studied the matter?

Zeke blushed. *I'm learning to be a husband.*

Aah, his dad replied. *Say no more.*

A deeper voice boomed through the link. *Is there a problem with the ocean on Earth?*

I'll look into it, Zeke promised.

Anything else to report? Deep Voice asked in a harried tone.

Zeke's kneejerk reaction to feeling like he might be wasting anyone's time was to start spewing minutia. *Let's see. Thanks to global warming, the Earth's getting hotter every year. Our economy always seems poised on the brink of collapse. International powers can't agree on how to disperse the hoarded drinking water. And our planet is receiving a once-in-a-lifetime meteor storm. Big chunks of meteorite are whistling through our skies.*

The link quieted from gentle murmurs at the other end and then without warning burst into a frenzied uproar. Zeke cringed as the shouting filled his head. In the din, he couldn't hear his dad's voice at all. He didn't know how many Tamans listened to his transmissions, but at times like this the number seemed quite large.

Deep Voice quieted the noise. *Tell us about the meteors.*

They're calling it the Great Meteor Storm. Unlike our routine meteors, this crop is from deep space. Astronomers have been aware of its approach for decades. Some of the material is entering our atmosphere now and putting on quite a flash-bang show.

These meteors – they're different?

Only in point of origin. No one seems alarmed about them. We get tens of thousands of meteor strikes each year.

The noise on the link increased again.

What? Zeke asked, impatient to learn what they knew. *What do you suspect? Are we in danger?*

His dad spoke above the roar. *Easy, Son. As you say, space is full of debris. You plan to check the water and the fish?*

Yes.

Use stainless steel sampling containers. No glass. And weigh your containers before and after sampling. Check for rare trace minerals, along with your standard tests.

What aren't you telling me?

No need to get alarmed. Meteors are commonplace. But worlds between the Taman home world and Earth experience unusual distress following a certain type of meteor.

Zeke felt the chill and the seriousness of the matter invade his thoughts. *We just repelled an alien invasion not long ago. Can't we catch a break?*

Being Earth's Guardian requires vigilance. Your job doesn't have regular hours. You must be prepared to respond when threats arise.

Is this what it was like for you, Dad? Were you constantly being pulled into intergalactic skirmishes?

8

I had periods of busyness. Sometimes it seemed we careened from one disaster right into the next. Other times, I did a lot of fishing.

I had no idea.

I didn't do it alone, Son. Remember that. Use your support system and the dolphins. We're here, and you have a network of helpers through the Institute. And your mate will ease the way for you.

His mate... His wife. *Something I should mention. Jessie's pregnant with our son.*

The link burst into cheers, claps, and whistles.

Good job. Keep a close eye on her. Some Earth women have a difficult time in the first trimester with our progeny. Make sure she gets plenty of rest.

Why? In Zeke's crash course on his alien heritage, he'd learned one of the benefits of being a Taman was having the unusual ability to impregnate a human. The two species were similar biologically, to a point. In a previous conversation, his late father had explained the sameness as related to the "Great Dispersion," in which a master race seeded the universe.

Gestational differences. Jessie and the baby must be protected at all costs during this vulnerable period. What about your cousin?

Angie? She's off doing something for Uncle John. I haven't seen much of her lately.

Don't worry. That will change soon.

The link faded. As usual, Zeke resisted letting go until the last possible second. Questions pulsed through his mind about the unusual water sampling stipulations, about extra safety measures for his family, and about his cousin. One thing he knew about his ancestors. They would be great at writing books. They parsed out barely enough information to keep him coming back for more.

Chapter 3

Jessie opened the medicine cabinet for the third time, looked at the bottle of pain relievers, and changed her mind. Taking any medication in the first trimester of pregnancy was asking for a birth defect. She wouldn't do that to her child.

She fingered the glittering platinum band on her finger. Her wedding ring. With her and Zeke both being orphans, and with her only sister pumped to the gills with alien drugs, their quickie wedding and honeymoon at Zeke's house on the island had been a thrill ride of togetherness.

She'd been so wrapped up in getting settled she hadn't realized how isolated she was on Tama Island. Times like this, she'd give anything for a woman friend. But at least her problems were of her own making.

This was her house and her husband and her baby. Not Bea's. She finally had a life. Not just any life, but the life she'd dreamed of forever. Except she'd hoped to share this slice of heaven with her sister. The pounding in her temples intensified.

Turning from the sink, she held the ice pack to her head again and wobbled off to the shuttered bedroom. She hadn't mentioned the headaches to Zeke. She didn't want to spook him with medical issues or make him think she was a complainer. The poor man was so fixated on having a son, she wouldn't do anything to jeopardize their precious baby.

If a thundering headache for a few days was the price of the baby's wellbeing, she'd bear that pain easily. She'd subsumed her needs for years to keep Bea's career afloat. Doing it for the baby would be minor in the face of her previous sacrifices. Her middle name should've been Take-one-for-the-team.

Her stomach rumbled and clenched again. Jessie flashed hot and cold, the room spun. Crap. Morning sickness stunk. She stumbled to the bathroom, dry heaved, crawled back to bed, pulled the covers tight around her, and closed her eyes.

Christmas would be here in a few weeks and at this rate she wouldn't be ready. They had no tree, no decorations, no gifts purchased or made. She'd downloaded tons of her favorite holiday music to Zeke's house system, but right now she couldn't tolerate flashing tree lights or syrupy music. Peace and quiet—that's what she needed.

Her thoughts drifted as she sought a mental hiding place where she felt no pain. Names. They hadn't talked about names. Should she get one of those expensive tests to check the baby's genetics for disease? Would she abort a malformed child?

No. No testing. No abortions. She loved this child already. Maybe a gender-neutral name like Chris or Lou would work. Except those didn't seem special enough. There would be nothing ordinary about Zeke's child. The man was friggin' brilliant, and she was no dummy.

She shifted on the bed, nestling deeper in the soft pillow using deep yogic breathing to calm her mind. Their child would grow up here on this remote island, safe from the pressures of the world, isolated from violence, drugs, and deceit. And she would have a dog. No, two dogs.

The thought made her smile. Jessie'd always wanted a dog or a cat, but that had been impossible in foster care. Later, while working as her sister's manager, she traveled all the time, and it wouldn't have been fair to keep a pet boarded so long.

A pet. No reason she couldn't get a pet now. She'd talk to Zeke about it.

Her thoughts drifted to her handsome husband. He'd turned down several speaking engagements since they married a month ago. She understood his reticence and his desire to spend the majority of his workday in the lab. However, to advance professionally he had to network and make public appearances. One thing she knew cold was how to manage a career.

She smiled to herself. She'd pull her weight in this marriage, no two ways about that.

*****

"Jessie?"

Zeke's voice drew her out of a dream. She blinked herself awake, his concerned face filling her gaze. "Hey." She studied his narrowing eyes, noticing his subtle air of discontent. Things must've gone wrong in his lab today. She struggled to sit up in bed. "What time is it?"

"Nearly seven."

"Oh." The flaccid ice pack slid to her lap, and her cheeks flamed. "Oh, dear. I forgot dinner."

"That's okay. What's wrong? Are you sick?"

"Not sick. Definitely not sick. Feeling a little pregnant is all." Aware her breath didn't smell the freshest, she tried to escape to the bathroom to freshen up. "I need to use the bathroom."

He made no move out of the way. "Shall I start dinner?" he asked.

"That would be great. I'll join you in a minute."

Jessie eased off the bed and took careful steps. Fortunately, her stomach had settled after the nap, and her headache had subsided to a mild roar. She could smile and charm her husband. That's what wives did, right?

After showering, brushing her teeth, and donning fresh clothes, she joined Zeke in the kitchen. A feast of dishes lined the counter. "I wasn't sure what you wanted, so I made everything."

He'd prepared enough food to feed twenty people. She smiled. "How thoughtful. Everything looks delicious." She helped her plate and followed him to the table. "I was thinking it would be nice if our child had a pet. A dog, for instance, would come in handy for eating leftovers."

He carried two glasses of water to the table and then grabbed a second platter of food for himself. "We don't have dogs on the island."

"Why is that?"

"I don't know. Barking possibly. People come and go at odd hours. I'd hate to wake the neighbors on one of my middle of the night rambles."

Zeke only slept three hours a night, a fact that had taken some getting used to. Some nights she reached for him and found a cold pillow. Oftentimes, he wasn't even in the house. He could be at the lab or the beach or anywhere in between, but he always came home to her.

Jessie realized the idea of a dog was a no-go. She switched gears. "What about a cat? Could we get the kid a cat?"

He didn't say anything. He might have actually shuddered. Her gaze sharpened. "What's wrong with a cat?" Jessie asked.

"Cats don't like me," Zeke said, passing her a platter full of food.

Jessie tried not to inhale any of the pungent aromas. She set her fork down on her still-full plate. "Nonsense. It's a matter of imprinting and routine. I could work on the training while I'm waiting for the baby to be born."

"Isn't there something about pregnant women avoiding cats?"

Her head started pounding again. "That has to do with cleaning the litter boxes. With all the sand here on the island, a cat wouldn't need a litter box. Owning a pet would give me something to do."

"A cat," he repeated neutrally.

Why was he so resistant to a cuddly pet? "Cats aren't alien invaders. They're domesticated, and they like living with people. We could get a cat on a trial basis."

"I'll think about it."

His curt dismissal stung. Her patience frayed, and a wellspring of emotion flooded her system. She lashed out at him with words. "While you're thinking, chew on this. Your uncle called here again about that unexpected vacancy for a Keynote Speaker at the International Water Symposium in Rio. I accepted for you."

His fork clattered on the plate. "You shouldn't have done that without consulting me. Cancel it. I'm not going to Rio."

"Why?" She shot back. "This opportunity will be good for you professionally."

"I'm not looking for career advancement. I prefer to stay here, on the island."

"You haven't gone to the mainland once in an entire month. You'll turn into a hermit at this rate."

"Fine with me. I don't need to travel. I'm a homebody."

"I thought I was a homebody, but I miss traveling. Rio is fun. I've visited there three times with Bea. I could show you around town, take you to the best places to eat. Rio could be the honeymoon we didn't take, and the Institute would pay half of our tab."

He downed more food. "Not going."

"If you won't do it for me, do it for your uncle. He says it's important."

"Uncle John always wants something. Are you taking his side?"

"I'm taking your side. I have a stake in your career now. You have a wife and soon will have a child to support."

"Why go to Rio when I have everything I need right here? Besides, those conferences are all alike. The paid speakers are flattered to the point of ridiculousness by the sponsors, and it's much ado about absolutely nothing. Issues aren't resolved at conferences. Scientists have no enforcement authority, so what's the point? Talking to the walls here would have the same net effect."

He was acting like Bea. A familiar frustration welled. This was their first fight. She had to stand up for what was best for their family. Jessie dug deep, ignoring the louder pounding in her head. "Be reasonable. No one exists in a vacuum. Your uncle knows you prefer to stay at home. He wouldn't push if it wasn't important. If you don't fulfill this obligation, your absence will reflect poorly on you, on me, on your uncle, and on your employer."

"A guilt trip? That's your strategy to convince me?"

The cloying aroma of beef made the room start to spin. Fighting nausea, she pushed back from the table. "Do whatever you like. But I'll tell you this. I won't cancel for you. The information's on the counter."

He rose, his brow furrowed. "I'm sorry. I'll take care of it. Please stay."

She shook her head. "I can't. The food. The odor. My stomach." Her tummy lurched, and she ran for the bathroom.

Afterward, when she came to bed, a fresh glass of ginger ale sat on the nightstand, a new ice pack rested by her pillow, and the covers were neatly turned down. Zeke stood to the side, wringing his hands. "You should have said you weren't feeling well," he said.

She climbed in, let him tuck her in. "It's nothing. Pregnancy stuff."

"It's everything. You're everything." Zeke spooned in behind her caressing her head and rubbing her knotted shoulders.

Jessie sighed with contentment. If she'd have known a back rub was in the offing, she'd have picked a fight weeks ago. Her headache eased, and she drifted into sleep, Zeke's palm splayed over her tummy.

I'm not alone.

I have Zeke.

Chapter 4

"Got 'em. Done and done," Forman crowed, his neural processors humming with satisfaction. He pumped his million dollar arms in a victory salute, the toucans on his lime green aloha shirt doing a jig. "Eat my dirt, NASA."

"The space cams, the sat cams, and the drone cams?" Zeke looked up from his work station. "How'd you get past the data blockers so quickly?"

"Simply the best, that's me." Seeing Dr. Z's puzzled expression, Forman added, "I, uh, anticipated your request for meteor tracking. Started decrypting and hacking weeks ago so they wouldn't notice a little extra draw this morning. To the casual eye, our feed is another encrypted backup routine."

"How far out in space did you go?"

"As far as the cameras, telescopes, and satellites would let me. However, the early footage is extensive and teeth-gnashingly tedious to view. I'll partition the footage of rocks floating in space into a separate file and create an accelerated time-lapsed view."

"Good idea. But that's low priority. I'm most interested today in the extra-planetary strikes from space. Focus on the impact zones planet-wide, gradually narrowing the focus to our area. I want to locate a meteor, for research purposes, of course."

Forman noted the flushed face of his boss indicating embarrassment. His boss also had dark circles under his eyes and a day's growth of beard stubble. Was his distress caused by the ongoing international drinking water dispute, meteors, marriage, or his wife's pregnancy? Whatever the cause, Forman would fix it so his boss could focus on his work.

Smoothing out issues for Dr. Zechariah Landry was his job, after all. In the short course of their association, Forman had used every one of his four programmed identities, and he loved the flexibility of being Zeke's assistant. He was the luckiest android in the world.

"What timeline?" Forman asked, creating an air bridge for virtual streaming between his processors and the lab's computer enclave. In a millisecond, data flowed from the com's hub into his system. "The storm visually began last night but microscopic dust from this meteor cloud has been falling for seventeen days."

Zeke looked up from his screen again. "You're right. I've been distracted these last few weeks. Good thing I have the only four-in-one robotic assistant on the planet. My brain's turned to mush since I got married."

Ah, exactly the topic Forman wanted to pursue. He dipped into the wellspring of his entertainment module for data. "Are you employing the techniques I suggested in your lovemaking? If those are stale by now, I have hundreds more, all designed to bring a woman to the brink of pleasure—"

"Stop," Zeke interrupted, rising to pace the room. "My love life is not open for discussion. We're discussing meteor showers."

"At least you have a love life," Forman grumped, less than thrilled with his romantic status. "Not all of us are so lucky."

"Please. Focus on the meteor issue. Uncle John will be calling shortly on the other matter, and I need to know we're making headway on this off-the-books snooping."

Spoilsport. Forman refrained from vocalizing his lament. His boss had more privacy points than most humans, but his intellect and talents more than made up for his secretive nature. Working for Dr. Zeke at the Institute was the best job ever, not that Forman's programming went back to previous clients. His personal memories had been erased the day he'd left Supply Central for his gig on Tama Island.

Glimmers of something occasionally surfaced. Flashing lights. Screams. Forman had stopped trying to remember. He truly didn't want to know about his past. He'd thought about having his love for Bea Stemford erased. The hole in his virtual heart wouldn't go away on its own, but he couldn't bring himself to blot out the love of his life. What if she was his only shot at feeling human emotions? He couldn't part with a single memory of Queen Bea.

Data hummed, sorted, and aligned. He tapped a few keys and shunted the virtual map to the large screen. "Here you go. Twelve hours of meteoric bliss condensed into three minutes. Hmm. Look at that."

"What?"

"Few strikes on the other side of the world. The vast majority came down over here."

"Play the entire sequence."

Forman replayed the loop, twice.

The view changed from rubble in space to flaming vectors shooting across the sky. There was no sound, but Forman remembered the sizzle and hiss from the night sky all too well. At the beach last night, he'd checked on his boss, discreetly, and nearly interrupted a private moment.

"A bit unusual," Zeke said. "How can there be such specificity in a meteor shower? That defies random distribution. What's more, I see a pattern. "Run that again," Zeke said, stepping closer to the screen, "but zoom in on the Atlantic basin this time."

"You see something?" Forman started the patched feed again, wishing he could sharpen the residual graininess from the images.

"Calculate land strikes vs. sea strikes for the planet."

Forman did the computations. "Sea strikes win by an amazing 78.3896 percent."

"Earth has more ocean than land so that makes sense."

"Show me the sequence for the South Atlantic basin on screen and then the North Atlantic. Make it easier to see."

Numbers and data streamed through Forman at a blinding rate. He converted the data to show impact positions rather than the actual images. "Ready, Freddy." The map resolved, then dots began filling in. Clusters of data appeared.

"Amazing. Most of the strikes were in the Atlantic Ocean. How is that possible? Such specificity doesn't follow known distribution patterns. Add the graphic for the Mid-Atlantic Ridge."

Forman added the reference point. Impact sites lined up along the ridge. His guy was smart. He added in the tectonic plate boundaries in the other oceans, showed those graphics. More impacts at plate margins.

"Hmm," Zeke said. "The meteors showed a marked preference for those zones. What about size? Did the meteors follow the same dispersion pattern when compared by size?"

Forman manipulated the data, color coding by size. A new pattern arose. Larger strikes were nearer shore. Few large strikes were on land.

"I need one of those meteors to study. Show me a 100-mile radius around Tama Island, land and sea, with the island in the center."

"None on land, but there were ten strikes directly east of us." Forman showed the splash pattern on the screen. "However, a large meteor hit dirt not too far from Rio."

"Rio? Another coincidence. I don't trust coincidences."

"Are we talking alien invasions again, boss? Should we be worried?"

"Nothing we know of could survive that sort of entry into our atmosphere. What we don't know concerns me."

"We could go to Rio and network with the other scientists."

Zeke swore as the com beeped. "My uncle. Check the output from the water analysis I ran while I handle this."

Forman stepped out as asked. He didn't know what his boss was up to, but whatever the project, he hoped a trip to Rio was involved.

Chapter 5

"Uncle John. Good morning," Zeke said, clearing the vid screens behind his cam link. John Demery was his mother's brother and his Cousin Angie's stepfather. More importantly, he was also Zeke's boss at the Institute.

His uncle's weathered face filled the screen. "Morning to you. Well? Jessie said you'd go to Rio. Does that mean you've come to your senses?"

"Jessie didn't consult me. I'm not interested. I could video-conference in, if you like."

"I need you at the conference. I thought your travel disorientation was better, and you have Forman to lighten your workload at the lab. What's the problem?"

Thanks to his father's keystone necklace which Zeke always wore, he could now travel off-island without the severe disorientation that had plagued him in the past. But he hated traveling. He preferred to stay home and work. The island, it centered him.

"My spatial disorientation is improved, but I'm busy. And married. I want Jessie's first trimester to be stress-free."

"I'm delighted about the baby, but you can't put your scientific career on hold. Couples have been reproducing for thousands of years. Heck, Jessie can stay home if you're worried about her traveling."

"She wants to go to Rio. Getting her to agree to that stipulation would be impossible if I were going, and I'm not. I have more important things to focus on. Can't the Institute send another scientist?"

His uncle's bushy eyebrows met over his nose. "You're the man for this job."

Zeke snorted. Not likely. Was something else afoot? "I don't understand."

"Finally. You may be a brain, but brains need money to effect change or the gig is up. This invitation couldn't have come at a better time for the Institute. We need the good PR. In addition, you'll cement your credibility as the world's premier water expert, which will come in handy during the upcoming drinking water negotiations."

His head kicked back with surprise. Quickly, he tried to connect the financial dots. "Is the Institute in financial trouble?"

Uncle John nodded. "I've heard rumblings. Several backers are making noise about pulling out. They don't see us as exerting the right amount of global influence. One of those wafflers is sponsoring the conference in Rio. He specifically asked for you to keynote after Sanchez's cancer treatment landed him in the hospital again."

"If the Institute has to put on a dog or pony show, send someone who wants to go. I can provide the slides and the lecture notes. I don't want to be in the limelight. Send Angie. Or Forman. Or even Browning Charles."

"Nope. Angie lacks the credentials. Charles is a loose cannon. And Forman doesn't pass the human test. You're it."

Zeke swore. He didn't want to be it. "Technically, I'm still on my honeymoon."

"Good try, but no."

"What's in it for me?"

"How'd you like a chunk of meteor to study?"

Heat crept to Zeke's face. "You know of my interest?"

"Not much I don't know about you, boyo. Besides, a scientific anomaly like the meteor storm was bound to attract your attention. Dr. Sidra McIntyre is already down there, and she's negotiating for a piece of the rock for the Institute. If you speak at the symposium, I'll arrange for some of her sample to come your way. The Institute doesn't mind if you indulge your curiosity about meteors, as long as you speak at the water symposium."

It was natural for an astrophysicist like Sidra to be involved in studying meteors. No one expected a hydrologist like Zeke to have more than an intellectual curiosity about meteors. Not that anyone knew he was an alien or had a keen interest in potential threats from outer space.

His competitive nature warred with his need to shun publicity. "Nothing's changed in the global water picture since I gave my last water talk."

"Even better. Your presentation is already written. Say yes to Rio.

If that isn't enticement enough, an admiral requested a private meeting with you in Rio. Something about intermittent deep sea anomalies picked up by Navy subs."

Zeke's interest flared. The talk with the Navy guy might shed some light on the peculiar groupings of meteor strikes. And maybe he could talk Sidra into coming back here and helping him decipher the meteor puzzle.

All told, the Rio trip would take four days out of his life. Less, if he didn't have to use public transportation. "Would I get the company jet?"

"If that's what it takes, you'll have it."

"Done. I'll go to Rio."

Chapter 6

Water.

At last.

Xstle imbibed the solution. The sleep had been long. So long he was exhausted from the sheer effort of awakening. Needed water. Food. Companionship.

Companions.

Many began this journey from Yar.

In this weakened form, Xstle knew not of the others' fate. His pod vectored toward the planet with water as it was supposed to or he wouldn't be conscious now. His kind flourished in water, but he needed helpmates to join him in order to survive.

He activated the summoning call.

That effort exhausted him. He floated under the surface of the water, away from the strong light, but suspended in the narrow band of microscopic food, hungrily engulfing all food sources he encountered.

Needed more water.

Fluid seeped in the narrow apertures, and he sipped deeply, reviving the long dormant matrix. Nutrition entered with the water, doubling, then tripling his revival rate.

He mimicked the shape of the food, extending fragile flagella first, then trying the whirring circle shapes. That worked better. As he imbibed more nectar of life, the increased motility helped him encounter more food.

Another of his kind found him, glomming onto Xstle's exterior. He repositioned the first unit away from the feeding portal with a flinch. It settled into place, absorbing into his exoskeleton, and began to sing the joining song. Another joined Xstle, and another.

The feeding portal widened to input more life-giving liquid, shunting more of the micro-sized life forms into his hungry gut. Larger shapes appeared in the water. Sleek, elongated shapes. Xstle hitched a ride on one, absorbing a fragment of genetic code before dislodging.

Soon, his shape flattened to resemble the streamlined creature, moving through the water more swiftly. His maw increased proportionately, and larger creatures became his prey.

Better.

A giant creature swam by, paying him no mind. Must not have the shape correct if I'm unrecognizable as prey, Xstle thought. I need more of my helpers to grow as big as the life forms here.

He vibrated the Yar song of life, summoning more of his countrymen, the specks. More found him, and the increased body mass caused Xstle to sink lower in the depths. With each addition, his mass increased and he required more sustenance. His locomotion ability improved with each successive size change.

More systems activated as he approached growth milestones. He began producing *auku*, terraforming the waters to best suit the larval form of his species. The sea rocked and nurtured him, an infant in its salty womb. Soon, the mighty Yar would be a force to reckon with on this planet.

He crossed the signal of a Drch and recoiled. The raucous dissonance cancelled Xstle's calling song. He barely swam out of range in time to avoid being drawn into the Drch's lethal snare.

A Drch.

His people's mortal enemy.

A Drch should not be here.

Impossible that a lying, cheating Drch convinced the elders to let it join the expedition. Something was very wrong with the colonization plan if a Drch was on this frontier planet, growing unchecked. No telling what size the Drch was now. With Drch's faster growth rate and more charismatic call, Yars were at a reproductive disadvantage.

Xstle couldn't battle a Drch until he was fully matured. No Yar could.

The only way to survive was to stay out of the Drch's path by hiding in the depths. He would return to fight this war another day.

Would that be soon enough?

Chapter 7

Sunny Acres put Jessie's call about her sister's welfare on hold. Seemed to be the way things were going in her life these days. Step to the side, Jessie, life is passing by and you're not in it.

She loved being married and Zeke was great, but in the process of becoming Mrs. Zeke Landry, she'd lost a job she enjoyed. Organizing Bea's performance schedule and making it happen had brought her satisfaction, though other aspects of that job had been downright awful.

Between Zeke, his uncle, the islanders, and the robots, she had little to do, and she needed a project to keep her hands and mind busy. She'd had an offer from a fan-zine to write Bea's life story, not that she would air her family's dirty linen. She could use her knowledge of the music industry to book tours for other performers, but she didn't want that level of aggravation again.

What did she want?

People who needed her. A project that made her feel useful. What would it be? Would she return to college for her PhD so she'd be on a par academically with her husband?

Nope. She had no desire to start graduate school when she couldn't finish before the baby arrived. Besides, even with a PhD, she wouldn't be on a par with Zeke. The man could think circles around a room full of brilliant scholars.

She didn't want to compete with him. She needed to find her own thing. Teaching? Social work? Why did the islanders wear orange tunics most of the time? Was there a clothes shortage? She liked sewing. Maybe she could supplement their wardrobe choices.

"Mrs. Landry?"

Jessie startled out of her reverie and stared at the vid screen nurse. "Dr. Loomis is available now," the nurse said.

A wiry man with thin hair and a white lab coat came onscreen. "Mrs. Landry. Good to see you again."

"Nice to see you, doctor. How's Bea? May I speak with her?"

"I'd prefer to show you a montage of video clips of her activities over the last few days. She's showing improvement on this last medicine."

Jessie's hopes flared. "Can she come home for Christmas?"

"Not this year. Bea would be a danger to herself and others. But if things keep trending this way, I don't see why you couldn't visit her in a few weeks."

She wasn't going anywhere until she got past the morning sickness part of her pregnancy. There was much to be said for the comforts of home.

"All right," Jessie said. "How soon will you know? I should probably make travel plans in advance. The tubes will be jammed with the holidays upon us."

"Hold off until next week. I'll feel more confident with the dosage and her reaction with a little more time under our belt."

Twice before, Bea seemed nearly back to her old self, but the slightest disturbance reactivated that alien chemical cocktail in her bloodstream. Jessie silently cursed the rocker who'd caused her sister's descent into hell. Now Bea lived in a padded room in a locked facility, and the rocker was dead.

"Sure. May I see the video footage now?"

"Yes, and I've made a note to call you next week."

"Thank you."

Images of her sister flickered on Jessie's screen. Her sister read quietly in the shade of an oak. Her sister strolled down a landscaped sidewalk. Her sister fed herself a bowl of oatmeal.

Jessie watched the slide show three times. At first it was good to see Bea doing normal things. But Bea didn't like to read books. She didn't amble aimlessly around. Not one image showed her sister's eyes, but Jessie knew they'd look zoned out still. The doctors didn't know Bea like she did. If this was *normal*, Jessie wouldn't get her sister back.

But Stemford girls were tough. Sooner or later, the alien chemical would purge from Bea's body, and she'd have a shot at living again. Bea was in there somewhere. Jessie wouldn't abandon her.

She rose from the vid screen and padded over to the fridge for the marinated chicken and veggies she planned to grill for dinner. She'd wrapped dinner tight with foil when she assembled the packets at lunch time.

This time of year the sun set early, and she needed to cook now while she still had natural light. Artificial lighting, even in the very mild coastal Georgia winters, drew a smorgasbord of bloodsucking insects. She could grill the food now and keep it warm in the oven for Zeke.

A movement in the backyard caught her eye. A visitor. How lovely. She opened the door.

Baggy waved hello. After exchanging pleasantries with the friendly islander and getting him a glass of iced tea, Jessie sat with him on the porch and asked about the traditional robes worn by the islanders.

"The ladies wear the robes, though some off-island men started wearing them around here for a while," he said. "Throughout the world, our robes are known as island orange."

"Yes, but what does it mean? Why orange robes? Why not another color?"

He shrugged. "Tradition."

"How long have islanders been following this tradition?"

"My mama and grandmamma, and theirs before them."

"A couple of generations?"

"More than that. Back further than I can remember."

"Interesting. Is there a book about the island's history where I can learn more about the robes?"

"Lotsa books about the coast, but the robes aren't mentioned."

Curiouser and curiouser. "Why?"

"Dunno."

"Hmm." Sensing the conversation had stalled, Jessie shifted to a new topic. "Sure is quiet on the island."

"More quiet than usual."

Trying to talk with this man was like pulling teeth. "And?"

"And I was coming around to talk to Zeke about it. He here?"

She shook her head. "Still at the lab. I can call him if you like."

"No need to bother him at work. But change is on the wind. And it isn't good."

Jessie rocked a bit, enjoying the company. "Can you elaborate?"

"Can't find any squirrels. Can't find any 'possums. No raccoons either. They should be here. They were here a few weeks ago."

She glanced at the empty blue sky. Many of the trees on the island had burned in a fire a few months back, so the tree line was sparse. There'd been a limping raccoon begging for scraps at her door ever since she returned to the island. She was surprised to note she hadn't seen Bandit in days. "You're right."

"Zeke needs to look into what's happening. Our critters shouldn't be missing."

"Maybe aliens took them."

Baggy's Adam's apple jumped. "You think?"

Jessie felt a wave of remorse for her flippant remark. Despite his simple-mindedness, Baggy and other islanders had helped Zeke quash the Maleem invasion. She shouldn't tease him about aliens when she didn't know what was going on. "Kidding. I'm sure Zeke has a perfectly good explanation for everything. You're welcome to stay and eat dinner with us."

"No thanks, I need to continue my rounds."

Baggy was the island's unofficial caretaker. He walked from one end of the seven-mile-long island to the other each day. Thunderstorms were the only thing to keep him from his self-appointed rounds. The man hated thunder.

"What if I got a cat?" Jessie asked as he rose.

He appeared to study the matter. "Should be all right. But not now, when small animals are disappearing. Get yourself a kitty in a few months."

"Is there a reason no dogs or cats live on the island?"

The islander shrugged. "Nobody wanted one?"

"Well, I do. Want one."

"How's the bambino?"

How Baggy knew about the baby was a mystery to her. Her pregnancy wasn't a secret, but they hadn't announced the news either. She wanted to make sure she got through the first three months before she told people outside the family.

"She's fine," Jessie said, with a smile.

Baggy's brown eyes twinkled. "*She* better have a boy's name. Only boys in Zeke's line."

"Ha! Only girls in mine. We'll see who's right in seven months."

Chapter 8

"Babies should breastfeed for the first six months," Forman said when their hover boat slowed.

Zeke groaned. For days now, Forman had been spouting off baby lore, driving him crazy with parenting tips. "Seeing as how I don't have the equipment for breastfeeding, Jessie will decide if and how long she wants to breastfeed my son."

"Nine out of ten pediatricians advocate breastfeeding over other choices. Natural is better."

Zeke grunted in answer. A pointed glare at Forman yielded no response. Lately, Forman's uncharacteristic behaviors had concerned Zeke, but he was reluctant to mention the oddities to Uncle John or Angie. They'd shut Forman down and muck with his neural net. Zeke would hate anyone doing that to him, and so would Forman.

His robot was nearly as smart as he was. He'd work out the glitch, eventually.

Since his assistant wasn't moving to collect the water samples, Zeke hopped up from the captain's chair and grabbed this batch of water samples. This was their fourth stop offshore. The boat bounced in the four-foot swell as Zeke sent the automated sampler down twenty feet, sampling sea water every foot. In the scheme of ocean depth, twenty feet wasn't much, but to sample deeper would require specialized equipment Zeke didn't have. Yet.

"This is futile," Forman announced from his chair. "Given the Gulf Stream current and the wind, the likelihood of anything from a meteor remaining in suspension in the water column at the splashdown site approaches zero. We'd be better served to hop a Navy sub and cruise down to the Marianna Trench where the majority of the strikes landed in this ocean."

"I'm sure the Navy or an intelligence agency is searching those deep sea sites. This is my backyard so to speak. I need to make sure I don't miss an opportunity for research."

Zeke hauled the sampler aboard, stashed the stainless steel vials in a cooler, and loaded the next set of vials. "Besides, our investigation of the meteor storm isn't public knowledge. As far as anyone knows, we're out here sport fishing."

"Your uncle knows of your interest, so he must be okay with it. Say, does it strike you as odd that we haven't seen the first sign of life? No sharks, no dolphins, no pelicans, no jumping fish. We're alone in a desert of water."

Zeke hoped his dolphins were faring okay. "You should've been a poet."

"Would you like to hear poetry? I can recite entire volumes of poetry for you to charm your lovely wife. What style would you like? Sonnets? Haikus? Limericks?"

"No poetry." Zeke plopped into the captain's chair and rubbed his eyes. The depth finder darkened momentarily. "Did you see that?"

Forman removed his sunglasses and studied the screen. "Is the instrument malfunctioning?"

"You tell me. Look. It's happening again."

"Unusual. The depth indicator zeroed out." Forman detached the instrument from the panel and fiddled with it.

"Can you do an air bridge diagnostic?"

Forman shook his head. "Too risky in an uncontrolled environment like this. I must insist we return to the island until we know if this is a malfunction or if something so large it disrupted this circuitry is down there." He tapped the housing against the side of the boat. "There. It appears to be working now."

Zeke snorted a bark of laughter. "I could've done that."

Forman placed his hand on the throttle. "We must return to the island."

"We've got six more stations to monitor."

"Another day, another fishing expedition. Until we know what's going on with the instrumentation, we're not staying out here alone. It's too dangerous."

"Weak, besides, I have more to do out here."

"The entire island believes your parents drowned at sea, not far from this location. You have responsibilities to Jessie, your child, and the entire island."

Responsibilities. Zeke swore under his breath. Life was simpler before he became the Guardian of Earth, before he became a married man. But the advantages to having a wife had so far exceeded the risk of his secret getting out. No one on the planet, not even Forman or Jessie, knew he was an alien, and he planned to keep it that way. Jessie respected his need for privacy, and she was a darn good cook, too.

Love had upended his logical existence, but now he couldn't imagine his life without Jessie. Zeke bobbed his head. "I'll concede, but if anything unusual is in the samples we've collected, I will definitely be back out here tomorrow."

Forman cocked his head. "You're thinking about her. Your voice turned dreamy."

Zeke grinned at the word dreamy. No one had ever used that term to describe him. "Hard not to. Jessie's a big part of my life."

"More important than science?"

The fate of his family line rested in Jessie's womb. "Definitely. She's the most important person on the planet. I'd do anything for her."

"As it should be. I worried you might screw this up, but you and Jessie appear to be getting along fine."

"For the most part." Zeke stopped, feeling it was unwise to talk about Jessie with Forman. He wasn't a gossip.

"But?"

"She's restless now that she has the house decorated like she wants it. What if I'm not enough for her?"

"She's a caretaker personality. Find her someone to take care of."

"Like a husband and a child?"

"Like a person in need, right here, right now. Or a cat. Didn't you mention earlier she wants a cat?" Zeke grunted, and Forman took that as assent. "If you gave her the cat, she'd have something to fuss over while we're in Rio."

Zeke's shoulders sagged. "She thinks she's going with us."

"You haven't told her she's grounded?"

"I meant to, but Rio's all she talks about. What we'll do. What we'll see."

"Dude. You have to tell her. Or she has to come with us. You can't have it both ways."

The boat lurched as a swell hit them on the side. Zeke busied himself with repositioning the bow to nose into the waves. "Jessie's happiness is important, but my gut tells me she should stay here. She'll be safe on the island. I asked Angie to help her with Christmas decorations today."

"Angie's back?"

"A few days ago. Why?"

"I have a love/hate relationship with your cousin. She treats me with the respect due a sentient being, then she changes my programming."

"At least she won't break your heart."

Forman thrust his sunglasses on his nose and stared at the horizon. "Give her time."

Chapter 9

"Company," Forman said the next day.

"Get rid of them." Zeke studied the data feed from his sample analyses. Nothing unusual in the profile. He'd been so sure he'd find something. So sure the water held clues everyone else had missed.

Wait. Something about the trace element panel didn't look quite right. He reset the gain and ran the samples again. He punched up the beachhead samples he'd taken yesterday and compared them to the offshore samples.

Salinity decreased closer to the mainland, but that was to be expected given the freshwater input from the Altamaha River. Trace elements were slightly different between locations, but all were within acceptable ranges.

Determined to leave no avenue unexplored, he set the computer to make pairwise comparisons of all elements among the median results for each site.

"Company," Forman reiterated, making a throat clearing sound.

Zeke pushed away from the vid console, a grumble lodged in his throat. He hated interruptions, and Forman generally respected his need for privacy while he was working. *Must be important*, he thought. Probably Uncle John or someone from the Institute.

"Baggy." Zeke shot Forman a dark look before turning to the man. Why didn't his assistant screen out the island's watchman? "What can I do for you?"

The man nodded in greeting, energy radiating from him in palpable waves. "My gator's missing."

The thin islander in ill-fitting pants didn't own a gator, but Baggy called the one who'd staked out a mud bank near his place "his."

"Maybe he's gone for a swim?" Zeke suggested.

"Gone for three days now. Very odd, since he's never disappeared before. Then I visited the other gator wallows. Couldn't find a single gator today."

Alligators were apex predators. They ate anything they could fit in their mouths, edible or not. For the island's population of nearly a dozen gators to go missing at the same time was unlikely.

"What's going on?" Zeke asked. "Are we talking poachers?"

Gators were federally protected species. Unless gators were in season, none could be killed, and even during the season, only a limited number of hunting licenses were issued. Gator season had already passed.

"Haven't seen any poachers on my rounds. All of our people are accounted for, and we've got no strangers on the island. That's why I came to you, Mr. Guardian. You need to look into this."

Islanders knew of Zeke's title, but as far as Zeke knew, no one on Earth besides himself knew what being the Guardian of Earth entailed. "Forman? You have any theories?"

"Gators need to eat. Would they have relocated?"

Zeke thought for a moment. Gators didn't need to eat every day. Based on the random incidence of their last individual feedings, the likelihood of a unison feeding event was nil. "Tags." He turned to the computer and accessed the tracking system for local wildlife. Pulled up the gator channel. Nothing. "Odd. No signals."

"Other critters are gone, too," Baggy added. "Squirrels, 'possums, raccoons. I told Ms. Jessie about them the other day."

Zeke's back teeth ground together. Something was happening on the island, and Jessie'd kept it from him? Then, just as quickly, he remembered her morning sickness and realized she'd most likely forgotten to mention it. "First I've heard of it. Sorry, I didn't know of your concern." Nothing to be gained from sitting in the lab when the problem was outdoors. Baggy walked the island every day. He knew where everything belonged. "Show me the empty wallows."

Baggy nodded, his furrowed brow deepening. "I drove the mudpuppy."

Zeke gestured to Forman as he strode to the exit. "Join us. The more eyes on this the better."

The noonday sun glinted off the creeks on the back side of the island as they traipsed from one empty marsh locale to another in the all-terrain vehicle. In the distant sky, a solitary hawk glided on a thermal. Zeke was struck by the unnatural stillness of the island. "Feels like the calm before a storm."

"Thought you'd pick up on the vibe," Baggy said.

"The meteorological service reports no storm systems in our area," Forman said.

A man of science, Zeke didn't put much stock in hunches, until lately. And his current hunch told him he needed to run the missing wildlife scenario past the Tamans. The chances of his slipping away to the lighthouse transmission chair during the day were small. Too many people kept track of his whereabouts, but it would be an acceptable risk if he could shake his assistant.

Or, he could go swimming and transmit through the dolphins, but the dolphins were avoiding the thickened seawater. Something *was* going on, but what?

"A metaphorical storm," Zeke corrected, figuring out how to get free time. Eight empty gator wallows so far, four more to visit. "I've seen enough, and I need to walk the beach to think this through. Please let me out here. Forman, return to the lab and initiate a search of other low country areas to see if this missing wildlife situation is localized or widespread."

"Should I post our observations on any discussion boards?" Forman asked.

"No. We don't want a horde of people descending on the island to study the data abnormality. Let's keep our observations private for a while longer. I'll update Uncle John after my walk. That should suffice for notifications."

"I should stay with you," Forman said.

Zeke didn't want his android to track him or to go into bodyguard mode. That would defeat the purpose of his need for privacy to access the secret transmission chair. "Baggy said we have our normal complement of islanders and Institute employees here on the island. My safety isn't at risk. I need you to make those inquiries and to continue the analyses we began on the water samples."

Forman hesitated. Zeke knew his assistant was calculating the odds of Zeke's safety. He'd have a narrow window of opportunity to use the chair before Forman came looking for him. The transmission would have to be brief.

"That's an order," Zeke said, as he climbed out of the four-wheeler.

"You're the boss."

34

Zeke strode along the path to the beach without looking back. After a few minutes of caution, he sprinted the rest of the way to the lighthouse. Fumbling with his key-shaped necklace, he accessed the hidden ladder inside the lighthouse and descended to the transmission chamber beneath the structure.

The muted lights brightened automatically as he climbed down the rungs, illuminating the wall of books and papers amassed by Guardians before him. The leather-like dental chair beckoned, and he hastened to it.

He stilled his thoughts, then quested into the mindlink, hurtling through space to Tween, the place where he met the Tamans.

Something wrong? his father asked.

Don't know. It's daytime here, so I have to keep this short. Wildlife has gone missing on the island. Small mammals. Gators. Birds. It's unusual to say the least.

Yes. Most unusual.

A deeper voice came into the link, sounding sleepy. *What's this?*

Did Tamans sleep? Zeke repeated what he'd shared with his father.

Your planet hasn't learned to keep the air and water clean? Deep Voice asked.

We have standards and rules about discharges, Zeke added. *Besides, pollution issues usually happen gradually. This happened over the course of a few days. My island is far from any industrial source and privately owned. The likelihood of this being a manmade event is small.*

Harrumph, Deep Voice stated. *What else you got?*

Nothing, which is baffling. But...

What?

Have you ever heard of a sentient meteor storm?

A roar erupted in Tween. Zeke cringed at the onslaught of noise. Finally, the shouting died down. *Explain yourself,* Deep Voice commanded.

It sounds crazy, but last week's meteor storm had a disproportionately high number of water strikes as compared to land strikes. I've checked the water, and my elemental findings don't indicate anything out of the ordinary in the water chemistry.

If it's from the water, his father said, *what do the dolphins say?*

They say the water is different. Thick, and they don't like it. But everything is in normal ranges, even the density.

Whispers started. Zeke heard words he'd never heard before. Then he heard one he knew. Pretenders. What were they?

Look, he said. *I can't stay long. If our problem hails from space, I need to know.*

You'll know when we know, Deep Voice intoned.

Cryptic mumbo-jumbo, Zeke thought. What'd he expect from a bunch of disembodied aliens? They must have nothing to do in Tween but imagine they're twiddling their thumbs. Definitely a serious downside to having no physical body.

We can hear you, his father said in a wry tone.

If it was possible to blush in a thought-state, Zeke colored at his blunder. *Sorry. I'm in a hurry. Do you have anything for me?*

There are any number of possibilities. Until you have more information, it's impossible to discern what type of infestation your planet has.

Zeke brightened. *You're saying it came in on the meteors?*

Or some other way, his father said. *The number of opportunistic species in the universe is astounding.*

How do we get rid of them?

Have to know what you've got first. Capture a specimen.

Easier said than done. I don't know what I'm looking for. What's a pretender anyway?

Another rumble sounded at Tween, deep voice quieting them down and speaking. *No point worrying about pretenders when you might have something easy to deal with like Grzz. A little UV radiation and Grzz disintegrate.*

Grzz are vampires?

Such craziness. Never mind. Until we know the culprit, we can't help you. Bring us more information.

Zeke retreated from the link, awakening in the transmission chair. Earth was infested with something extra-terrestrial? Not good.

Worse, he had no idea how to address the problem until he defined the scope. Back to the drawing board.

Chapter 10

When Jessie took the lid off the pot of stew she'd been simmering all afternoon for dinner, her stomach rebelled. *Not now*, she thought. Zeke will be home any minute.

She clapped the lid back on the pot and set the spoon aside. From networking with other women, she knew morning sickness was normal and expected in the first trimester of pregnancy. Some women reported that morning sickness occurred throughout the day, so that was normal too.

Her stomach lurched again. For good measure, she hurried to the bathroom in case her lunch came up. She was wetting a cloth for her brow at the vanity sink when her vision whirled. She clung to the sink, the onslaught of nausea in her gut adding to her distress.

Hang on, she thought. *Hang on, and it will pass.*

She gritted her teeth as sweat beaded down the channel of her spine. This had to be normal. Her baby had to be normal. Just because she had a trace amount of Maleem drugs in her system when she'd conceived, that didn't mean anything was wrong with her baby.

Her cheeks dampened. Drat. Crying again. And she couldn't spare the energy to lift a finger to dash them away. *Give me strength*, she prayed silently.

The back door opened and closed. "Jessie?" Zeke called.

Oh, no! I don't want him to see me like this. "Just a minute," she managed, dampening her thoughts so he wouldn't pick up on her distress. Zeke's telepathy was much stronger than hers.

The effort cost her. Lunch shot up her throat and out God knows where. Her vision tunneled to black. She clung to the sink as her lifeline. *Come on, light. Don't abandon me. I need to be able to see.*

"Are you okay?" he asked from somewhere close.

She could lie. But she didn't want to lie. She needed help. "No."

His hand touched her shoulder. Warmth and calm radiated from his touch. Tension in her head ebbed. Her field of vision stabilized.

Jessie made out parallel shapes, hers and his, in the mirror before her. The stench of vomit permeated the air.

"I'm calling Uncle John," Zeke said. "We need a medic."

Doctors. They might stick her in a clinic, somewhere far away from Zeke. In a padded room like her sister. "No doctors. Morning sickness is normal for pregnant women. I don't want to be any trouble."

He turned her around and enveloped her in a tender hug. "It's evening, and it's no trouble at all."

She nestled into the creature comfort he offered. "Morning sickness can stretch out to the evening. I checked. Some moms are queasy all day long."

He nuzzled her hair. "I don't want anything to happen to you or our son. At the very least, I should have Uncle John send Nola over to monitor your vitals."

"Daughter. I'm having a girl-child. And my vital signs are fine. I checked them myself. My pulse and blood pressure are right where they should be."

"You look pale to me."

"You'd look pale if you tossed your lunch."

"Good point. Let me tuck you in bed. I'll come back and clean the bathroom."

Jessie took stock. Now that she'd emptied her stomach, she felt better. She could see again. And the room no longer spun in tight circles. "I can do it. I made the mess."

Zeke steered her out of the room and toward the bed. "Lay down and put a pillow under your knees."

"I feel much better."

"Please. Do it for me. Let's get the color back in your cheeks."

"Or what?"

"Or it's off to the hospital you go."

"In that case, I'd be delighted to rest in bed while you clean up my mess."

She let him get her settled. A deep lethargy came over her as she closed her eyes and relaxed.

*****

Zeke rubbed the back of her hand. "Wake up, sleepyhead."

Jessie opened her eyes. Checked the time. Two hours had passed.

She bolted upright. "Oh, my. Dinner. Let me get our dinner served."

"Relax. I ate already. Your stew was delicious. Thought you might prefer ginger ale and toast."

She gazed in the direction of his finger to see a tray on the bedside table. She sipped the ginger ale liberally, swung her legs over the edge of the bed. "That trick with the pillows under the knees knocked me right out. Thanks. I'm feeling much better."

"Take it easy, okay? We could take the tube up to Savannah or Atlanta tomorrow for an exam. I know some people, and it could be off the books, if you like."

"No need. I'm a new woman."

"Seriously, Jess. I'm concerned about you. We should cancel the trip to Rio."

"Your uncle would kill you if you did that. This opportunity is a big deal in his world."

Zeke shrugged and fed her a piece of toast. "He'll get over it."

The last thing she wanted was for her pregnancy to hold his career hostage. "But I won't. You need to go to Rio."

His cheek twitched. He didn't speak. She hastened to fill the silence. "I can stay here, in our home. I don't need to throw up all the way to Rio and ruin your trip."

"I'm not worried about Rio. You, on the other hand, are more precious than gold. There's only one Jessie Landry."

Jessie smiled at the compliment. "Goes both ways. There's no one like you. So we're even." She sighed, regret filling her over the missed travel opportunity. "I really wanted to go, but we can hit Rio together another time. Are you disappointed?"

"I am." Silence again. "You should've mentioned your discomfort. I thought the morning sickness had passed."

"I thought so, too, but this week, I felt more nauseous than ever."

"Anti-nausea meds will help."

"They have side effects. I'm not pumping any drug into my body, not unless it's a medical emergency. Bad enough about the Maleem drug…" Oh, dear, she hadn't wanted to mention that.

"What about the Maleem drug?"

His sharp tone bit into her guilty thoughts. "I, uh, was concerned a trace of it was in my bloodstream at conception. Yours, too. Oh, Zeke, what if our baby has two heads or something? We'll love it, of course, but the rest of the world will be afraid."

"More likely the baby would be Maleem green instead of two-headed, but my son is strong. The Maleem drug won't affect him."

"How can you be sure?"

He shrugged in a totally maddening arrogant male way. "I just am."

"I want so much for our child."

"He'll have it, love."

Jessie punched him lightly. "She'll have it."

He grinned. "What do you say to a vid, and then early to bed for both of us?"

The thought of being with him and not sleeping hummed through her thoughts. She needed to refuel first. And brush her teeth. "I'd say fine, especially if that vid comes with a bowl of stew. I'm starved."

"Coming right up."

She heard him talking while she was in the bathroom and questioned him about it when she came out.

"I returned my uncle's call from earlier today," he hedged. "Nothing major."

"I'm fine," she reiterated. "No need to call in the cavalry. See, I'm walking around like a normal person. I can take care of myself. I can feed myself."

"I will protect you, Jessie."

An odd thing to say, especially since she wasn't being threatened in any way. "It's okay, Zeke. I'm pregnant, not ill with some dread disease. Women have survived pregnancy for thousands of years."

He spooned the stew into her, despite her protest she could do it herself. Then he hauled her off to bed. But not to sleep.

Chapter 11

Xstle sensed the powerful presence from the depths. Not a Drch. Not his fellow Yars. Something else. In the flattened shape of the largest bottom swimmer he'd brushed up against, he vectored up from the sea floor. Were Ancients here? How was that possible?

After attaining a full complement of specks a sunrise ago, Xstle had silenced his calling song, allowing the remainder of his kind to collect and join with other Yar explorers. Reconstituted and fully functional, Xstle continued to feed and horde resources. When the time was right, the dozen Yar Primes on this expedition would reproduce, and their spawn would colonize this planet.

They would arise from the sea as one and battle the Drch to the death. Until then, his mission was to gather intelligence, which included checking out the possibility of an Ancient above the water. As Xstle neared the surface, he slowed and rounded into a copy of the smallest creatures he'd consumed on this planet, allowing himself more opportunities to observe the open pod above.

One life form, atop the water. Hmm. Xstle quested to the thought plane and brushed against the consciousness of the Ancient. He retreated to safety, drawing in on himself to form a small inconspicuous sphere, silencing his telepathic probe to avoid detection. Wait. How could that be? He expanded and sent out another pulse. Confirmation was immediate.

Definitely an Ancient.

Yars had filed the necessary colonization requests prior to commencing the expedition. Surely, the Yars weren't in violation of colonization procedures. Unless … Had the Ancients learned of Drch's treachery? Were they here to make sure the Drch were vanquished once and for all?

He had to know. Withdrawing and reforming into a small finned sea creature, he followed the water-going vessel back to shore. He shot out of the water in swimming shape and quickly stalled out on the wet sand. This shape had no locomotion ability on land.

What rotten luck.

All he had to do was wait. Something would come along to scavenge the sea creature. Time passed slowly. He absorbed the heat of the sand as the tide withdrew and left him exposed. He expanded his consciousness, singing the Yar song of freedom.

Just as he thought he might fare better from mimicking the substrate material, a winged creature circled overhead. Perfect. Patience always paid off. That's what he told his recruits at the Academy. To wait for it. Being in a hurry got you dead quicker than anything.

Sharp talons grabbed him, lifted him into the sky. Xstle pondered how he would handle this assimilation. Best, he thought, to absorb the genetic code of the creature from the exterior and reform, leaving the creature intact and none the wiser.

The view from up here was stupendous. Open space as far as the senses could quest. Clean air. If he allowed the creature to survive, the winged beauty would battle him for feeding territory. Much as he enjoyed fighting, the time for fighting had not yet arrived. His current mission depended on stealth and information gathering.

Therefore, the predator animal had to die.

When the creature alit and began pecking at him, Xstle secreted *auku* along every contact point. The creature shrieked, a high piercing sound, and flapped its magnificent appendages. With enough of the life-absorbing adhesive mud clinging to the hawk, Xstle disincorporated from the fish shape and transformed into the shape of the sticks and twigs in the nest. As he sang the victory song of Yar, his collective penetrated the skin of the hawk and began absorbing and copying the internal organs.

Chapter 12

"You got her a real cat, not an AI?" Forman asked, eying the vid screen in Angie's living room while twisting his hands together. Jessie meant everything to Zeke. If she wasn't happy, Zeke would be miserable. With so many eyes on them in Rio, Zeke's wellbeing was paramount.

Angie toggled the view to inside Zeke's house where Jessie reclined on the sofa. "Jessie would have noticed if she had a fake cat. Besides, Sanjee comes highly recommended."

Sanjee had hissed and spat at both Zeke and Forman in the lab earlier, but the fluff ball had purred contentedly in Angie's arms. Conventional wisdom indicated a feline's preference for females was typical behavior for cats, though why anyone would want one was beyond Forman's reckoning.

"Zeke's nearly there with the carrier. What if she doesn't like long-haired felines? We should have offered her a choice."

"You're a tad anxious for an artificial lifeform. Next time you're due for a tune-up, I'll adjust the gain on your emotions."

Forman recoiled as if he'd been struck. "Please, don't. I have so few genuine emotional experiences. Even a bucket of bolts like me can tell the difference between the sterile ones I've been given for reference, and the ones I've formed. I treasure every memory I've made. If you care a whit for me, please don't touch sector 46w5k99c."

"As long as your budding emotions don't interfere with your prime directive of protecting Zeke, I promise not to touch them. But we can't have you going off the deep end again, like you did over Bea. The emotional component is to equip you with empathy, not to take over your life. My cousin needs a research assistant, a bodyguard, and a social facilitator. He doesn't need an emotional wreck on his hands."

"Understood." He'd had it bad for Bea, the pop superstar, but she'd moved on to dally with another man right after dumping Forman. Though Bea's rejection was painful, it showed he was capable of strong emotions.

Onscreen, Zeke opened the door, called his wife's name. Jessie rose from the sofa, curiosity stamped on her face. *She isn't as pretty as Bea*, Forman thought, but she's light years more stable. His heart ached for Jessie's superstar sister. It always would. He'd made sure by embedding the feelings deep in every subroutine in his multiplex processor system. No amount of reprogramming would let him forget her. He'd even uploaded a backup file, coded, of course, into the lab data system in case Supply Central wiped his memories again.

"This isn't about Bea," Forman said. "And I'm fine, in case you're wondering."

On screen, Jessie opened the cage, and the white kitty leapt into her arms like it belonged there. "Oh, Zeke, he's perfect!"

Beside Forman, Angie sighed happily. "And that, my friend, is how it's done. Jessie will have Sanjee for company while we travel to Rio."

Forman shot a worried glance at his boss's cousin. "I thought you were staying home with her."

"No offense, but Uncle John decided sending two robots with Zeke was one too many. One of his Nolas will monitor Jessie remotely while I accompany you guys to Brazil."

He cocked his head to one side. "I'm fully capable of protecting Dr. Landry. My track record bears witness to this fact. My four-in-one upload makes me uniquely qualified to keep him safe from harm."

"No matter how strong, smart, or wily we make you, others have co-opted you in the past. Uncle John wants a human bodyguard for this trip. That would be me."

Her patronizing tone rubbed salt in his virtual Achilles heel. "We overcame that glitch."

"We did, but who's to say a determined programmer can't hack your subroutines? Now that Zeke has international visibility, he requires additional security when traveling."

"Dr. Z won't like that. He barely tolerates my presence in the travel pod. How will you explain your presence?"

"I'm going under the heading of visiting with Sidra McIntyre who will also be attending the symposium. We became friends when she came here last month. And we won't be using pods for this trip. Uncle John has put his fastest transpo at our disposal, and I get to fly the bird."

In micro-seconds, Forman analyzed Zeke's cousin's words, checking the nuances in her voice, the tiny muscle twitched in her face, her altered respiration pattern. Angie was lying to him about something, but flerk if he'd let on he was wise to her tricks.

More than once she'd ambushed him and reprogrammed him. Though he had the software modules of four androids, and although he maintained the handsome façade of a Gary entertainment model most of the time, his default mode of thinking was that of a Bob super nerd. From his Brutus bodyguard module, he could perform every known method of hand-to-hand combat, and knew how to test for and treat poisons. His experimental Holmes disguise module was top secret and known only to a few key individuals.

Best to keep this conversation light and breezy. "Shazatt!" He grinned as if he didn't have a care in the world. "Score on the transpo, girlfriend."

Angie returned his high five, then clicked the vid screens back to whole island perimeter mode. "I saw something odd earlier today as I reviewed the security tapes. The red-tailed hawk at the north end of the island? It did the oddest thing this morning. Wait. I'll find the footage."

Though technically it didn't matter where he was positioned in the room for best acuity, Forman leaned forward to mimic human behavior. His best offense was to act as human as possible, despite the AI identification necklace international law forced him to wear.

"I've seen him around. He's the only hawk on the island."

Angie queued up the segment. "I flagged this sequence earlier because it was weird. What do you think happened to him?"

Forman watched the hawk take a nose dive out of a tree, flapping his wings like a chicken. Due to the panning of the cameras, he didn't see the bird lift off from the ground. Instead, he saw two more failed attempts at flying. "Maybe he ate some bad berries."

Angie snorted. "You think he's drunk? Is that even possible?"

To answer accurately, Forman accessed the console with a streaming data bridge. "Not only is it possible, the effect is well documented throughout human history. In 836, an entire flock of birds was seen flailing and flopping around a monastery and all revived later that day. In 1648, a Spanish galleon captain reported his parrot got into the rum, passed out, and was better after sleeping it off. So, yes, it happens."

"What could the hawk have eaten?"

"Any number of plants on the island are poisonous. Oleanders, pyracantha, holly, pokeberries. Some residents purchased Christmas poinsettias for the season and brought them to Tama Island. Should I go on?"

"Nah. I got it. But the hawk must be hurting to scavenge for berries."

"Wildlife seems to be in short supply on the island." He took ten seconds to compare other areas in the region. "The phenomenon has been reported along the Eastern Seaboard over the last two months."

"What's happening to our wildlife?"

"We're working on the puzzle in the lab," Forman said. "All I can say at this time is that the water chemistry is within normal ranges."

"Are people in danger? Perhaps we should evacuate the island before the Rio trip."

Forman accessed health databases at hospitals in Georgia and her neighboring states. He checked missing person records. "No localized illnesses or epidemics have been reported. No abnormal levels of missing persons have occurred. Whatever happened to the wildlife, humans have not been affected."

"That's a relief. What's Zeke's working theory?"

"That would be for him to tell you."

"Good answer, but you can tell me. We're on the same team. I promise to keep my lips sealed."

He glanced at her pouty lip expression, puzzled by her sudden display of courting behaviors. "Even so, Dr. Z doesn't like his theories bandied about, especially if he hasn't proved anything."

"He has a null hypothesis?"

"He has anecdotal data from Baggy and other islanders about the small animals and now the gators no longer visible."

"Visible? He thinks they went invisible? That's so sexy."

"Dr. Z is a reputable scientist," Forman shot back. "Don't put words in my mouth. He has no wildlife to examine to determine if there is a disease vector, though one that would harm so many species across the board is unprecedented."

"Did something eat everything?"

"We don't know the fate of the wildlife, but invisibility isn't on the table."

She stretched, arching her back and thrusting her breasts in his direction. "Your passion on this subject makes me hot."

With her change in body language, Forman accessed his courting behavior files and joined the sensual game. Leaning back, he gave her a flirty sidelong glance. "Angelika Courtney, are you flirting with me?"

"What if I am?"

"Zeke would kill me if I slept with you. He's already warned me to stay away from you."

She chuckled seductively and rose, extending a hand to him. "What my cousin doesn't know won't hurt him. I'm primed for a hookup. No emotions need be involved."

Forman hesitated. "I shouldn't. I still have feelings for Bea."

Angie's face clouded. "Bea didn't honor you or put you first. She doesn't deserve your abstinence or faithfulness. At best, she will have long-term psychiatric issues from the drugs she absorbed. If you want to pine for her the rest of your life, fine. But I've seen you mooning over Zeke and Jessie's togetherness."

"I haven't."

"A pseudo blush. How cute. You are so lifelike. No wonder women buy these Gary entertainment modules and forget about human males. Let's talk frankly. I'm looking for a good time. You excel at intercourse. I like you. You like me. Why make our coupling difficult?"

Indecision teeter-tottered in his brain. He was attracted to Angie, but Zeke had warned him to steer clear. Zeke didn't need to know everything. "You're beautiful, Angie. You could have any man you want."

"I want you."

"Then I'm yours."

Forman channeled his entertainment mode. He complimented and pleasured Angie until her eyes glazed over. When she roused, he went through the intricate dance of lovemaking again, this time allowing himself to draw pleasure from the activity. Third time around, he caressed her gently rounded belly.

"You have the figure of a Madonna," he murmured against her

glowing skin. "Your classic figure is every man's ideal." He cupped her hips. "Especially these loins. So perfect for childbearing."

She roused, reached under the pillow. "What'd you say?"

"You're a statuesque lady. Fertile and glowing with overt sensuality."

Angie sat up, pushing away from him, a disabling device in her hand. "Did you store our lovemaking in your long term cache?"

He smiled smugly. "I did. We created pleasurable emotions."

"Good. I'd hate for this to have been a complete waste. Only the last few minutes will be erased."

Shock melted his demeanor of male satiation. He could overpower her and take the device. His brute strength was four times that of a human. But Angie was family. They'd shared intimacy. Why would she betray him this way?

"Why?"

She raised the device, activated it. As his systems lost power, she said, "No one can know."

Chapter 13

Flying in Uncle John's transpo definitely beat the commercial alternative. With Angie piloting the deluxe plane and Forman fiddling with the water data set again, Zeke could sit, stand, or pace all the way to Rio and no one would care.

Jessie would care.

He'd hated to leave her. It felt as if he'd left part of himself behind. He stared out the window at the graying sky. When he met Jessie, she'd been just another person, a female stranger. She hadn't pushed him as some women did when they wanted to bed him.

"Mooning over the wifey?" Forman asked.

Zeke startled. "No. Uh. I mean. Well. Yes."

"She's worth it, dude. Everything about her is true blue, and she makes you happy."

The mystery of her affection astounded him. "How did it come to this? One minute I was myself, and the next I was a besotted idiot. I should be reviewing my presentation, refreshing my memory and emphasizing Uncle John's mandated talking points. Instead, I'm wondering how she's making out at home, if she's missing me."

"You could call her on the com."

Zeke snorted. "I've been gone two hours. No way am I going to be *that* guy. I need to focus."

"Me, too." Forman paced up the aisle as if he were going to the cockpit, then whirled and headed back to Zeke. He pitched his voice low. "Ever wonder if your thoughts are your own?"

Uncle John's heavy-handed fingerprints in Zeke's presentation came to mind. Zeke didn't like being told what to think or say. But how was that any different from his intergalactic communication with the Tamans? At times, he seemed to exist to live out other people's plans.

Zeke drew in a slow, considering breath. "I dislike playing the part of Institute puppet."

49

"You'll get back to your man of science M.O. soon enough. I'm talking about something different. I have nanosecond gaps in my memory. In most cases, the memory seems intact, but the time signature is off a smidge."

"Someone's tampered with your programs?" Zeke rose in alarm. "I'll ask Angie to run a diagnostic."

Forman shot a worried glance to the front of the plane. "Angie may be the problem. My gaps are in a more, shall we say, personal area. The timelines are consistent in every other aspect."

Zeke's expression darkened. He didn't like where this was headed. "Angie? And you? When? How?"

"The usual way."

"We spoke about this. I asked you to stay away from my cousin."

"She came on to me, Dr. Z. I was lonely. I caved. Don't hate me." Forman slumped in the adjacent seat and held his head in his hands. "I miss Bea. The six weeks she's been in rehab have been the longest six weeks of my life. Knowing my gift of chocolate exacerbated her illness makes it worse. I still love Bea, but she's changed. Worse, she never loved me. I was a plaything for her. Otherwise, how could she have thrown me over like that?"

"Bad enough that emotions are corrupting *my* thoughts." Zeke scowled at this new concern. "You're the most advanced android ever built. Your emotion chip is supposed to make you compassionate, not destroy you. You need a system overhaul. You might consider having the emotion component removed."

Forman recoiled. "No. I need to feel. These sensory inputs are my intellectual property as much as anything else I've computed, analyzed, or experienced. Feelings and emotion are normal, and I desire to have them. Someone surgically removed fragments of my feelings. Are you behind this?"

"No. I wouldn't do that to you. You have my word on that. However, I could set a trap for whoever is deleting your feelings. We could divert your memories to other, more mundane sectors for starters."

Forman shook his head. "I'm sure I thought of that last time this happened. I looked and found nothing."

Concerns swirled in Zeke's thoughts. Who would tinker with Forman? Was his research at risk? What about his personal safety?

Zeke released the tension in his jaw. "How long has this been going on?"

"Not sure, big guy. I've had some hard times since I came to work for you."

Between being reprogrammed by a secret society and being ripped to shreds by a powerful alien invader, Zeke's android was lucky he had any contiguous thoughts and a shred of humanity. "Understood. Still, Angie could shed light on this for us."

"Angie's using me, same as Bea did." Forman's expression darkened. "Only this time my emotions aren't involved in the coupling. I'll figure out what she's doing to me and find a way to circumvent her meddling in my head."

"You won't go rogue on me?"

"Nah. I save that for my sensual encounters. Some sexual partners like it rough."

Zeke raised a cautionary hand. "I don't want to hear your exploits. Especially where my cousin is concerned."

"Gotcha." Forman looked like he was working hard to contain his laughter. "That cat turned out to be perfect."

At last, a less disturbing topic. "If anything about a cat is perfect."

"You disagree?"

"The cat hates me. As soon as that feline saw Jessie, it wanted nothing to do with me. Darn thing hissed at me when I kissed Jessie goodbye."

"Sanjee may never have a pair bond with you, but as you occupy the same living space and have designs on the same female, the cat will develop a tolerance of you."

"Enough pop psychology. I'm glad Jessie is happy with him, but I'm concerned about our lack of progress with the seawater analysis. I can see a physical difference in the water, but the water chemistry doesn't capture a difference, unless you count an increased sediment load in the water."

"Turbidity is a physical parameter," Forman said.

"I hoped for something else. A trace element out of whack. A new element. A microorganism bloom. Something to explain why the sea isn't herself."

"With so many meteors entering our atmosphere in such a short period of time, is it any wonder we're seeing an effect?"

51

"I get that, but I want more. I'm hoping Sidra will let us bring her entire meteor back to Tama Island for study."

"Too bad you're married, dude. That chick's into you."

Zeke's gaze narrowed. "I did not need to hear that."

Forman chuckled. "What did you do before I came along? Females must have been hitting on you for years, and you never knew it."

"I'm very happy with my mate." Zeke grimaced at the politically incorrect term favored by the Tamans. "My wife. I'm happy with my choice of wife."

"I love it when you go all tribal on me. Reverting back to early man's behaviors where women are concerned is a step in the right direction for you. Contrary to rumors that you're the android and I'm the scientist, I'd say you're officially one hundred percent *Homo sapiens.*"

Except he wasn't.

Chapter 14

Jessie inhaled the sea air wafting across her front porch where she gently rocked. She felt pensive. Zeke, Forman, and Angie had flown to Rio and she'd stayed behind. She could've gone. No one said she shouldn't go, but the collective sigh of relief when she'd volunteered to stay behind had been unmistakable.

She may be Zeke's wife, but she wasn't his equal when it came to symposia or public relations trips for the Institute. Bummer. When she managed her sister's career, she'd been happy to work behind the scenes, to troubleshoot to her heart's content.

Zeke had his own brilliant assistant to help him problem-solve. And his uncle and his cousin. All the family Jessie had to fuss over was Bea. And the cat. And soon, the baby.

In her dreams, Jessie starred as Jacqueline Kennedy to Zeke's John Fitzgerald Kennedy, where everything seemed golden and a fairy tale existence. Rotten ending in that particular Camelot, though. She wanted to live her entire life with Zeke, not lose him after a few love struck years.

The cat bounded onto the porch and leapt onto her lap. "What in the world?" Jessie asked, petting Sanjee's soft white fur.

The cat arched into her touch, purring, and stretching. Then it crouched in her lap, tiny claws sharp through her jeans. "This won't do," Jessie said, lifting the animal and massaging the claws into the cat's soft pads. "Mama doesn't like you to hurt her. Be nice."

Though the cat allowed the cuddle, Jessie sensed tension in the animal's stiff posture. She followed the cat's gaze. Someone approached. In the late afternoon sunlight, dust motes haloed Baggy's dark head. "It's all right," she murmured to the cat. "Baggy's our friend."

"Afternoon, Miss Jessie," Baggy said as he climbed the stairs, sitting down on the topmost one. "How's the kitty cat?"

Jessie stopped rocking to dig the claws out of her thighs again.

"Fine, well, fine until he heard you coming. Then he climbed up here and got us both stirred up."

Baggy nodded his head in affirmation. "He's protective. That's good. He'll let you know if anything's amiss."

Jessie shook her head. "I've never heard of a watch cat."

"Now you have. Sanjee comes highly recommended from my second cousin on the mainland. We wouldn't have allowed any old cat over here."

Surprised that so much effort had gone into her pet selection, Jessie beamed with delight. "Thanks. We seem to be a good fit, though he could be nicer to Zeke."

"Don't worry. Those two will make their peace in time. How're you feeling?"

"The baby's fine. I feel good most of the time, but when morning sickness strikes, there's nothing to do but ride it out."

"I heard you didn't want to take anything for the discomfort. Homeopathic herbs will help. No need to suffer when you should be feeling joy."

Jessie sighed and petted a purring Sanjee. "I started thinking about outfitting a nursery this morning, and I had a panic attack. Where will I find what we need? How will I make choices? Zeke doesn't have an opinion about furniture or theme. It's a lot for one person to decide."

"When a trouble is big, break it down into doable steps. Start by making choices that please you."

"But I don't even know where to start."

"Tell you what. Zeke's crib is stored at Mrs. Dee's. I'll have a friend bring it by, and you can decide if you like it. That's a fine place to start."

"Wouldn't it be easier to take me to the crib?"

"Her place is a bit of a jumble," he cautioned.

Jessie beamed. "I like jumbles. Can I visit her tomorrow?"

"I'll check with her and get back to you." He glanced at his shoes. "Would you look at that?"

"What?"

"I stepped in some mud on the far side of the island. Barely covered the toe of my shoe. Now look. I'll be darned if the mud isn't covering my shoe and now it's on my sock. How'd that happen?"

54

Jessie rose, depositing the cat in her rocking chair. "Let me wipe that mud off. Sit tight."

She dashed inside, for a wet cloth and a dry one, stopping to grab a glass of water for Baggy. "Here," she said. "Have some water while I clean your shoe."

"I can do that," he said.

"Nonsense. Sit tight and I'll wipe this stuff off." She scrubbed the mud, but it didn't budge. "You sure this is mud?"

The cat thumped down from the rocker, nose in the air, sniffing Baggy's shoe. "What in the world?" Jessie asked as the cat lapped the mud clean from Baggy's shoe. "Should he eat that? Won't it make him sick?"

"Odd, indeed. But helpful. Very helpful. Nice kitty," Baggy murmured. The cat removed every trace of mud from Baggy's clothing.

Baggy rose and handed her the glass of water. "Thank you, Sanjee, and Miss Jessie. I enjoyed your hospitality."

The older man shambled away to complete his rounds of the island. Jessie looked down and saw the cat licking the cloth she'd rubbed on Baggy's shoe. "You are a strange one, kitty. A bit weird. Didn't your mama tell you not to eat dirt?"

She carried the glass inside and thought about fixing a sandwich for dinner. Nothing hot for her tonight. And ginger ale. It was liquid gold to her delicate stomach. According to everything she'd read, she was on track with her pregnancy. Just a couple more weeks and she'd feel comfortable telling her sister and their friends about her news.

A harsh question arrowed through her head. Would it matter? Would anyone in her world care that she, Jessie Stemford Landry, was having a baby?

For a moment, she couldn't catch her breath. Other than her music industry acquaintances, no one other than her sister even knew she was alive. Zeke knew. She mattered to him. And the islanders knew and cared.

Stop feeling sorry for yourself, and start thinking about being a mom, about decorating the nursery. She detoured to the spare bedroom, eying the room in a different light. Turquoise would be good in here. No pale pinks or baby blue for her daughter. She'd have the rich color of the sea. And dolphins. Oh, this was good. She'd discovered a theme.

Now to write her ideas down. Would she paint the dolphins on the wall or craft them from weathered wood? Wood, definitely. And there should be replicas of all the special dolphins. Zeke had shared their names with her – Tunis, Nicola, Boz, and Klickie.

Zeke would be so pleased.

Her belly tightened and eased. *Look at that. The baby is pleased, too.*

From outside came the unmistakable sound of retching. Sanjee. Jessie hurried out to see the cat spit out a wad of dirt and a matt of hair. "Poor thing. That'll teach you to eat dirt, even if it tastes like cat nip. Come on inside, and I'll feed you dinner."

But Sanjee wouldn't come inside with her. He sat there watching the contents of his stomach in the sand as if it held the keys to the universe.

Jessie took a firm stand. She was in training to be a parent, after all. "I'm not bringing dinner to you. Come inside when you're ready."

She propped the screen door open and fixed a peanut butter sandwich for herself along with a glass of ginger ale. Today she'd solved two problems. She'd located a baby crib on the island. Not just any baby crib, but Zeke's crib. How could she not love a family heirloom? And she'd decided upon a dolphin theme for the nursery.

She sat quietly on the sofa, making notes and sketching. Then her tummy acted up. She hurried to the bathroom to unload her dinner. The cool tile floor drew her, and she lay down. Soon the purring cat curled beside her.

Jessie roused enough to draw the cat closer. "We're a pair, aren't we?"

Chapter 15

Zeke's hand strayed to his father's Taman necklace as the transpo circled Rio. He wasn't disoriented from being so far from home, but he felt off, as if part of him was missing. The Jessie part. Touching the keystone pendant centered him. He could do this.

"I see it," Forman crowed, pointing to the statue with outstretched arms. "Christ the Redeemer is the number one tourist attraction in the city. It's 130 feet high and weighs 700 tons. How magnificent."

Zeke acknowledged the tall statue with a grunt, looking beyond Corcovado Mountain to the tight sardine arrangement of waterfront hotels and beyond to the sea. From this altitude, he could see for miles. Instead of a brightly flashing sea, he beheld a dull body of water. Almost wren brown. His hands itched to take samples. Something was amiss in the ocean, and he was stuck giving a dog and pony show for politicians and their flunkies.

Life was indeed cruel.

The transpo landed at Galeão International Airport, and the customs agent came out to them.

"I could get used to this VIP treatment," Forman said as they filled out the necessary forms.

The customs agent balked over the stainless steel containers Zeke had brought along for his meteor and water samples. Zeke listened mutely as Forman explained in Portuguese the purpose of the materials. Finally, all was squared away, and they were free to deplane.

Angie strode back to the passenger compartment looking energized for someone who'd just piloted the aircraft for hours. "Ready to head to the hotel? We have a courtesy car at our disposal."

"Seems strange to see all the travel aboveground here," Zeke said as he stepped onto the tarmac, carry bag slung over his shoulder. He didn't trust his presentation files to anyone.

"No place in all this granite for underground tubes," Forman crowed, his skin tone darkening to resemble the native complexion, as he paced beside Zeke. "I can't wait to hit the beach. Should we visit Copacabana or Ipanema Beach first?"

"Beaches." Zeke mulled the idea over in his head. Bikini-clad women held no allure for him, but he needed to sample the water. He glanced over his shoulder to make sure the rest of the luggage was following them. "What was the problem with the sampling containers?"

"The container material. Seemed the customs agent thought they might be used for making incendiary devices."

Outrage boiled up in Zeke's throat. "Bombs? The agent thought I'd carry bomb materials into a foreign country? What idiot scientist would do that?"

"Relax, Z-man. He understands now that he knows you're a big-wig science geek. We're cool."

"I'm not feeling cool. I need some serious downtime in my hotel room. But first, I want to hit the beach. Any beach."

Forman's lip trembled. "Not the famous ones?"

"I need to sample the water. The mini-analyzer we brought along won't tell us much, but we can measure the turbidity level."

"All work and no play? Not fair. We're in Rio, man. We should hop into a chopper, cruise the beaches, and go shopping."

"Those activities aren't on my itinerary. I'm here to do the presentation, finagle a corner of Sidra's meteor, and collect water samples."

Steam seemed to shoot out of the top of Forman's head. After a moment, he grinned. "You don't know much about being married. We need to get Jessie a present. For that, we have to go shopping."

Jessie. Yes, she'd like a present. Why didn't I think of that? "Fine. You may pick something up for her when you go shopping."

"Can't do that, seeing as how I'm your bodyguard. You'll have to accompany me or no one goes shopping in the Marvelous City."

"Great." Forman started whistling a peppy tune, much to Zeke's annoyance. "What're you doing now?"

"Getting into the local scene. Choro instrumental music was born here. This melody from "Atraente" is my favorite. We'll listen to the original by Gonzaga and Lacerdo on sax and flute in the hotel. Don't your feet itch to move to this beat?"

"My feet are moving."

"Boy, you're a grouch today."

"Sorry. I'm focused on the ocean and not on soaking up the local color. I appreciate the effort you've made to bone up on everything Rio. You're a good friend."

"Thanks for the love, boss man." Forman lightened his skin tone from that of the locals to match Zeke's permanent tan. "How about if we go with the brother look here in Rio?"

Forman's Holmes disguise module frequently came in handy in their off-the-books investigations. Even so, Zeke wasn't keen about having a robot look-a-like. "The mandatory AI necklace ruins the similarity, don't you think?"

"I could ditch it."

"No. We don't need that kind of heat down here. We're here to play by the rules."

Forman sighed. "I'm starting to wish Jessie had come along."

At last. Common ground. "Me, too."

A short ride later and Zeke stepped onto bright white beach sand, two sample containers in hand. A few tourists sunbathed up near the beach access point, but none were in the water or near the water. Zeke took a deep breath and immediately wished he hadn't.

He gagged on the vile smell. "What's that?"

"Rio de Smellio, that's what," Forman quipped. "This is not right. There are no putrid smells listed for Rio in any of the archives."

Zeke kicked off his flip-flops, rolled up his khaki trousers, and stepped into the shallows with a sample bottle. "I agree. Let's get right on this analysis after we check into the hotel."

"You're not getting in my limo smelling like that water, are you?" Forman asked.

"You're a machine. You'll survive." Zeke handed his assistant the capped sample container and bent down to collect another. The water's increased sediment load was visible to the naked eye. But increased turbidity alone wouldn't account for the noxious almost sulfur-like odor. No boats were bobbing in the gentle waters. No apparent red tide or dead organisms lined the water's edge. If the noxious sea kept people away, the tourism economy must be in trouble here.

"I do not like this, Zeke I am."

The odd sentence structure stopped Zeke. "What?"

"I made a literary reference to a children's book written last century by a Dr. Seuss about green eggs and breakfast meat."

Zeke waded out of the shallows with the second sample bottle and toed on his flip-flops. His eyes watered at the pungent scent. "Who'd eat green eggs?"

"Exactly."

"Enough with the vague references. I need to think."

"You need to shower."

Zeke took a whiff of himself and nearly passed out. "Agreed."

*****

The mini-analyzer confirmed the higher turbidity level. Zeke shunted the data to Forman and messaged them to his lab in Georgia. He refrigerated the remaining liquid and hit the shower.

After a quick vid call to Jessie to assure her he'd landed safely, Zeke settled down to review tomorrow's presentation. He noted a place where he could insert the thickened water issue and made a note to add a comment. A discussion starter like that could turn a boring meeting into a brainstorming session and make this trip worthwhile.

Sidra had been vague in the message she'd left at the hotel for him. She had the sample. She was in hiding to protect her meteor. She'd find him.

Of more interest was the terse summons from the admiral in his electronic message queue. *Report to Admiral Russell Valenkamph at 2000 tomorrow.* No mention of where. No return address. No nothing.

Prior to the trip, Uncle John had mentioned an admiral wanted to see him, but his uncle hadn't mentioned a name. A quick records search into official databases showed Vice Admiral Valenkamph had a host of commendations and medals including the Navy Cross, the Presidential Medal of Freedom, and the Navy Distinguished Service Medal. There'd been a furor over misconduct of his subordinates at a training facility, but he'd weathered that storm.

His current posting as Chief of Naval Operations raised Zeke's eyebrows.

What did the CNO of the U.S. Navy want with him?

Chapter 16

In his winged form, Xstle studied the dwelling from the treetops. He recognized a faint subsonic signature of the ancient ones in the *gurt*. Not *gurt*, he corrected himself. The word here was house. To survive on this frontier posting, he had to adapt to the new ways and speak the new language until the Yar collective took over.

But Ancients.

They'd died out centuries ago.

How was it possible one existed in this far corner of the 'verse?

And the furred creature that guarded the female. Why was Xstle unable to overcome it from inside? For generations, he had successfully defeated many species in that way after they had consumed him. Yet, the furry one repelled him and blocked absorption of any coded material.

The female called the creature Sanjee. He'd never encountered a Sanjee before. There seemed to be only a single replica of a Sanjee on the island, but there were many bipeds. During the eight moons he'd been here, he'd pinged every biped. No others had the unique Ancient signature. The strong Ancient he'd followed here had left the area.

Hence, the female commanded his attention. If he was correct about her incredible heritage, the true power resided in her. He hungered for her divinity. But it would be a bold move to assimilate an Ancient.

Meanwhile, the biped that patrolled the island interested Xstle. He'd been in the process of assimilating the patroller when the Sanjee thwarted his effort. Xstle shuddered. As a bird of prey, he should be superior in all ways to the Sanjee, but the thought Sanjee might intervene again prevented him from eliminating the hideous creature.

He'd been eager to assimilate a biped, but his failure cost him many of his countrymen. Consequently, he'd taken to flying to a buoy in the sea, alighting there, and changing back into swimming form each afternoon. Sometimes other Yars were there. Sometimes his effort was for naught, and he spent the dark cycle producing more *auku* and feeding on marine life. The more *auku* he produced, the more of his larvae would survive when it was time to spawn.

But he couldn't give up hope at this minor setback.

A score of Yars had made the voyage to this sector. In past colonizations, about half the volunteers had made landfall. With this journey so much farther than anything a Yar ever attempted before, the survival rate would be less.

And there was a Drch to contend with.

Xstle needed more helpmates to conquer these bipeds and vanquish the Drch. He must have them if he was to claim this territory for Yar.

As long as Yars answered his call, he would rebuild and observe. Bipeds held power and authority on this planet. They'd evolved beyond the sea to conquer land and air. He needed to assimilate a biped to integrate into their society. He'd been rash to start with a mature biped, but the man with loose trousers had been easy to ambush.

He'd seen juvenile bipeds on the island, knew where they went outside. He couldn't risk an assimilation indoors yet – he'd be too vulnerable until he'd undergone the change several times. Stealth was his friend.

Xstle soared to the buoy, scanning the sea and sky for predators. Clear. He plunged into the choppy waters, changing into a finned form. All through the moonrise, he called and called, singing the song of Yar. A few specks came, and as they joined him, their calling song magnified.

At sunrise, he leapt from the water, assumed his winged form, and flew back to the island. He felt stronger. Strong enough to go for a biped again. This time he'd select a juvenile to be certain he got the job done.

Long live Yar.

Chapter 17

"Dr. Landry?" A woman in a crisp Navy uniform stood at attention beside Zeke's dinner table. Her name tag said Hinson. Her insignia indicated she was a Lieutenant. "Admiral Valenkamph will see you now."

Zeke knew the time for his appointment had arrived, but he hesitated to leave the decadent torte filled with raisins, nuts, and apples and topped with cream and ice cream. Jessie had recommended the Torta Hollanesa as the best dessert in all of Rio, and after two bites he agreed with her.

"Give me a sec," he said, spooning up another delicious morsel. The general had been cryptic about this meeting, and Zeke refused to be penalized for the other man's secrecy. "I need to finish this. Please, sit down. Would you like a bite?"

"No, sir. My orders are to escort you to the admiral." Lieutenant Hinson assumed a military stance. Her rigid posture and military bearing, along with the crisp khaki uniform, were quite the contrast in a room full of colorful, sunburned tourists.

Zeke shot Forman a pointed look as people in the restaurant stared their way. He didn't normally have a sweet tooth, but Jessie would ask him if he ate every bite, and he wanted to say yes. He spooned up another mouthwatering bite of the torte and melting ice cream.

"Perhaps you'd care to wait outside," Forman suggested. His subtle movement showed a ripple of biceps beneath his flamboyant aloha-style shirt dotted with blue macaws and yellow canaries.

The naval officer didn't blink. Didn't twitch or even seem to breathe.

Huh. Must be serious. In any event, the silent treatment and disruption to the intimate restaurant had the desired effect of rushing him.

With a shrug of his shoulders at Forman, Zeke hastily downed the rest of the delicious dessert and chased it with coffee.

"I have to pay the bill, and I'll be ready."

"It's been taken care of, sir." Though she was still immobile, an air of expectation surrounded the young officer.

"In that case, let's go." Might as well get this over with.

Zeke followed Hinson outside where a two-person transpo awaited. His feet dragged to a full stop. Three to ride. Two seats in all. Obviously, Forman wasn't invited.

He'd been separated from Forman on other trips, and parting ways never went well. Zeke had chafed initially at Uncle John's idea of a robot bodyguard and assistant, but now he relied upon Forman to accompany him. "Sorry. No can do. If my assistant doesn't go, I don't go."

"The request was for you personally, Dr. Landry." The lieutenant shot a dismissive gaze at Forman who looked harmless in his "Gary" entertainment persona. "Your A.I. may await your return at the hotel."

"I'd like to accommodate the admiral's request to meet, but this travel arrangement won't do."

"I am a highly decorated officer, sir. You have my word that no harm will come to you."

A look at the thick patch of hardware on her uniform confirmed she'd achieved success through combat situations. Still, Forman knew every fighting style known to man. "No thanks. I'll pass. The admiral knows where to find me."

Zeke turned from her and strode toward Forman.

"We should visit a dance club," Forman suggested. "The evening is just starting to come alive."

Zeke snorted. He barely danced and when he did, he slow danced with his wife. Would his bluff work? Would the military spirit him off in full sight of the crowd of Rio tourists?

"Please. Wait," Lieutenant Hinson said, following him. Her heels clicked a staccato beat on the pavement. "I've arranged for a larger transpo to accommodate us and your A.I. companion. It will only take a few minutes to arrive."

From the snide way she said A.I., Zeke knew she thought Forman was his sex toy. Which meant she hadn't done any background on him. That much was good. Zeke pivoted to face her. "What's this about? Where's the admiral? Why all this secrecy?"

She met his gaze with serious, cop like eyes beneath her brimmed uniform cap. "All will be explained."

*****

Zeke followed Hinson down another level into the ship. Seemed like he should be on the bottom of the harbor by now with all these stairs. He was shown into a room with an aquarium, which took up a whole wall. In front of the tank, a knot of people conferred, one of whom he recognized from the PR photos as Admiral Valenkamph.

The admiral's voice boomed cannon-loud across the chamber, swearing about something. Though the man was at least thirty years Zeke's senior, he looked to be fit enough to climb all those stair sets in record time. Everything about the officer screamed toeing the company line, but the grim set of his mouth bespoke something was amiss.

"What can I do for you?" Zeke asked after introductions had been made.

Valenkamph took in Zeke's casual attire and flip-flops with a pained air. He didn't spare a glance at Forman. "I know you're not a fish-guy per se, but my Institute connection said you're the go-to guy for water and for unusual. This qualifies as both."

Zeke's gaze followed the man's hand gesture to the glass wall. In the murky water, a large fish swam. He could barely make out the narrow elongated blue body shape and fanlike dorsal fin. A sailfish? Maybe a fifty-pounder. The fish wobbled past the front of the tank, and Zeke glimpsed the tail.

He did a double take and looked again. The tail looked like it belonged to a big brown grouper. How was that possible that this fish was of two different species? He drifted closer to the tank, Forman on his heels.

"I've never seen anything like this," Zeke said.

The admiral joined him at the tank, his subordinates trailing after him. "My boys pulled this anomaly out of the depths, but they've seen this craziness at sea for the last few weeks. Never caught one until a few days ago. The darn things dissolve into nothing, if you're not careful."

"There are more fish like this?" Zeke asked. Was this a carnival oddity or a genetic modification?

"Yes. The ocean is teeming with odd looking fish, as if a genetics experiment had gone wrong."

"How bizarre. I see two distinct body types on one frame. As a point of evolution, this offshoot would be a dead end. No way could it outcompete either of its parent species. How did this anomaly survive to adulthood? Why didn't it get eaten by something bigger?"

The admiral nodded sagely. "Excellent questions. We're hoping you can answer them."

"Sorry. Without closer examination, all I can offer is speculation. I need a specimen to necropsy in my lab. And the water. I'd like some of the aquarium water to take home with me. In stainless steel containers, please."

"I can't spare this living specimen, but stainless steel? Do you have inside information about this water or the fish?" the admiral barked.

Zeke couldn't reveal his off-planet network of alien advisors, or his hunch about the meteoric origin of the fish. "No, sir, I don't. But we have a similar cloudy water situation in the upper Atlantic as well. Have you made any behavioral observations from the days you've had this thing? Does it eat?"

The general gestured to a short twitchy sailor in an oversize lab coat in the corner. The man's Adam's apple quivered as he stepped forward. "We haven't observed it eating, but the feeder fish we drop in there disappear, and the creature has doubled in size."

Zeke nodded. "That wouldn't explain the dual modalities. Got anything else? DNA sequences? Chromosome typing?"

"We can't catch the darn thing to test it," nervous guy said. "We tried putting a euthanasia agent in the water and it had no effect, even at double strength. Unless we electroshock the water or drain the tank, we can't get our hands on the fish."

The admiral waved the man back. "Our orders are to keep the fish alive, for now. We don't know squat about the critter. That's why I called the Institute. John Demery said you tested the ocean and found off-the-chart turbidity. We have that in spades, and it's highest around these odd fish."

The fish were causing this dirty ocean phenomena? Zeke's curiosity amped into overdrive. Why would an aquatic species change the water profile? He needed to talk to his dolphins. "My analysis of the water didn't reveal a cause for *how* our oceans hold more particles in suspension. The specific gravity didn't change, and the relative ratio of minerals in the water remained constant. There's just more of everything staying in the water column. If this trend continues, we run the risk of shutting down photosynthesis, which will domino through the entire food chain and the water cycle."

Admiral Valenkamph looked askance at his aide.

"Dr. Landry is saying the ocean will die, sir. The brown water will wipe out the blue water," Lieutenant Hinson said.

The admiral shook his head. "We can't have that." He glared at Zeke. "Fix it. Your man said you could figure this out. You can use anything in this ship to get started. I want you on this round the clock. And if it's not here, I'll get it for you."

Zeke shifted uneasily on his feet, torn between leaping feet first into a new scientific challenge and keeping his job. How did one tell an admiral no? "Uh, Admiral Valenkamph, sir, I'm here in Rio to present a keynote speech tomorrow. I've been told the Institute's funding for the near future is dependent on my presentation. As fascinated as I am with this entity, I have a prior obligation tomorrow. I will be at your disposal after the event, though my preference would be to study the fish back at my lab in the States."

The admiral cursed a blue streak. "GD politicians. Nothing but a wolf-pack of misguided do-gooders, brown nosing idjits, and land sharks. If it was up to me, I'd toss those dickbags in the brig."

At least the admiral wasn't mad at him, Zeke thought with relief. He was exceedingly glad he wasn't a politician. The fish in the tank slowed in front of him, then circled around and came back.

"Looks like you've made a friend," Hinson said.

The fish's dull eyes lingered on Zeke. Curious. Why did it single him out? He stepped away from the others. The fish circled again and stopped in front of Zeke a second time.

"You sure you don't know anything about this fish?" Admiral Valenkamph asked. "This one zeroed in on you. It hasn't singled anyone out before, preferring to stay in the back of the tank."

The fish's odd behavior made Zeke uncomfortable. Did it detect his alien ancestry? If so, was the fish extra-terrestrial? Whatever the answers, he needed to examine this fish in the privacy of his lab.

"I've never seen this specimen before, never thought anything like this was remotely possible." Zeke turned from the tank to face the admiral. "What's your proposal for getting this thing to my lab in

67

Georgia?"

"Gonna catch you another one. A baby one. Got my best crew on it right now."

"Just so long as it fits in my private air transpo. We return to the states day after tomorrow."

"Lieutenant Hinson will personally oversee the arrangements."

"Good deal."

Chapter 18

After ascertaining Zeke was sleeping soundly, Forman answered Angie's late night summons by stepping across the hotel corridor and into her open arms. She smelled of woman and desire. For him.

He was lucky this beautiful woman sought him out, even if her interest was merely for sexual release. He hugged and kissed her, but try as he might, Bea's image persisted.

He wasn't betraying Bea by engaging in sexual congress with someone else. She'd kicked him to the curb and screwed up her life. Time for him to move on. He banished the superstar's image and focused on pleasing his current sexual partner.

A quick scan of his memory elicited the techniques Angie preferred. This was their eighth coupling, so he had a solid baseline of performances to draw from.

When he trailed his fingers down her spine and massaged her buttocks, she leaned into him. "Ooh. Yes."

"Like that, do ya?" He kissed her exact pleasure point on her neck, and she tugged him toward her rumpled bed.

"Come here," she said.

"We should go slow," he murmured as she tugged off his palm tree aloha shirt. "We have all night."

"Don't want slow. Want it hard. Fast."

He hesitated. This was Angie. His boss's cousin. "How hard and fast?"

Angie's robe opened to reveal black lacy undies as she straddled him. "Like this."

Playful, then. Forman's Gary entertainment programs clicked into overdrive as he complied with her directives. Her satiated image imprinted in his processors as he concluded his performance. "Like that?"

"I did, pretty boy."

Her face loomed over his. "Thanks. My apologies in advance."

He felt an electronic surge. His circuits frizted.
She'd done something to him.
Again.
Why? Had his lovemaking been substandard?
His thoughts faded to white static.

Chapter 19

Zeke gazed over the crowd of VIPs the next day as he concluded his remarks at the Rio Symposium. His international water crew was there. Dr. Claudia Gruber of Austria and her boyfriend, Dr. Stephan Ivanov of Russia, sat on the right side of the room. Italy's Cosma Rossi and China's Ming Li sat on the left. Great Britain's Gareth Davies sat on the front row, a seat away from Forman. Brazil's bearded leader was there, surrounded by a phalanx of bodyguards. The dapper Jose Rivera-Nieto, president of the Mexican/Central American Alliance sat in the corner of the room, away from the doors.

Men and women from the University were there, along with holy men in their various black, white, or red garb.

An eclectic assortment of participants, until you considered an alien with an android bodyguard was giving the keynote address.

Loud applause followed his closing statement. He'd given this talk to the water people in this room twice before, but they seemed incredibly eager today, as if they hung on his every word, as if he were divining answers from heaven. Fat chance of that.

The moderator, Hugo da Silva, rose on the dais, mike bud prominently displayed on his lapel. "Are there any questions for Dr. Landry?"

"If the water distribution scheme has been agreed upon by the nations of the world, why isn't the drinking water being distributed?" the cleric in red asked.

"Thank you, Bishop Curry," da Silva said as he repeated the question into the microphone for the record.

Zeke raised his hands in a surrender motion. "That's up to the governing authorities. I'm merely a scientist who helped with the plan. Don't shoot the messenger."

Polite laughter ensued.

"You should be more than that," Curry said. "You make sense and cut through all the political wrangling. I say we nominate you for

71

head of the United Nations."

Zeke flashed his palms and quelled the alarm in his gut. "No, thanks. I'm quite comfortable working in my lab. Nothing beats going to work in flip-flops and shorts each day."

A man in the back raised his hand and spoke in a booming theatrical voice. "But, Dr. Landry, your lab is an extension of the U.S. military, is it not? Aren't you their puppet? You're spending tax credits on frivolous projects while people around your country are starving."

Zeke studied the dark haired, intense man in the rear of the room. Forman stirred uneasily in the first row. Angie edged toward the man from her position on the side of the room. Zeke wanted to avoid a disturbance if at all possible.

"I work for the Institute. Not the military," he said in a clear, strong voice. "We're a nonprofit organization, and my field of study is water research. The Institute's mission statement and her findings are all a matter of public record. My research papers are published in scientific, peer-reviewed journals."

"But your *secret* projects. Those aren't," the man persisted. "People say you were the one who stopped the Maleem, that you have superpowers."

How the hell did that information leak into the public sector? Zeke's battle against the invading aliens had indeed been epic. But his part of the fight wasn't public knowledge. He eyed his heckler with shrewd concern. This kind of wild talk was dangerous in the extreme.

Zeke tried an easy grin. "I'm a scientist, and I guarantee you, I put on my pants the same way you do, one leg at a time. No superpowers."

More polite laughter, but an edgy sense of expectation filled the room. People craned around to see if the guy would respond.

The man shouted from his seat, "Don't belittle your efforts to save the world. Let me live on Tama Island with you. I want to be your acolyte."

The bishop's face turned bright red at such heresy. Zeke squirmed in his fancy shoes, not knowing what to say to this delusional devotee. He opted for humor. "I'm not that kind of man, and it's not that kind of island."

Two security guards approached the shouter. "Unhand me," the man yelled. "I rebuke you. Get behind me, Satan."

The entire assemblage turned to witness the scuffle. The man swore and resisted, then went limp after the guards pulsed him. Moments later, he was gone, and Angie stood sentry at the closed double doors.

Da Silva rapped on the podium to gain the crowd's attention. "Sorry for the interruption. Dr. Landry gave us an excellent presentation on the freshwater distribution plan, and the floor is still open for questions and further discussion on the subject matter."

A woman raised her hand, identified herself as the local press. "Is the delay in releasing the drinking water worldwide because of China's new agridome? Will that addition cause the water distribution to be reshuffled?"

Zeke noted Gruber of Austria and Ivanov of Russia exchanged a sour look. They'd wanted that dome for their countries. China's gain had been their loss.

"That's for the politicians to decide." Zeke hoped the reporter didn't press the issue. China's strict policy on birth control was slowly being integrated throughout the free world. Many viewed this award of a dome as a strike against the pro-life movement. "Our worldwide population is growing, so we must produce more food. Water is an integral part of dome operations. However, the water draw for the new dome will not exceed the allotment already set aside for the Chinese. Even with the dome, they will have a net surplus of water."

One of the university students with a bright, clean-scrubbed face raised her hand. "Shouldn't they get less water if they have an excess allotment?"

"The algorithms for distribution are too complex to explain in this brief Q&A session. I'll be glad to meet with you afterwards to discuss those in more detail," Zeke said.

The young woman nodded.

Great Britain's Dr. Gareth Davies cleared his throat, puffed out his knighted chest. "What we all want to know, Dr. Landry, is what's happening with the ocean? Why's the water so brown?"

The silence in the room was absolute.

People leaned forward, silently beseeching him to share the answers. No one here doubted he had answers. His lack of knowledge would be a disappointment.

Zeke took his time answering. "At this point, I don't know any more than the rest of you. History gives us no precedent for this dirty water syndrome. I've run water samples through my lab and have found nothing untoward to justify the heavy sediment load."

"Is this the end times?" a female university student asked. "Will the death of the ocean be as foretold in *Revelations*? A third of it turning to blood and a third of it turning to Wormwood? We've already seen the locusts in the domes. What's next? The four horsemen? Will a great beast arise from the sea?"

Zeke knew enough about Biblical prophecy to know he didn't want to answer this question. "Theology is out of my realm of professional expertise, and I'll pass that question along to the bishop in a moment. However, the recent locust plague was an act of terror by mankind. Bishop Curry? And thoughts regarding the end times?"

The bishop rose to his feet, a portly vision in flame red. "We know not when the bridegroom may come. Each of us should live every day as if it were our last. Carry the Ten Commandments in your hearts and be at peace."

Da Silva said "amen," echoed by other Christians in the room. "Our session is concluded. We'll have a short break before our next speaker…"

Zeke quit listening as the facilitator itemized the schedule for the remainder of the day. He gathered up his things, stowed his presentation in his satchel. Forman stepped up to assist him.

"Close call, boss man," Forman said in a soft voice. "You were nearly outed by the crazy dude."

"Crazy is right. Sounded like he thought I'm the new religion."

"Nothing wrong with worshipping at the Church of Landry. You are indeed a miracle of an answer man."

"Shh. Don't even joke about such a nightmare. We're trying to keep a low profile, remember?"

Zeke shook hands with attendees as they crowded around. Angie stood behind him, Forman to his left, so people came through a receiving line from the right. Bishop Curry held his hand for longer than Zeke was comfortable with. He wanted to yank it back, but the holy man had him in a squeeze grip. Was this a test? Would he pass or fail?

"To him who has been given much, much will be expected," the bishop said.

Zeke recognized the passage as being from one of the gospels. Luke, maybe? "Thank you, Bishop."

"Vaya con Dios," the bishop said as he lumbered away.

Go with God. Not an entity that Zeke spent much time thinking about. He'd attended church with his mother as a boy, but when the island church disbanded, that had been the end of his formal religious education and exposure. He'd yet to reconcile his alien heritage and long distance Taman telepathic communication with his early theology exposure. But if he had to say he believed in something, it was a loving God instead of a vengeful one.

As the crowd thinned, astrophysicist Sidra McIntyre appeared, her nursemaid companion Ronni by her side. Like a blue-haired imp, Sidra waved at him from the back of the room. The security people immediately started toward her.

"It's okay," Zeke called. "Dr. McIntyre is a friend. She is my guest here."

"Darn tootin' I am," Sidra bounced around the strongmen with agility, then hurried over to him. Her neon pink zigzag striped outfit shifted with each movement she made.

Angie hugged her first. "Look at you. I need me a pair of those stylish boots."

"Good to see you, too." Sidra hugged everyone, saving Zeke for last.

He couldn't resist reaching out to her on a telepathic level. *Missed you, little minx. What you been up to?*

Everything and nothing! Can't wait to dish.

The meteor? You have it?

Angie cleared her throat. "English, please."

"Oh, right." Zeke shot a worried glance at the security staff in the room. "Let's adjourn to my suite."

"Good idea," Sidra said. "Can I help carry anything?"

"We've got it." Forman ushered the group toward the door.

Zeke hoped Sidra's jubilation was due to the meteor in her possession. He could feel her revving energy in his mind, and it took extreme willpower to talk about mundane topics in the crowded hallways, the packed elevator, and the hotel corridor. Finally, they reached his room.

"Fill me in," he said, setting his case on the low-boy dresser and turned to the teenaged savant.

"I've never seen anything like this!" she gushed. "It's totally mag."

Chapter 20

Insistent banging on the door awakened Jessie from her afternoon nap. She clutched her robe to her throat and hurried to the front door. Had something happened? Was it Zeke? Dear God. She should have gone to Rio with him.

Baggy's wrinkled face scowled at her. "You all right?"

"Pregnant. That's all," Jessie said. "What's the matter?"

"A child's missing. Mayhree's daughter. Have you seen her?"

"Little Paige?" Jessie sagged against the paneled door. She'd last seen the young girl two days ago. Paige's image appeared in Jessie's head. Spiky blonde pigtails, a gap-toothed smile, and enough raw energy to fire a power plant.

"I haven't seen her. Give me a moment, and I'll get dressed to help search."

Baggy shook his head. "I can't wait. Have to keep spreading the word. The search parties are meeting at the Alliance Hall. I've got to tell everyone. Come when you can."

"Understood."

A sense of purpose filled Jessie, driving the vestiges of morning sickness away. A beloved daughter, missing. Her hand went to her tummy. She couldn't stand it if anything happened to her baby. No mother could.

She had to help.

With the continuing warm spell, jeans and a light jacket would suffice, despite it being early December. She grabbed a water cylinder, an energy bar, and her hat. Then she glanced down at her sneakers. They'd have to search the marsh. For that, she needed her boots. Quickly, she changed shoes, ran outside, and climbed in the red mini-transpo Uncle John had given them for a wedding present.

Sanjee leapt up to sit on the seat beside her. "Stay here," Jessie said. "I don't know how long I'll be gone."

Though she lifted the cat out of the transpo twice, it jumped back in. "Suit yourself," Jessie said, unwilling to spend more time arguing with a stubborn cat. If Sanjee wanted to come home before she did, he could certainly find his way. The island wasn't that big.

The outside benches were crowded at the hall. Jessie parked and hurried over to join a group of women in orange robes. Tension filled the air as Mayhree explained she hadn't seen her daughter since breakfast. Four hours ago.

Island children were given the freedom to roam, but they didn't go far. And this seven-year-old didn't have a tendency to wander. She'd much rather run circles around the other children. Her disappearance was unusual.

"I checked her favorite places outdoors. Called the neighbors. Asked all the kids. The last anyone saw her was three hours ago." Mayhree's worried face streaked with tears.

Jessie wished Zeke were home to ask the dolphins to search for the child in the water. She'd seen Paige swimming not too long ago, her lips blue with chill from the wintertime water temps. Even a good swimmer could have an accident in the water.

Baggy took charge while two islanders comforted Mayhree. "We need to search the island. Every inch of it. Paige likes to climb trees. She likes to hide. She likes to visit with everyone. We know she's not at any of the houses, but we can't rule out any place as she could still be mobile. My plan is to have four section leaders, and folks can join those search teams as they like. Who else wants to be a section leader besides me?"

Three men spoke up before Jessie could get her hand in the air. Baggy nodded. "Aaron, you take the east side of the island. Ty, you take the south side around the Institute. Randell, you've got the west side of the island. I'll take the north. There are a lot more marshes and hammocks on the west side, so Randell needs the most help."

Jessie stood and started toward Randell, but Baggy stopped her. "You would help us the most at the Institute, Mrs. Z. You know the people there and the buildings. That okay with you?"

The chance the child had gone to the research area of the island was unlikely, with so many other enticing places to play. Was Baggy trying to get her out of the way?

Stop thinking the worst of him. He's right. You do know the Institute people best. Jessie summoned a smile. "Sure."

Jessie joined Ty, two young women in island orange, and a senior waiting under a broad oak. A stooped, hatted man somewhere between seventy and infinity, Ty began instructing his team. "We'll check the creeks and marsh around the complex. Traci and Shaundra, you ladies start at the boat landing, Nolen and I will start at the other end and work toward you. Miss Jessie and her kitty will canvass the buildings."

Jessie's cheeks heated. Sanjee was strapping his tail around her ankles, purring loudly. She picked up the cat and cuddled him. "I tried to leave him home, but he insisted on coming. Maybe he thinks he's a scent cat."

When no one laughed at her attempt at a joke, Jessie wanted to crawl back in her four-wheeler and hide in the woods herself. Instead, she stood her ground and waited for a dismissal.

"Everyone's com link active?" Ty asked. When his group nodded, he continued, "Set them to emergency frequency alpha three. Contact me every fifteen minutes while you're searching. If something's afoot, we want to be on top of it."

Traci's turbaned head bobbed. "Something's afoot? Something worse than a missing child?"

"Paige is a healthy, active child. For her to go missing concerns me. I've served in three wars, and one thing I've learned is it pays to be diligent. Let's be smart about what we do, so on the off chance there's more to this, no other losses are sustained. Move out."

Sobered by Ty's militaristic take on the search, Jessie placed Sanjee on the seat beside her, and started for the autobahn, the nickname of the straight road bisecting the island's length. She hadn't cleared the group before Sanjee hissed and puffed up, the fur along the ridge of his spine standing up in a Mohawk.

Sensing a potential for danger, Jessie slowed and scanned the area. She saw nothing out of the ordinary, but Sanjee leapt from the moving transpo and raced off in the opposite direction from where she was headed. "Come back here!" Jessie shouted as she hit the brakes.

Should she get her cat or search her designated area for the missing child? The child had higher priority, of course. Sanjee would turn up sooner or later.

Another transpo halted beside her. Baggy. Gosh, could this get any more awkward? "My cat ran off," Jessie mumbled.

"Did he?" Baggy looked thoughtful. "Which way did he go?"

"Last I saw, he was headed into Randell's section. I'll come back for him after I search my sector."

Baggy stared after Sanjee. "You and I will follow the cat."

"Won't we be duplicating effort?"

"I'm open to the powers of the universe. The cat wanted to come. The cat ran a certain direction when we broke up to search the island. I'm following the cat. Come or don't come, it's up to you."

Jessie contacted Ty via com. "I'll be a few minutes," she said before she clicked off.

Baggy powered ahead of her, turning onto the narrow track that led to the marshiest section of the island. Jessie followed. She marveled at her go-with-the-flow attitude. So unlike her. She'd always been the adult to Bea's child. How the world had changed. Just this once, she'd see if the universe was sending her a message.

As she bounced over the sandy trail past pines dotted with Virginia creeper, clumps of wax myrtle, noisy cabbage palms, and spiky marsh elder, she marveled at her impromptu decision. Growing up, Bea had criticized Jessie for her lack of spontaneity. After they were orphaned, they'd gone through the foster system together, Jessie always protecting her younger sister. That habit stuck through adulthood, with Bea becoming more irresponsible and Jessie locked in parental mode.

Until Zeke.

He'd set her free.

Jessie Stemford had been a certified stick-in-the-mud.

Jessie Landry went with the flow of the universe. She stopped behind Baggy in the salt pan, stood up on her transpo bumper, and studied the tall, dark needle rush and beyond. With the low height of winter-tanned glasswort and saltwort leading to the taller cordgrass bordering the tidal creek, she could see quite some distance.

A flicking white tail at the edge of the cordgrass snagged her gaze. She pointed at the spot and hopped off her transpo. "He's over there."

In the few days Jessie'd had the cat, Sanjee hadn't frequented the tidal part of the marsh, not unless he cleaned all the mud off before he came home. His behavior today was not typical.

"Wait," Baggy said, barring her movement with his outstretched arm. "Let me look first. Just in case."

Jessie's stomach clenched. Just in case the child was over there. Just in case her cat wasn't stalking a rodent. Just in case the universe had dialed her number.

Chapter 21

"My meteor has a dust problem," Sidra said, as she triumphantly whisked the dark blue cover off the locked vault.

"Space is full of dust," Zeke countered as he stood beside her in the rudimentary lab, staring at the opaque container. Sidra's companion hovered near Forman by the door. "Why didn't you store it in a clean containment vessel?"

Sidra bounced with impatience. "I did. I've wiped out the vessel and dusted the space rock several times. The dust comes back no matter what I do."

"Interesting." Donning a glove, he rapped on the outside of the poly-resin box. Not one speck of dust shifted. He itched to get his hands on the dust, but he wouldn't take that risk here. "What did you do with the collected dust?"

"Saved it. Ran some tests. Nothing remarkable in the profile—"

"I need to see that composition profile," Zeke interrupted.

"You will. I'm getting to that." Sidra smirked. "Don't be a cranky pants."

"Give me an idea of the chemical composition."

"Oh, all right." She shot a glance over at her companion, Ronni, who nodded in agreement. "You'll have it on your com in a few tics. Mostly I detected iron, nickel, and cobalt. Some silicates. Oxides of magnesium, aluminum, and calcium. Iron sulfide. Precious metals. Typical stuff. Nothing noteworthy or novel. Rather disappointing, if you want to know the truth. Anyway, I stored the dust in those sample jars."

Zeke peered at the two dozen empty glass containers on a nearby bench top. "And?"

"Isn't it obvious? The dust isn't there anymore."

The hair on the back of Zeke's neck stood on end. No dust of Earthly origin could pass through glass. What kind of space dust was this? "Did someone tamper with the jars?"

Sidra picked up a container with her gloved hand and pointed to the magenta tape with her initials on it. "Seals are still intact. Damnedest thing I ever saw."

A chill shivered down Zeke's spine. He scanned the lab, looking for an accumulation of dust. It had to be here somewhere. "Put the next batch of dust in stainless steel cylinders."

Sidra arched an eyebrow at him. "You know something I don't?"

Zeke was tempted to answer her question in the literal context, but seeing as how that might piss her off and deny him continued access to the space rock, he refrained. "I know less and less each day."

"You're funny." She elbowed him in the side. "I'm not touching this rock again until we have better equipment."

"Whatever you need, I can have it set up on Tama Island by the time we fly back. I need this meteor in my lab."

"I'd love to visit your island again, but I have certain requirements. I planned to cut you off a chunk of meteor, but guess what? I couldn't dent the darn thing. I need something old school, maybe a quantum cascade laser. I don't want to vaporize any gases trapped in the rock."

"Done." Zeke caught Forman's eye. "Anything else?"

"I need a P-4 lab, analysis instrumentation, and unlimited access to Forman and your brain. And maybe your dolphins."

"I can deliver on everything but the dolphins. That's up to them." He studied her for a long moment. "You think this dust profusion is related to the murky seas around the world?"

"Can't prove it, but given the pervasive dustiness of this rock, and the advent of the muddy seas after the meteor storm, I'd say the probability of a positive correlation is high."

Zeke surveyed the drab high school science lab where Sidra had set up shop. She was lucky nothing had happened to her prize.

This place wasn't secure. Too many doors and windows. No stainless steel anywhere.

Zeke turned to Forman. "Will this fit in our rental transpo?"

"Negatory, Doc. We need a larger vehicle and another Brutus A.I. to lift the darn thing. According to Ronni, they used a forklift to get this rock in here."

"What's the weight capacity of our air transpo? Will the rock push us over our weight limit?"

"We'll make it work."

Zeke felt the pressure of time. The sooner he got started analyzing this dust, the better. "I want the vault loaded ASAP. We're headed home tonight."

"Gotcha," Forman said. "I'll locate Angie and inform her of the departure time change. She planned to dine with friends from the meeting today."

Zeke shook his head. "My cousin's personal network amazes me. Tell her I'm sorry. I've got the military and Uncle John breathing down my neck about the meteor problem. We need answers fast, and my lab has the security and equipment options we need to get started."

He turned to Sidra. "Can you leave tonight? We have room for both of you in our private transpo."

Sidra propped a hand on her hip and adopted a vacant look. "Gosh, I'd planned to dance the night away in Rio."

"Sidra," Ronni growled from the doorway. "Play nice."

"You geezers have no sense of humor." She heaved a dramatic sigh. "I'm ready to go now. As long as you promise me a party when we solve this space dust mystery."

Forman danced across the floor, whirled Sidra into his arms. "I like your style, gal."

"No dancing." The words flew out of Zeke's mouth before he thought about them. Forman and Sidra looked taken aback. *I am old. I need to lighten up.* "We can't risk bumping into anything. Make sure those empty sample jars come home with us. I want to run some additional tests on them."

You're not old, Zee, Sidra shot into his head. *You act mature. Is that better?*

Doesn't matter. Next to this teen-aged prodigy, Zeke felt more than twice her actual age. But she was brilliant and a telepath. He needed her on his research team.

"Wheels up in two hours," Zeke said aloud.

"One more thing," Sidra said. "I've named my meteor. Her name is Rio de Dusterno, Dusty for short."

Zeke fought a laugh, then let out a grin and leaned in close to the vault to prove he wasn't a complete fossil. "Dusty, your secrets are not safe with us."

Chapter 22

Baggy waved Jessie forward. Heart thumping all out of sorts, she picked her way across the sloppy marsh footing. In only a few steps, her worst fears met reality.

The girl lay in the mud, one foot twisted at an unnatural angle. The cat feverishly licked the child's muddy face. As Jessie drew nearer, she noted the child was breathing. She stopped to access her com and broadcast across all emergency channels simultaneously.

"We found Paige," Jessie said. "Tell Mayhree she's alive but unconscious. A busted ankle, looks like. Send a stretcher and a med team, stat. We're on the west side, just beyond the walk-out to Blackberry Flats."

Jessie ended the call, squatted, and reached for Sanjee. The cat hissed at her. Jessie drew back in alarm, glanced at Baggy. He nodded and circled around to the other side of little Paige, while Jessie called her cat. "Here, kitty, kitty, kitty. Come on, Sanjee. Let us help Paige."

The cat crouched and licked faster.

As Baggy approached from the creek side, Sanjee hissed and swiped a clawed paw in Baggy's direction.

Stunned by the cat's protective display, Jessie froze. "Keep your distance. He's getting that gunk off her face. He's not hurting her."

"Look at the color, Jess," Baggy whispered from where he'd stopped. "The mud's the wrong color. Yellow, not black or brown. Same color as was climbing up my leg the other day."

Jessie remembered when her cat licked Baggy's pant leg clean. "Yellow mud made Sanjee sick before. Should I stop him?"

"Your cat seems determined to clean the child's face."

"I have to do something." Jessie crawled on her hands and knees through the gloppy mud, which was much darker than the substance on Paige's face.

"Easy," she murmured, gentling her voice for Sanjee. "I want to take a closer look."

The cat eyed her and continued licking.

Jessie took Paige's cold left hand in hers, searched for a pulse. Found a faint one. She cradled the tiny hand in hers. "Paige, can you hear me? Paige? It's Jessie. I'm here with Baggy and my cat. Help is on the way. You had an accident, but you're going to be okay."

Baggy watched from a safe distance, standing in the cordgrass. "Look at how methodical the cat is. He isn't leaving a speck of the mud behind."

"He is being thorough," Jessie said, careful not to make any sudden movements and talking softly. "Why? Won't the mud make him sick again?"

Only a small patch of the light-colored dusty mud remained. Sanjee showed no sign of letting up from his task. Paige still hadn't roused, unusual for a twisted ankle or broken leg type of injury, but she was breathing easier.

The skin the cat laved clean appeared blistered. How odd.

"Jess," Baggy said. "You see yellow mud anywhere in this marsh?"

Jessie looked. "No. All the mud around here is blackish brown. Where'd the yellow mud come from?"

"I don't know."

"What about when you had yellow mud on your shoes and pants? Did you see yellow mud that day?"

"No." Baggy stared off in the cloudless sky as if he were thinking back.

Jessie followed his gaze to where a lone hawk soared in the sky, the bird's dark outline crisp against the deep azure. Not a muscle moved as it sailed over the winding creeks beside Tama Island. To the west, across the sound, she saw the hazy shoreline of the mainland.

"I slogged through several puddles of water near the north end that day. There was flooding from the rain because it was high tide."

"Did the water look different? Was it laden with silt?"

"I didn't notice."

Huh. She needed to tell Zeke about this. He'd know what to do. Too bad he was in Rio. Jessie glanced down at Paige. For the first time, she noticed the same mottled red appearance on Paige's other hand. What if the mud had been on the child's hand and then she'd rubbed her face? The cat found Paige before they did. It might have started the cleanup on her hand.

Jessie nodded at Baggy. "Check out her right hand."

He leaned in. "Red. Like her face. She must have stuck her hand in the mud first."

"My thoughts exactly."

Abruptly, Sanjee lifted his head and streaked toward the woods.

Jessie glanced down at Paige's clean face. Though the skin appeared red, she seemed better. Her respirations were deeper. Jessie gently squeezed the child's left hand. "Paige. It's Jessie. You had an accident. Help is on the way. Hang in there."

In the distance, they heard the unmistakable sound of retching. Baggy's brow furrowed. "Whatever that mud is, it isn't good for anyone. We need to warn people that the yellow mud is bad news. It should be avoided at all costs."

Jessie held his worried gaze. She shared his concern for the residents and for her cat. Sanjee couldn't keep making himself sick. "We need more cats."

Chapter 23

Xstle circled the sky again. In this winged form, he could see forever, and most importantly, his crisp visual acuity provided intel with minimal risk of detection. From the heights, he saw the Ancient kneel beside the juvenile recruit at water's edge.

Worse, her four-legged companion, Sanjee, was reversing the absorption process by licking the *auku* from the biped's hide. He'd never encountered a Sanjee before, but a protector species boded ill for Yar colonization attempts on this planet.

Yar colonized in stealth mode. First, they targeted small aquatic species, then increasingly larger ones as each prime collective grew in mass. A dozen primes had volunteered for this exploration. Traditionally, each prime set up their colony in a different region of the new world to ensure even food distribution.

When territories overlapped due to resource shortages, the weaker prime would terminate to strengthen the remaining collective.

Xstle had no intention of terminating.

He'd claimed this space.

It was his.

He'd slept in the ocean each night, singing the Yar calling song. Not once had another Yar signal crossed his receptors. So why this unannounced incursion? No other prime should be so brazen.

Initially, he'd thought the recruitment was the work of a Drch. A territorial ploy to draw Xstle out before he was ready for battle, but he'd spied the juvenile lying prone in the mud and landed nearby. One whiff of the breeze, and he recognized the scent of the Yar who'd invaded his island.

Kvn.

Young. Reckless. Hothead. Those were a few of Kvn's tags before he became an explorer. Burning with exploration fever, Kvn courted the council until they relented. To get rid of him.

Now the upstart was Xstle's problem.

If Kvn survived the reversal process.

Since Xstle had been through a similar dislodging, he knew how disoriented Kvn felt at being thwarted. And how horrible it felt to be trapped inside a species it couldn't absorb. He shuddered instinctively.

More bipeds arrived at water's edge.

The four-legged protector ran off into the tall grasses, away from the crowd. Xstle circled lazily in the sky, distant, but fully present, with his sharp gaze trained on the small animal. Kvn would be frantic inside the beast because his only means of defense, his *auku,* would not adhere to any surface. Xstle well remembered the terror he'd experienced when it happened to him a few sunrises ago.

Being unable to integrate his hostile environment, would devastate Kvn. The creature's internal caustic fluid would burn into Kvn's collective. Thoughts of termination would summon a backward glance at his lifelong accomplishments. Kvn would chant the warrior's song of death. Light would flash in his thoughts.

Would the biped protector absorb his countryman? Or would Kvn be expelled as Xstle had been?

Xstle watched as Sanjee lay in a pool of sunshine, immobile. The longer Kvn stayed inside Sanjee in the burning solution, the less likely Kvn would survive.

Xstle circled low, away from the bipeds, closing in on Sanjee. The animal glanced skyward, saw him, and jumped awkwardly out of the flight path. Xstle gained altitude, circled to track Sanjee's attempt to escape. It raced toward the tree line, stopping to retch.

Good.

Perhaps Kvn would survive. At least now, free of the animal, Kvn had a chance to recover his strength.

Sanjee heaved several times before scampering off. Xstle surveyed the surrounding area. No movement. The bipeds were gone. The Sanjee had departed. The threat level was low.

He landed beside the moist heap that was Kvn and spoke to him in the old tongue. A shaky Kvn whispered his thanks on the thought plane. Following Xstle's suggestion, Kvn formed into a small fish which Xstle carried to the creek. After dropping his countryman into the salt water for cleansing, Xstle soared to the tide line, stood in the shallows, and changed into a fish. He swam to Kvn, and they both dissembled to their elemental form of dust to ease communication.

This is my territory, Xstle began in mindspeak after greeting protocol was satisfied. *Tell me why I should not absorb you immediately.*

By our laws, you have that right, but I beg you to hear me out. Two Drch are here.

I know of a traitor's presence. But two Drch? That is bad.

Already, Drch have taken out eight of our primes. You, me, Oieg, and Nrz are all that remain.

Xstle sobered. *Four primes are barely enough to start a colony. We must preserve our strength to battle the Drch.*

I heard your calling song and responded, bringing forth my meager collective to your location. The Drch have amassed many of our kind, stealing our future. Those independent Yars are forever lost to us.

Without a large collective of specks to pull from, the number of times a Yar Prime could change shape was limited. Xstle bristled at the unexpected constraint. *We need those Yars.*

You won't get them. Oieg and I made the choice to find you and Nrz. I answered your call song. We should unite. Only strength will defeat a Drch at this point. We both know each of the Drch easily has the strength of two primes, maybe more. Individually, a single prime cannot vanquish them.

Agreed. Xstle paused. *Why did you attempt to recruit the immature biped in your weakened state?*

The youth was playing in the puddle where I rested. Her size would fuel me for many moons. I coated her hand and was on track to absorb her. Another hour more and she would've been mine. Instead, I nearly lost my life. What was that furred creature?

The four-legged one is called Sanjee. It belongs to an Ancient.

No. The shock in Kvn's thoughts cut deep. *An Ancient, here? How is that possible?*

It is possible, and I am staying close to the honored one. The Drch must not be allowed to find the Ancient before we align with such a prize. It is imperative we defeat Drch.

An Ancient. I can't believe it. Of all the duties, protecting an Ancient is the highest honor a Yar can ever achieve. I claim the honor.

You claim nothing. Xstle fought to control his emotions. All he'd worked for during his distinguished career. All he'd accomplished came down to this instant. He would not yield. *I found the venerable one. It is my duty to protect her.*

I would fight you for the honor, but you already surpass me in followers. Your complement of Yars is three times what I amassed.

Kvn would yield to him. Thank Yars. He tried to lessen the blow to Kvn's ego. *I was fortunate. Many Yars answered my initial call, and I fed at will in these fertile waters. I have mastery of water and air. As for the third element, land, my accomplishments are minimal. I must continue to recruit living material from the earth.*

He paused. *I also tried to absorb a biped, with the same null result. The protector removed me. Like you, I nearly died. Fortunately, I had access to a flier shape, which allowed me to escape and regenerate in the sea.*

We need to stop the Sanjee.

Tempting, but until the Drch are dispatched, the Ancient will need multiple protectors. Our mission goal has shifted. The Sanjee stays to protect the Ancient until we are also masters of the land. Then the creature can be terminated.

Merging our collectives will give you a full complement. You must not call others or risk discovery until you are reborn into your ultimate form.

Kvn would sacrifice his life for the cause? The thought of losing a colleague saddened Xstle, even as he keenly anticipated the influx of more Yar independents to his assemblage. *Agreed.*

You will honor my memories?

I will.

Then I accept. Kvn began his song of death. Xstle felt his sadness, but it had to be this way. The familiar, melancholy notes washed over him. So many had sacrificed for Yars to travel this far from home. Xstle would honor their memories and preserve the old ways.

He knew his enemy, knew him well.

They had clashed before.

This time Xstle would triumph.

As Kvn's life faded, his Yar components dissociated and surrounded Xstle. He welcomed them with effusive praise. Much strengthened, he melded into a large fish and darted through the warm coastal waters.

Behind Xstle's island base, the air breathers swam and surfaced, feeding on small fish. Xstle much admired the air breathers and wanted to assimilate one. Dolphins, the bipeds called them. When he'd tried to get close to the dolphins before, they'd scattered too fast for him to start the absorption process.

The small one was the slowest. That juvenile also strayed the farthest from the group. Emboldened by his new plan, Xstle changed into the shape of a feeder fish and waited for his opportunity. The air breather's mass would provide needed nourishment for his new recruits. It would bring Xstle ever closer to his full strength and the restoration of his powers.

First, he had to acquire an air breather in the sea.

Then a small biped on the land.

With mastery of sea, land, and air creatures, Xstle would be unstoppable. By all that was holy, he would triumph over the traitorous Drch or die trying.

Chapter 24

Zeke tried to reach Jessie when they changed craft in Atlanta. She didn't answer her com link. Odd. He'd tried to reach her twice en route with the same result. Where was she and why wasn't she answering the phone?

"Problems in paradise?" Sidra asked, standing and yawning on the busy tarmac.

Zeke glared at his wrist com unit. "No problem. I wanted to tell Jessie I'd be home a day early. I can't reach her."

"What about Forman? Can he access the cams in your home and office from here?"

"I don't wish to invade her privacy."

"Don't look in the bathroom then. Check the rest of the house. She might be listening to music. You want to make sure she's safe, right?"

"No cams in the bathroom anyway." He nodded to Forman. "Do you see her?"

"The house appears to be empty. Wait while I check the lab." He manipulated the com screen. "It too is empty."

"She's not home," Zeke said.

"She must be out having fun with islanders. No worries," Sidra said.

"She should answer her wrist com." He'd missed Jessie during this trip to Rio, but until this moment, he hadn't doubted her welcome when he returned. Her absence from the house and her lack of communication availability made him uneasy.

Something wasn't right.

"We'll be there in an hour. Relax," Sidra said. "What can happen in an hour?"

*****

As the chopper lifted off from the Institute helipad, Zeke left Forman and Sidra to transport the meteor and water samples to the lab. The

Navy hadn't come through with another mutated fish before their journey, so that would be delivered later. He jogged the mile home, needing the exercise to work out the knots in his travel-weary body. The uneasy feeling in his gut intensified. Something was different here. The island's atmosphere felt tense. Coiled, as if in preparation for an approaching disaster.

He expanded his thoughts. Caught the faint pulse of Sidra's thoughts. Couldn't reach the dolphins. Couldn't reach Jessie.

He picked up the pace, running full speed up the steps to the home he and Jessie shared. "Jessie? I'm home."

"Zeke?" His wife emerged from the bathroom. Her face a pale moon-white, her right hand cherry red.

"I missed you so much." He swept her in his arms and twirled a tight circle. The gnawing anxiety in his gut didn't subside. "Thank goodness you're okay. I was worried when you didn't answer my com page."

"Oh. I took my com off earlier. I've been trying to get my hand clean and didn't want to splash water on my personal com."

"Your hand?" he asked. He tipped her chin up and drowned in her adoring gaze. Times like this he couldn't believe he'd found a mate or how protective he felt about Jessie. "What's with the hand, love?"

She held out her arm. "I thought I could get this mud off, but it's stuck fast. I need Sanjee to lick it off but he's nowhere to be found."

Her voice thinned as she spoke. Zeke took a long look at the dark areas of her reddened hand. When he went to lightly rub a dirty area, she pulled away from him. "Don't touch it. This ick spreads by touch."

"Where'd it come from?" Anger surged. He wanted to pound something. Why'd he leave Jessie even for a minute? Nothing could happen to Jessie. Or his son. He wrestled with his emotions, feeling so out of kilter he couldn't quite pull it together.

"Paige."

"Mayhree's daughter? How?"

"While you were gone, Paige went missing for several hours. We found her unconscious in the marsh, with this yellow mud on her face and her right hand. I didn't touch her face, but there must have been some residual mud on her left hand where I touched her."

A child. In danger on his island. Unthinkable. "Is Paige okay?

What happened?"

"Reports from the hospital indicate she's recovering. She's weak and doesn't remember anything, though."

"I'd like to know where she came in contact with the yellow mud. We need to make sure no one else gets contaminated."

Jessie waved her reddened hand in the air. "Too late. I already did."

"Wait. You said something about your cat. How does your new pet fit into this?"

"Twice now Sanjee has removed the yellow mud from people. Once from Baggy and now from Paige. I didn't want him to lick Paige clean because the mud makes the cat sick, but Baggy convinced me the cat's actions were necessary. At the time, I doubted Sanjee did anything that anyone else couldn't do, but now I can't get this stuff off my hand."

Zeke took a deep considering breath. "Must be something in the cat's saliva. Where is the cat?"

"I haven't seen Sanjee since he cleaned the child's face. There was a lot more mud on her than on Baggy. The cat's somewhere trying to recover from the retching. I'm sure he threw it all up again."

Zeke's head ached at the lack of data. He wanted more intel on the child. He wanted to know about Baggy's experience with the yellow mud. He needed a sample of the mud for the lab. And he must take care of Jessie. She was his top priority.

He couldn't divert Forman because those meteor samples had to be properly stored. "Where's Baggy? Why didn't anyone let me know about this incident with Paige?"

She shrugged. "Wasn't much you could do about it from South America, and everything happened today. Baggy's gone off-island to the hospital with Mayhree. He feels responsible for the child's accident since he didn't sound the alarm when he first came in contact with the creeping crud."

"I need to talk to him."

"Fine, but do it while we search for the cat. Not only does this mud burn and sting, I don't have much feeling in my hand now, and I can barely move my fingers."

"Come on. Let's take the four-wheeler." He guided her toward the door. "We can cover more ground that way." Understanding dawned. If she couldn't work her fingers of her right hand, no wonder she didn't answer when he buzzed her.

She balked. "What am I thinking? You must be exhausted from your trip. At least grab a tube of water and a power bar before we head out. How was your trip? Did you get a meteorite? Is Sidra here?"

He hesitated. "I'm good food-wise. Should we take something along for you?"

"Yes. I feel better if I eat every two hours, and who knows how long it will take to find the cat."

Zeke hurried to the kitchen, dumped the whole case of water and a dozen power bars into an insulated tote, and returned to Jessie near the door. She nodded and allowed herself to be swept along to the transpo. Zeke fired it up and began calling the cat.

"Not like that," Jessie said. "He'll think you're mad at him. Say 'here, kitty, kitty' in a soft voice."

"I am mad at the cat. Why isn't he here?"

"I'm sure he's resting. Probably curled up somewhere between here and the walkout to Blackberry Flats."

Zeke headed straight to the marsh side of the island.

"Hole!" Jessie said, bracing on the seat.

The transpo bucked as it plowed through the hole in the rutted lane. Zeke's bottom lifted off the seat. *Uh-oh.* He let off the throttle. "Sorry. I wasn't thinking about your condition. I was hurrying to find the cat."

"Won't be any need to find the cat if you hit another bump like that. I nearly went through the roof."

Zeke sucked air through his teeth. "I'm sorry. I can't say that enough. I barely know how to be married, much less an expectant father. All I can think about is finding that cat for you. I'm killing you with my good intentions."

"No one is dying today. I won't allow it," Jessie said. "We're finding Sanjee, and we're getting my hand cleaned. Then we're going to have a normal dinner, and I'm going to welcome you home as a proper wife should."

He ruffled her hair. "I like the sound of that, but make no mistake, your health is my chief concern." He powered the transpo and moved at a more sedate pace, calling the fluffy white cat as she'd instructed. They drove out to Blackberry Flats, and all the way back home. No cat.

Jessie's face was drawn with pain. Shadows lengthened across the road.

Zeke needed help. He pinged Angie on the com. She appeared almost instantly. "I've got a cat emergency. We can't find Sanjee anywhere. It's imperative I locate him immediately."

"You heard about Paige?" Angie asked.

"Just now. The cat. Have you seen him?"

Angie stepped back from the com to reveal a frazzled cat in her arms. In the background, he noted the speckled blue cabinets of her kitchen. "I've got him. He needs TLC after the incident today."

"Hang onto him. We'll be right there. I repeat. Don't let that cat out of your sight. Jessie's life may be in danger."

Angie's eyes went wide. "Jessie?"

"The mud on Paige transferred to Jessie. We're coming to you. I repeat. Don't let the cat out of your sight."

Chapter 25

When the samples and the meteorite were safely sealed in the containment lab, Forman realized he hadn't heard anything from Zeke. Probably making love to his wife, the android thought. *Lucky dog.*

Between accessing the house cams to verify Zeke's whereabouts and comparing the data Sidra collected with Zeke's prior sampling efforts, Forman nearly missed the fact Sidra was suiting up for the containment lab.

He exchanged a worried glance with her nursemaid Ronnie. "Whoa. Should you be doing that, Dr. McIntyre?"

"I don't know if I should or not, but I'm doing it. Something's changed. Look at Dusty."

Forman followed her hand gesture. After they'd used heavy equipment to convey the shipping crate in the lab, he'd powered the lift outside for pickup. No sense in tripping over excess equipment in the lab. Meanwhile, Sidra had programmed the crate to auto-open after they exited the air lock. From this external vantage point, the plastech container with the meteorite was crystal clear, the space rock, a shiny burnished mahogany. He shook his head and stared again. "What the flerk is going on?"

"I don't know, but I'm going to find out. I want to double-check that tamper seal. What if someone in Rio accessed the shipping crate and stole my dust?"

Forman considered the possibilities. Rejected them. "Impossible."

"Nothing's impossible. Besides, the evidence is staring us in the face. The dust was there before the trip. Now it isn't."

"Doesn't mean it's missing. Maybe changing altitudes did something to the rock. All that dust couldn't have stayed on Dusty's exterior on her journey through space. It would have been lost forever. Perhaps the unpressurized compartment on the transpo triggered a physicochemical response of sorption once we attainted a certain altitude."

"Or perhaps Dusty is alive. In which case, I want to be the first to make contact."

He trailed after her to the air lock. "How can dust be alive?"

"Seems to be alive in my house," the teenaged astrophysicist quipped. "It accumulates by the walls and then starts rolling around. Dust bunnies. Surely you've heard of them."

Forman scowled at her poor humor. "Dr. Landry should be here."

"You know as well as I do that Lover Boy needs private time with Jessie." Sidra elbowed him. "Are they doing it yet?"

A thousand snarky retorts rolled through Forman's thoughts. He rose above them all. "I haven't checked."

"Exactly. Look. I love Zee like a brother, and he is smart and super talented with the telepathy stuff. But my world doesn't revolve around him. The meteor is mine to study, and it's in the appropriate facility to maximize my physical safety. Stop nagging me about what I should and shouldn't do. I'm busy making the greatest discovery ever. First contact with a new species."

Forman analyzed the probabilities. Other than physically restraining the visiting scientist, the best he could do here was damage control. For that, he needed to accompany Sidra into the containment lab. If he went in without a special suit, he could risk contaminating his housing. A dumb move, since his dual mission was to assist and protect Zeke Landry.

He suited up.

"Watch her," Ronni said.

"I will. Say, if you're tired from the trip, go ahead to your quarters."

"I'll stay a little longer. For Sidra. This is a big moment for her."

Forman shrugged. "Your call."

He heard the crackling sound through the com link when Sidra stepped on something in the next room. "Damn. A roach," she said.

No matter how many times the lab was sprayed for insects, those things continuously appeared. The joys of island living.

Though he didn't need air to breathe, the breathing apparatus for the suit served to maintain positive air pressure and to keep potentially tainted air from entering the protective gear. He hated the loss of tactile sensation in the double gloves of the suit, but he understood the need for protection.

He nodded to Sidra's companion, Ronni, who had been watching mutely all this time. Ronni was the quietest, most low-key person he'd ever met. She'd perfected the art of fading into the woodwork, which worried him. As long as he could remember, he'd wanted to be human. To be human and act like a machine as Ronni did was such a waste.

Machines were disposable in the eyes of humans.

Ronni didn't value her humanity.

He'd have that conversation with her another time. He hurried through the airlock, following all the sequential procedures to contain contamination.

Zeke's not going to be happy about this. He wanted to be here when the meteor vault was unsealed. Forman switched into full record mode. That way, Zeke could view the entire process whenever he liked.

With duty on his mind, Forman accessed the nearest wall com to scan the security cams secreted in Zeke's house. No one was at home. Hmm. He pulsed Zee's wrist com for a physical location. On the island. Near Angie's. Not sure what that was about but Zeke was in good hands with Angie. Zeke's cousin was a fierce warrior.

"Where did the dust go?" Sidra asked after she'd circled the plastech vault. "The containment seals are intact."

"Could someone have resealed them?"

"No. These are the symbols I personally drew in the sealant."

"The container isn't stainless steel," Forman observed.

"It's a standard plastech shipping container. Big whoop."

"Zeke's been adamant about using stainless steel containers for the sludgy ocean water."

"Get real. I can't wave a wand and make this one stainless. There's no visible dust in the container."

"Visible dust. Yes. That's a good tangent."

"What?"

"Maybe the dust is currently invisible."

"Boy, we could make a fortune if we learned how to make dust invisible. But I bet the housecleaning lobby would put out a hit on us."

Forman dug a UV light out of a drawer and energized it. "Room lights off."

"Cool." Sidra's white coveralls glowed. She laughed, and her teeth glowed as well.

Forman waved the light over the meteor containment box. "What a bunch of nothing."

"Lemme hold it." Sidra grabbed the instrument from his hand and waved it over the box, over herself, over Forman. "Disappointing scientifically, but fun in a creative way." She danced around the room, shining the light source on various machines, counters, walls, and doors.

Forman tracked her progression, amused at her youthful ebullience. Would it be maddening or fun to work full time with Sidra? "You're like a firefly, the way you wave that instrument all over the room."

"A remnant of the dust should be here. Why can't we see even a speck of it? Nothing in our universe goes invisible at will."

Forman considered her statement a challenge. His circuits hummed with activity. "Technically, your statement is false. Several magicians claim to achieve invisibility in their acts."

"The subsets between science and magic are few and far between. Wait a minute. Look at that."

A barely luminous spot appeared on the floor. Nearby another spot briefly appeared then vanished.

"What do you make of this, Forman the doorman?" Sidra asked.

"Something was here. Outside the box. I'll be damned."

Sidra picked up one foot then the other. A spot on her right foot glowed. "The spot on the floor came from me. I stepped on something."

"You stepped on something when you entered the area. Lights on 100 percent." The lab brightened. "Where's that cockroach?"

"Brilliant connection."

The roach couldn't be found. Not even an antennae or a stray leg. Not even a bug gut smear.

"Cruff," Forman said. "This is wrong."

"Whatever entered our atmosphere with the meteorite had to travel inside the meteor or it wouldn't have survived," Sidra said in an unsteady voice. "Science tells us that. We've seen the dust entity as a solid, and I'll wager a month of ice cream this thing was a gas on the space journey here. It might be a gas again. It might be in the lab with us. And if it can go through solid plastech, it can go through these flimsy suits."

Forman inched to the wall com port. Human safety was at risk. Time to summon reinforcements. "I'm calling the boss."

Chapter 26

"You don't have to hold me in your lap," Jessie said. "You're making the cat nervous."

"Oh, but I do need to hold you. And Sanjee better get used to me being around." Zeke smoothed her hair back from her face. "You're my wife."

Jessie thought it was cute the way his voice choked up over the word wife, as if it were difficult for him to say. She was definitely his wife. Thanks to Sanjee, the yellow mud was nearly gone from her hand.

She twittered nervously as the cat's tongue laved between her fingers. The urge to jerk her hand away hammered through her thoughts. No, I need to do this, she reasoned.

We're not moving until the cat removes every last bit of the adhesive substance, Zeke said.

Zeke? How'd you do that? Jessie met his level gaze. *Is this another of your Guardian moments?*

I'm not such a good Guardian if you got hurt on my island. Humor me, and the cat, and let's get this stuff off you.

I can't usually hear your thoughts. She searched his face. *Are the Maleem coming back?*

No people-eating aliens in spaceships are anywhere near our planet. Rest assured, this isn't the work of the Maleem. Whatever this light-colored mud is, though, I will isolate and identify it. Then we'll make sure it never bothers you or anyone else ever again.

You're scaring me. Is this an invasion? Wait. You said there were no spaceships. How'd this stuff get here?

I'm working on the transport mechanism now. The samples from Rio will help me better understand what's going on.

"Y'all are doing it again," Angie said. "Talking in your private language and shutting the world out."

"Sorry," Jessie mumbled, both guilty and annoyed her private conversation with Zeke had been interrupted. "We didn't mean to exclude you."

"I wish I could save a sample of this stuff to study," Zeke said. "But I didn't think to bring any containers with me."

"If the past repeats itself, Sanjee will vomit this stuff out," Jessie said. "You could collect it then."

"I could loan you a jar or a tube," Angie said.

"I need stainless steel," Zeke said. "Doubt you have any of that lying around."

Angie's face lit up. "You'd be wrong. Godja's old soup pot is stainless. I haven't used it in years, but it's in the back. Let me get it."

Privacy. At last.

Zeke's breath feathered her neck before he kissed her. "I missed you."

Jessie shivered at his touch, her aches and pains sliding away. "I missed you too."

"We need… I need…You. I need you, Jessie. I can't stand to think of anything happening to you."

"Okay, people," Angie said. "Remember you're sitting on my front porch. Anyone could walk by here and get an eyeful of you two getting frisky. I came out here to tell you I found my pot."

Jessie turned to face Zeke's cousin, not feeling the least bit sheepish at making out with her husband. "Thank you for that reminder. I didn't get a chance to welcome Zeke home before we hustled over here to find the cat."

Angie placed the pot in an empty rocking chair and stood with her arms crossed. "How's the hand?"

Jessie glanced down at where her hand rested on Zeke's arm. The yellow stain was gone, and the redness seemed to be fading. "Getting there." She looked around the porch. "Where's Sanjee?"

Zeke unfolded from beneath her and placed her in the chair. "I need that cat."

Angie chuckled. "Cats have minds of their own. Sanjee's been through a lot today. And nobody likes to throw up in public."

From the rear of the house came the unmistakable sound of retching. Zeke grabbed the pot and scampered away. "Music to my ears."

"I'm going to remind him he said that," Jessie said. "Lord, I'm tired of throwing up. I'm ready to move to the next phase of pregnancy, whatever that is."

"The waddle? The back ache?" Angie asked.

"I was thinking more of the flutter of life within."

"Zeke's son will be strong, not to worry."

"My daughter will be strong."

"Don't get your hopes up. Guardians have sons. It's their way."

"Zeke's not your typical Guardian, from what I've learned. I'm hoping we'll create our own traditions."

Zeke leapt back on the porch with an almost feline grace, pot raised in triumph. "Got it. Ready to go?"

Jessie rose with a smile. "One cat barf for the road."

Angie hugged them goodbye. "See you two tomorrow. Y'all take it easy."

Zeke sat the pot on the transpo seat between them. "Make sure that doesn't turn over. We'll drop it at the lab on our way home."

She held the pot as he fired up the transpo and departed at a leisurely pace. "If you'd asked me yesterday if today I'd be holding an old dented pot of cat barf in a transpo, I'd have denied it could ever happen. But that's what I love about living here. Every day is different, a shiny new adventure."

"I'm glad your part of the adventure is over. Stay away from the mud, okay?"

"Believe me, I won't touch anyone with mud ever again. I've learned my lesson. But what about you? How will we keep you safe from it?"

"I'll take precautions. My son needs his father around as he grows up so that I can teach him the ways of the island."

"Your daughter will take ballet and piano lessons."

His lips twitched. "We'll see."

"Baggy came by the other day and offered us your old crib for the nursery. That okay with you?"

"Sounds great, assuming it meets the current safety standards."

"I'll make sure it does, and I've decided on a dolphin theme for the baby's room."

He smiled. "Progress."

The trees overhead opened up to clear blue sky. Off in the distance, a hawk soared on a thermal, lazily flying in wide circles, as if it were a normal ordinary day. Speaking of normal, she hadn't asked Zeke about his travels. "How'd you do on your trip? Did you feel okay?"

"The travel discomfort is minor compared to what it used to be. It's hardly worth mentioning." He stopped the vehicle on the path and dug in his pocket. "Oh! I nearly forgot. I brought you something."

Jessie accepted the stylish box with wonder. Nerves set in. Was there jewelry inside? Her heart fluttered. Jewelry was a luxury she'd denied herself. Not that she'd needed jewelry. Bea had tons of the stuff, and she'd let Jessie borrow anytime she wanted. Jewelry of her own. How novel.

How exciting. "For me? But I didn't get you anything."

"I'm dense about many social customs, but I hope I got this right. Open it."

With fumbling fingers, she raised the lid. A necklace. A beautiful necklace. Tears misted her eyes. "It's stunning."

His eyes searched her face. "That's good, right?"

"Yes. It's more than good. It's fantastic. Thank you. Will you help me put it on?"

"Sure." His fingers were whisper light on her neck as he cinched the clasp. He cleared his throat. "It looks beautiful on you."

She leaned over the pot to kiss him. "If it weren't for the cat barf, I'd have my way with you right here, right now."

He grinned and powered the transpo. "I'll hold you to that, later, Mrs. Landry."

Her fingers caressed the smooth stones of her gift. "Tell me more about your trip."

"I got Sidra and the meteorite, but the mutant fish from the Navy didn't materialize."

"Mutant fish? First I've heard of that. How's it mutant? Two heads?"

"Nope. Two species glommed together in an impossible manner. The Navy's seeing these oddities all over the deep. They want me to study one. I didn't mention it when I called because our coms weren't secure. The Navy's keeping this finding hush-hush."

His com buzzed. Zeke answered it. "Forman, you still at the lab?"

Forman's voice boomed through the com. "I am. We have a situation."

"I'll be there in five minutes. What's happening?"

"Dusty's gone."

"Someone stole the meteorite?"

"The meteorite is here. The dust is missing. All of it. We hope it's in the lab. If not, it's loose on the island."

Zeke let up on the throttle, glanced at Jessie. "Give me a few minutes. I need to take Jessie home first."

"Jessie's coming with you," Jessie said. She'd had enough of being left behind. "I'm an expert on dust and mud."

"I need for you to stay safe," Zeke countered.

"I need to help. Don't shut me out of your work. I want to be part of your entire life."

He didn't respond to her, just went quiet. She couldn't hear his thoughts either.

Zeke spoke into the com. "Where are you and Sidra?"

"Still in the containment lab. Ronni's outside. Should I send her home?"

"If Sidra can't leave, Ronni won't go." Zeke glanced at Jessie then back to the com link. "We'll be right there."

Chapter 27

Urgency rode on Zeke's shoulders pushing him way past his comfort zone. Gritting his teeth, he slammed the throttle to the max. The transpo surged forward. "Hold on."

Jessie grabbed hold of a side rail and clung to the barf pot. "Will do."

Events were happening at a breakneck pace. Zeke had barely recovered from Jessie's contamination by an unknown entity when Forman called about the missing meteorite dust. He still needed to figure out what was happening in the ocean. To make matters worse, the Navy was sending a mutant fish for him to analyze any day now.

What happened to the good old days of solving one problem at a time? Is this chaos what being a Guardian was all about? Multitasking? If so, it sucked. How could he work so many problems at once?

Bottom line, he needed to talk to the Tamans. Now that he had more information about the dust in the water, surely they could provide information about its origin and what it wanted with Earth.

His dolphin friends – he hadn't thought of them in days. How were they faring in the thickened sea? He needed to check in with them.

First things first.

The roofline of the Institute came into view, then the tabby-faced buildings loomed large. Those thick walls of oyster shell, lime, and sand had withstood a hundred years of human habitation. Would they handle a dust infestation?

Especially when the dust was extraterrestrial.

He parked beside Sidra's transpo at his lab, a smaller, modern building on the near side of the complex. The lab's out-of-the-way location had drawn him to select this building as his domain. Now he was darned glad for the privacy.

"I don't know what we're dealing with here, so please be careful,"

Zeke said as he held the door open for Jessie.

"Understood. I will be on the lookout for any and all dust particles."

He slid the pot of cat barf into a fume hood, sealed the lid with a double frosting of lab gunk, and headed for the containment lab. He scanned the floors, walls, and ceilings. "I'm not seeing any dust," he said. "You?"

"No light brown dust. No golden adhesive crud. Only the common everyday dust that's everywhere. What's this lab coming to with dust problems? A month ago you were solving the problems of the free world, and now we're on a housekeeping misadventure."

"Not funny." He rounded the corner and there stood Sidra's nursemaid and companion, Ronni, wringing her arthritic hands. Tall and willowy, the older woman seemed paler and frailer than usual. "You okay?"

"I'm exhausted from the flight, but I can't leave Sidra," the nursemaid said, her eyes downcast. "She's in danger in that lab."

The woman couldn't stand still. A memory surged from the depths of his mind. When little kids moved like that, his mom had called it the pee-pee dance. Sympathy swelled. And Zeke more than understood travel sickness. "If you wish to return to your quarters, I'll see Sidra home safely."

"You sure?"

"Absolutely."

Ronni exhaled heavily. "Thanks. I'm not as young as I used to be." With that, she toddled off, leaving Zeke and Jessie alone outside the containment lab.

"What now?" Jessie asked.

"We gather data." He opened the locker and pulled out two full-air suits.

Jessie accepted the one he handed her. "Data? Sidra is a human being, and Forman is your wingman, uh, wing-robot. They aren't science experiments."

We're all science experiments. He muffled the even more incorrect thought, managed a wry smile, and suited up. "Poor word choice, but my meaning is the same. To postulate how the dust moved and where it went, we have to know as many specifics as possible." He shot her another pleading look. "You're welcome to search outside the containment facility. If the dust is truly mobile, it might be out here."

Jessie sealed her suit. "We stay together. There's strength in numbers."

She had a point. It took many to defeat the Maleem a little over a month ago. Whatever this threat was they'd face it together.

"Finally!" Sidra ran to Zeke and threw herself in his arms. "I knew you'd come and save me."

Zeke glanced over the top of the blue-haired prodigy at his wife's narrowing eyes. Not a good sign for marital harmony. He disentangled himself from the teen. "Go through what happened step by step. Don't leave out anything, no matter how insignificant."

Sidra bounced around, gesturing wildly with her gloved hands. "We don't know what happened. I used the automated instructions for removing the crate inside the lab. Once the crate opened, the dust was gone."

"Forman?"

His robot stood taller. "I recorded our movements so the entire timeline is available for your review. However, nothing on the record shows moving dust. It was on the rock in Rio, but the dust wasn't on the rock a few moments ago."

Zeke walked over to the clear vault, examining the intact seal. The rock inside the box had a smooth, shiny surface. Not a speck of dust remained. Could it have resorbed into the meteor? Did it bleed through the plastech? If the dust was in the lab, had it changed phase? How would he even know what to look for? The containment lab appeared spotless. Everything was tidy and in place, except for the UV scanner on the lab bench.

He mulled the problem out loud. "We know the dust wasn't physically removed before or during the flight because it was visible when the vault was crated and secured on flight. Was the crate left unattended at the dock?"

Sidra rapped her gloved fist on the vault. "The crate was in eyesight until we placed it in the containment lab. Then we stepped outside to suit up."

"We can rule out theft. How much time elapsed between when the rock was put in the lab and the crate opened?"

"Seventeen point three six nine eight minutes, Dr. Zee," Forman said.

Not much time, but if the dust was sentient, it might move quickly. The Tamans had hinted the meteor threat might contain dust that passed through most substances. Looked like that was exactly what they had on hand. Or used to have.

"Tell me about the UV lamp," Zeke said.

Sidra darted over to the instrument. "Forman had the idea to try an alternate light source, in case the dust fluoresced. But the only thing we saw light up was a trace of the remains of the bug I squashed."

"What bug?" Jessie asked. "First I've heard about a bug."

"A roach. I stepped on it, but all we found were traces of bug guts."

"Show me," Zeke said.

"Hit the lights, Forman." Sidra picked up the UV source, moved to the center of the room, and powered it up. As the overhead lights faded, a purple glow filled the room. "I stepped on the bug here. We both heard it crunch, but not even a trace remains. We saw the smudge on the bootie part of my suit at first, but it's gone now."

Sure enough, nothing fluoresced or popped. "May I see that?" Zeke ran the light over Forman and Sidra and then all around the lab. Nothing. "Lights one hundred percent."

"Where is it?" Sidra asked, her voice breaking as the lights brightened to full intensity. "Is it inside me? Is it on my skin?"

"You would feel it," Jessie said. "I had adhesive mud on my hand today. It burned like acid, and I couldn't get it off no matter how hard I scrubbed. Is your skin burning?"

Sidra shook her head rapidly. "No."

Jessie patted her shoulder. "You're okay then."

"As long as mud and dust are the same problem," Zeke added. "Let's head back to the other side and our street clothes."

"How many kinds of invading dust are there?" Forman asked.

The four of them stepped into the decontamination suite where lights and sprays deconned the outside of their suits. With the com links, they were still able to converse during the safety procedure.

"Now we're asking the right questions," Zeke said. "The water appears to be thick, but not from dust, from an increased natural sediment load. The child's incident and Jessie's brush with the wet dust stemmed from incidental contact. We have two entities here, at a minimum."

"What happened to your dust?" Sidra asked Jessie.

"The cat ate it."

Sidra burst out laughing. "No, really. Tell me."

"I couldn't wash it off, but Sanjee licked my hand clean."

Sidra dumped her used air suit in the sanitizing bin. "I need to examine this cat."

"No one's examining my pet," Jessie said. "There will be no necropsies, no anything. Sanjee is a hero. He saved me and Paige and Baggy too."

"I'll take a teeny sample. He won't notice," Sidra said.

"He will notice, and so will I. The answer's a big fat no. Nobody touches my cat."

"We don't need the cat," Zeke interrupted as the women's voices turned shrill. "We have the contents from his stomach after he cleansed the dust."

Sidra huffed out a blast of air as they exited the air lock. "Why didn't you say so?"

"The mud on my hand wasn't from your meteor," Jessie continued. "Does that mean we have lots of moving dust on this planet? We saw hundreds of meteors in our section of the sky. Multiply that times the entire planet for several days and the number of hitchhikers is truly scary."

"Meteoric?" Sidra quipped.

"Not funny," Jessie said.

Sidra laughed, her bright blue hair a shocking contrast in the austere facility. "Bring on the cat puke."

Zeke thrust out a palm. "Not tonight. I'm going home with Jessie, and you're taking care of Ronni's travel sickness. We'll reconvene here first thing in the morning."

"Do I get my own lab key?" Sidra asked.

"You do not. We will work the problem together. Tomorrow." He nodded at Forman. "A word."

After sending the women outside, Zeke spoke to Forman. "I need database searches tonight. Search for people missing near the Atlantic coast, people with clinging mud or dirt that makes them sick, crazy looking fish, crazy looking animals, missing wildlife, dead wildlife—basically anything that raises a red flag and is different from the status quo."

"Should I start testing the water samples?"

"No. We'll do that tomorrow with Sidra. Contact animal shelters on the mainland and tell them we have a pest problem. I need to determine if all cat saliva neutralizes the wet dust or if the desired result is unique to Jessie's cat. Arrange for the research cats to be on the early ferry, and keep them out of sight from my wife."

Forman mimicked zipping his lips closed. "Mum's the word."

Chapter 28

Refreshed, finally.

An hour before dawn, Zeke crept down the walled ladder into the Taman transmission chamber. Soft lights came on as he descended. So far, no one had suspected anything existed under the historic lighthouse, and due to clever, durable construction, the concealed passageway would serve centuries of Guardians.

Zeke's concern was with the present. These dust entities went through glass and plastech and then vanished. He had to know more about them. How dangerous were they? Could he stop them?

He didn't spare a glance at his late father's journals or any of the crumbling tomes from his ancestors. He needed a much quicker pipeline of information.

Settling into the transmission chair, he reclined in the soft leather-like seat, opening his mind and questing through time and space. Their voices called to him from Tween and beyond.

Where have you been? his father asked. *We've been sick with worry. We've heard terrible stories about Earth.*

His father's comments deflected Zeke momentarily from his information gathering purpose. *Yeah? Who else besides me is here?*

The dolphins contacted us.

They can do that?

They send us picture words. Dirty ocean. Bad fish. They sent more but the transmission garbled.

Are they safe? I haven't had a chance to look for the dolphins since I returned from Rio yesterday.

They're nearby, but the tone of their message implied Tama Island is in trouble. They don't want you swimming anytime soon. The ocean isn't safe.

Tell me something I don't know. The Navy has captured a strange fish, and they're sending me a smaller sample as soon as they catch another one. It's two species joined in an impossible way, and yet still alive. What do you make of that?

Are odd happenings occurring on land and in the sea? Deep Voice asked.

Yes. Zeke told them about the mobile dust and his lack of significant results with the water samples. *Please, help me out here. I don't know what I'm up against. What do you know?*

The boy's got Yars, Thin Voice trilled. *Evacuate the planet. Immediately.*

Zeke blocked out the other voices clamoring in the wake of those terse statements. Someone had spilled the beans, only he had no idea what any of this meant. *What's a Yars? And no one can evacuate. We don't have the technology to do that. Help me.*

People argued loudly. The noise hurt Zeke's head. He couldn't hear his father's voice at all. Should he disconnect from the Taman helpline?

Quiet, Deep Voice roared. *Let Quimby talk.*

Zeke, you still there? his dad asked.

He could refuse to talk, but what good would that do? He needed their help. Quimby must be one of the Tamans at Tween. *I'm here, Dad. What can I do to protect Jessie?*

Yars are like fleas. They nest and reproduce quickly. That's what they're doing in the ocean. From what I've learned they excrete something that makes the seawater retain more sediment. Sounds like your intruders have evolved past the water stage and have graduated to land animals. I've never run across them, but Quimby lived through an infestation on another planet. You're using stainless steel for sample containers?

Yes. But I haven't found anything extraterrestrial. Just more of what's already here.

I have the floor, Thin Voice shrilled.

Quimby? Please tell me what I'm facing, Zeke said.

Yars colonize quickly by absorbing DNA of living matter. They can then assume the shape of the pirated genetic code. They're pretenders.

How do they pass through glass and walls?

I don't know the how of it, I only know that they do. Stainless steel stops them.

Cats stop them, Zeke added.

What's a cat? Quimby asked.

A murmur went through the Tween crowd. They quieted as Zeke spoke. *A domesticated pet here on Earth. My wife's cat licked the wet dust off a child and the child survived the attack.*

Didn't the Yar assume the shape of the cat?

Not that I know of. The cat, uh, expelled the material he licked off the child. To my knowledge, the cat has done this on three separate occasions. Once when the dust was on an older man's clothing, on a child's hands and face, and on my wife's hand.

The cat survived?

It did.

And there are no copies of the cat running around?

Not to my knowledge.

What about people? You seeing any body doubles or missing people?

No.

Good. We need to know how the cat blocked the Yar. Your research could help people defeat Yars across the cosmos.

There are more of these things?

As your father said, Thin Voice continued, *Yars are like fleas. They reproduce at a fast rate of speed, and they wipe out all life on planets they invade.*

Everything? How is that possible?

I leave the science to guys like you, Quimby said. *Yars are everywhere.*

How come I never heard of them before?

Need-to-know basis, Deep Voice grumped.

I need to know how to beat them.

Not to worry, Deep Voice continued. *They are afraid of us, of you.*

Why?

Long story.

Give me the abridged version.

Our needs for expansion are similar. Often we're at cross-purposes.

But we beat them every time?

Not always.

The link started to fade. *Wait!* Zeke called. *I'm not done. What do*

I do? How do I beat these Yars?

You must return. There is a problem on your island. You must tend to it immediately.

Chapter 29

Xstle landed with a thump in his aerie high above Tama Island. His initial elation at assimilating Kvn's collective had long faded. This day's landmark events had turned him upside down and inside out.

He'd been stunned to learn that prior to Kvn joining his collective, a rogue band of Kvn's Yar collection had attached themselves to the female biped carrying an Ancient. They had refused to desist and demanded Xstle claim his prize. Their initiative was commendable, but they'd committed a cardinal sin.

Ancients were uncertain allies at best; however, they were ruthless opponents. Angering a powerful foe could sabotage the entire expedition. Xstle cursed the reckless strategy and certain retribution.

The Ancient's four-legged guard dispatched the indies, and now those specks were imprisoned in a locked dwelling. The bipeds had known of the secure containers to seal the renegade Yars. His compatriots' life signals were so dampened he could scarcely hear their pleas for help. Without a prime to unite them, those Yar specks would cannibalize each other and terminate by dawn.

Pity.

Xstle had absorbed enough planetary life forms that he could rescue them without raising an alarm, but the rogue Yars were the least of his problems.

Another Ancient moved about on the island now. A full-fledged, powerful male. The one which the rogue Yars attacked was embryonic. The female biped must be gestating it for the male Ancient. Figured. The bipeds were under the rule of the Ancients. Another setback for Yar. He must decide upon a strategy. To do nothing would lead to certain death.

Stories handed down through generations of Yars told of the destruction the Ancients could incite without moving a finger. Legend had it they could move mountains and part seas, and they could kill with a look. Some said Ancients could manipulate time and space.

He was so dead.

Should he cower in fear or throw himself on the Ancient's mercy? Would the Ancient kill him on general principle? Yars and Ancients weren't natural allies. They weren't enemies, but Yars generally avoided Ancients to ensure species survival. Which hadn't been a problem in Xstle's lifespan since the Ancients were rumored to be extinct.

Soon there would be two, on the very island Xstle had selected as his new base.

Out of all the land masses on this planet, what were the odds?

He had no way of warning the other primes on this mission, no way of informing his compatriots across the stars. Loss of communication with the interstellar Yar community was the price of founding a new colony.

He swore. And swore some more. *Ancients! What rotten luck!* Even if Yar established a viable colony here, Ancients had rules. Their colonization policies prohibited indigenous extermination and industrialized farming of the resident species.

Yars would be expected to live in harmony with the vermin on this place. If they wiped out the extant species, Ancients would retaliate across the cosmos, and Yar would be no more. Anywhere.

He swore again.

The Yar primes on this mission had suffered mightily already.

Which brought Xstle to his second point of terror.

The Ancient transported a Drch to the island. Xstle recognized the signature pulse of the Drch he'd battled before on V362KR91 and lost. This Drch used stealth and ensnarement to acquire targets. It adapted quickly to new terrain, copying powerful species without bothering to assimilate backup shapes.

Worse, this Drch violated every rule of Yar colonization. Sure, the end goal of planetary control was the same, but a Drch, this Drch in particular, delighted in the cruelest war tactics. One of Xstle's associates dubbed this baddie, Wrill, after the fiercest species they'd assimilated.

The Wrill of yore took no prisoners, and the namesake Drch lived up to their fierce reputation. Many Yars had died battling Wrill. Xstle shuddered at his continued bad fortune.

He settled in his bower, tucking his wings tight to his body. The sun sank lower in the western sky, providing a colorful aerial display. Bronzed wheat gave way to burnt orange, and for a magical moment Xstle felt as if he was at home under the familiar orange skies of Yar. He silently hummed the battle hymn of Yar to center himself.

With only three Yar primes left, soon to be two if his fellow primes Oieg and Nrz merged, the odds of crushing Wrill were poor.

The only Drch worse than Wrill was Queen. She could dissociate into multiple tactical units and acquire varied targets simultaneously. Xstle's colonization party, even at full strength, was no match for Queen or Wrill.

If Queen was here, that explained why so many of his landing party were no more. Worse, all that *auku* he'd shed in the ocean to create a Yar breeding site was the perfect media for his enemy's replication.

Twilight descended and in the thin curtain between night and day, the sad fact was indisputable. Alone and afraid, Xstle quivered. There would be no thriving colony of Yars here. Between Queen and Wrill, the indigenous species on this planet were doomed. As was his entire landing party.

Light years of travel in stasis. Decades of preparation. And for what? A spectacular failure. His only consolation was that if Queen and Wrill were here, the home colony had a better chance to reestablish itself elsewhere and to restore their species' good name.

But this place, Earth as the natives called this bit of rock, water, and air, faced certain extermination. The sea would die. The air would foul. Drch ruined everything before they moved on. Except the craft to get here had been unconventional and a one-way ticket. There was no escape plan, and from what Xstle'd seen of the technology here, no pod to steal and peruse the stars for a new home. It had been a crapshoot coming this far anyway.

And thanks to the stowaways, both Yars and Earthlings were on the brink of extinction.

Their only chance of survival was banding together to fight their mutual enemy.

Except his foot soldiers had attacked the female biped gestating the Ancient. He shuddered. He was so screwed.

Chapter 30

"I need a ride to the lab," Sidra said over the com. "Can you come get me?"

Forman scowled at the lab's vid link. He was starting to make headway with the water data sets, and he still had the cats to pick up from the ferry before the boss arrived. "You have a transpo. Use it."

"Can't. Ronni made me swear I'd have one of you escort me to work. Please. I can't call Zeke. This is so embarrassing to need a ride."

"How old are you?"

"Eighteen. You know that. But Ronni still thinks of me as the ten year old she took under her wing. She worries about my safety, and she's under the weather from the flight. She won't take her nausea medicine until someone picks me up. You'd be doing us a huge favor. I hate to see her suffer like this."

"A health and safety issue?" He defaulted to the automatic response. "Should I send a medic over?"

"No. She just needs to sleep and rest. I was stuck in the hotel with her for two whole days in Frankfurt about six months ago for the same exact thing. I beg you. Come right now."

In a microsecond, Forman ran the possible consequences of accepting or declining her request. Bottom line, Zeke needed Sidra in the lab. Forman's job was to assist Zeke. The computations and the cats could wait. The astrophysicist couldn't.

"Be right there."

*****

"Notice anything different about the island?" Forman asked.

Sidra propped both of her bright yellow sneakers on the dash. Her primary color palette complimented the Christmas package aloha shirt he'd chosen for this sunny December day. "What do you mean?"

"Does the place feel the same as last time?"

"Maybe, though I hadn't thought about it until right this second. Seems pensive, if that's possible. I'm anxious to study the cat barf, but I could be projecting my edgy mood upon the island. And I'm dying to solve the mystery of the disappearing dust."

"I checked the lab several times during the night. Dusty did not reappear in the vault."

"No rest for the wicked?"

"You wish."

She arched her back, stroked his arm, and purred in a sexy voice. "Hey, I'm of age now. We could have some fun."

She was only a few months older than the last time he saw her. With her colorful ruffled outfits and gleaming blue hair, she didn't resemble any adult he knew. "You are a kid."

"The government considers me an adult. But I've been older than my calendar years forever. The whole genius thing, ya know?"

She confused him, and he didn't have time to humor her. "Make up your mind. Are you hitting on me? Or do you want me to feel sorry for you?"

"Hmm. Tough choice. Sex or sympathy? Why can't I have both?"

Forman turned onto the ferry road, a blast of warm wind blowing in his face. "You can, but not with me. We have a professional relationship, and we need to keep it that way. Both of us are here to support Zeke's research."

"Not me. I'm here for *my* research. You'd best keep that in mind."

She annoyed him. That's all there was to it. He steered through a pothole, watching with satisfaction as her feet came off the dash, and she scrambled for purchase on the bench seat.

"You did that on purpose," she whined.

He didn't give her the satisfaction of an on-topic response as the dock neared. "We have a lot to do today."

Sidra ignored him until they stopped. "What's that noise?"

Caterwauling. The caged cats weren't happy. He grinned and pulled up next to the crates at the ferry landing. "Your next assignment. We have to figure out how Sanjee neutralized the adhesive dust."

"More cats? Shouldn't we test Sanjee instead?"

"We will do what Zeke asked. He wants us to test these cats. Help me load them in the back."

"I've never had a cat." Sidra let loose a flurry of sneezes as they moved the four vented cages.

"Allergic?"

"Don't know." She sneezed again. Her eyes watered. "But it's looking that way."

"Oh, joy."

Angie emerged from the terminal, stalking straight to Forman, her island orange robe snapping about her legs in the breeze. Her tight expression worried Forman. "Is there a problem here?" Angie asked.

Sidra edged closer to him. She must have felt the bad vibes too. "We've got this," Sidra asserted, tripping over nothing and falling into Forman's arms.

Angie glared at the two of them. She shot Forman a leer filled with heat, and not the good kind. "A word."

Forman set Sidra on her feet, released her, and leaned toward Angie. "Cherries."

"What?"

"You demanded a word. Cherries came to mind."

Angie shook her head. "I need a private word with you right now."

"I can take a hint," Sidra said. "I'll wait in the transpo with the unhappy cats."

Angie marched Forman over to the jetty. Beyond the protective wall, the sediment-laden water ebbed out of the tidal creek at a fast clip. In another hour or so, the tide would start coming in again. Did the tide ever get tired of going back and forth?

Forman did. His back and forth relationship with Angie confused him in the extreme. They seemed to be friends with benefits, but if that was the case why was Angie so steamed over Sidra?

"She's a child," Angie said. "You should be reprogrammed for dallying with her."

"Not anymore. Sidra's reached the age of consent, and she propositioned me, not the other way around."

"You can't sleep with her." Angie's remarkable eyes flowed through his memories in a collage of moments. "There are repercussions."

He sharpened his thoughts to the present. "I know enough not to sleep with her, but sex would be a fun encounter with Sidra. She's got a lot of spunk."

"I'm gonna spunk you if you so much as think about her in that way again."

"I don't see why it matters. Unless… unless you're jealous."

"Don't be ridiculous."

There it was again. That flush of fire and passion and outrage. Interesting. "I haven't seen you since we returned from Rio." Forman lowered his voice and leaned in close enough to detect her natural, pleasing scent. "Is there someone else?"

"I've been busy, and so have you. Saving the world is hard work."

Her level of emotion intrigued him. "I need to know where we stand. Are we friends or something more?"

"Does it matter?"

"Seeing as how my last girlfriend dumped me, went crazy on alien drugs, and now lives under lock and key, yeah, it matters."

"I'm not looking for permanent. Just an occasional good time. Can't you slip into your Gary entertainment module persona and cut me some slack?"

Forman snapped to attention. "I'm more than the sum of my individual parts. I may have the programming to be a boy toy, but I want more than a hookup. I desire to experience a relationship."

Angie snorted. "Look, you can practice your Real Boy wish with someone else, Pinocchio. I don't care to be your science experiment any more than you care to be exploited for your excellent sexual techniques."

"Huh. Never considered that angle, but I see where you might interpret my emotional exploration in that light."

"It's the only light. You're a machine, Forman. I can program you to do any flerking thing I want you to do."

Forman's processors hummed. Angie had unrestricted access to his electronics. Why would she tamper with his memories? Until he knew, he couldn't trust her. Zeke was the only human he trusted.

He bowed his head as if in defeat, his bright shirt at odds with this dismal day. "You're right."

Her frank gaze made him blush. "See you tonight. My place. You know the drill."

Flerk.

Chapter 31

Zeke sat at the conference table in his laboratory with Forman and Sidra. Uncle John was patched in on the big screen they faced, his bushy eyebrows and hair snowy white on his tanned face. "Tell me what you've learned."

"We divided the work," Zeke said. "I took the water samples. Forman analyzed cat saliva. Sidra worked on the dust the cat regurgitated. Sidra will go first with her report."

"All I have is bad news," Sidra said, her earnest eyes dominating her small face. "The cat barf had no moving dust. No unusual elements or combinations of elements. Nothing that said alien creature. Nothing that said I'm alive. It stank to high heaven, though, so I'm thrilled to be done with that analysis. Next time, Forman gets the vomit."

"You requested that work," Zeke said.

"Sure I did, because the cats made me sneeze," Sidra said. "I say we crack open the sealed meteorite vault and laser Dusty in half. The dust has to have gone back inside the thing."

"Not at this time," Uncle John cautioned. "We need to know what we are dealing with."

"Forman's report is next," Zeke said, nodding to his subdued assistant. He needed to have a private moment with Forman later to see what was troubling him, but work took precedence right now.

"Saliva was collected from each cat and analyzed. There was some variation by subject, but a multifunctional panel revealed amylases, mucins, lipases, statherins, cystatins, and histatins were present."

"English, please," Uncle John said.

Zeke leaned forward. "The components we isolated were known constituents of saliva. Each component aids digestion or protects the animal through antiviral, antifungal or antibacterial properties, along with tissue coating, lubrication, buffering, and mineralization."

"Is cat saliva different from people saliva?"

"The components are similar."

"So what is it about Sanjee that neutralized the dust?"

"That hasn't been determined. We tested other cats this morning."

"Not Sanjee?"

"Jessie didn't want him tested."

"You will test the cat. The test is non-invasive. I don't see what the problem is."

"The idea of testing the cat upset Jessie. I couldn't do that. I thought checking other cats would be a good first step, and it would establish a baseline for comparison."

"We have no time to waste. Get Sanjee's saliva in the lab immediately. That's an order."

Sidra tapped her stylus on the table. "For what it's worth, Mr. Demery, Sanjee's vomit showed no abnormalities."

Uncle John glared at Zeke. "I hope you have better news for me."

"The water profiles from Rio are statistically similar to those taken here. Whatever is in the water and making it hold more sediment appears to be a widespread phenomenon. I've been in contact with my water research friends around the globe, and they are reporting the same sediment load in their areas as well."

"What happens if the ocean dies?"

"That would not be good."

"We need to do something about this situation. I'm hearing reports of little to no fish in the Atlantic Ocean. The plankton layer is dying off. What theories do you have? What's our plan of attack?"

"Theories are hard to come by right now. The higher turbidity is blocking light and fouling the gills of sea life. Consequently, there are fewer organisms in the ocean now than before the meteor storm."

"This stems from the meteors?" Uncle John asked.

"We had hoped to prove that correlation with Sidra's meteor, but we don't know where the dust from her meteor went."

"What do your other sources recommend?"

His other sources. The Tamans. Uncle John didn't know the extra help came from across the universe, did he? Come to think of it, why didn't his uncle press him for more details about his sources? Unless he knew more than he was letting on. Certainly something to ponder when Zeke had down time.

"They view this incursion as an infestation," Zeke admitted.

"Like roaches?" Sidra asked.

Zeke nodded. "Something like that."

"I stepped on a roach in the containment lab," Sidra said. "Could the dust have somehow morphed into a cockroach?"

Zeke rolled her idea around in his head. "Seems farfetched to me, but I don't understand how that blended-species fish the Navy captured could swim. We don't know what normal is for this dust." He gazed at his uncle's face on the big screen. "Any word from the Admiral?"

"They can't catch another specimen," Uncle John said. "Last I heard, they were awaiting presidential approval to sacrifice the specimen they have in the name of research."

Like that would happen. "My sources say this dust is dangerous. They call the dust 'Yars.' It wipes out all life on the planets it encounters. So far it looks like it's on its way to killing the ocean. They asked if we'd seen any copies of things floating around."

"Copies? Like extra chairs and the like?"

"No." Zeke lowered his voice. "Body doubles."

Uncle John laughed. "How is that possible?"

"If Yars can imitate a cockroach and a fish, imitating a person or another land species isn't a total fantasy."

"Speak for yourself. Sounds like fantasy to me."

"My contacts were quite emphatic. They also said we had a problem on the island."

"I thought Sanjee took care of that."

"Maybe, but something's changed over here. This place felt different after we came back from Rio. As if it were brooding. We've been talking about it in the lab today."

"Without proof, we can't take a feeling to anyone. Do you recommend we quarantine Tama Island?"

Zeke frowned. "That seems extreme, given we don't know what the problem is. It makes no sense that they've targeted tiny Tama Island."

"Maybe it isn't the island that they're after. Maybe they know you're the Guardian and they're coming to get you first."

Zeke shrugged. "Anything's possible."

"Can you fix the Atlantic?"

Sidra snorted. "Not unless we flood it with cat saliva."

Zeke stared at her with wonder. "You know something?"

"Yeah. I did a little side experiment of my own. Sample size of one, so take my result with a grain of salt. I shot a squirt of Forman's cat saliva sample into one of your leftover water samples. The sediment flocked out and the water totally cleared."

"Excellent work, Sidra," Uncle John beamed. "Great initiative. What's your take on her findings, Zeke?"

"This is the first I've heard of them." Zeke didn't like being one-upped. "But if we can repeat her results, I foresee a huge demand for cat saliva. We'll need to isolate and purify the active ingredients."

"This is the best news I've heard all day. Back to work my brilliant worker bees."

"Sir, I'd really like to take a crack at the meteor," Sidra said. "If I can open it, I will better understand how the dust withstood the rigors of space."

"In time. We need a cure for the threat we're facing. No point in opening another potential Pandora's Box. We must focus our research efforts."

"Understood," Zeke cut in, drilling Sidra with a quelling glare. "We'll isolate the active saliva ingredients and scale up to save the oceans. Without a healthy sea, the planetary water cycle faces an uncertain future."

"We're counting on you." Uncle John's image faded from the large screen.

Zeke faced Sidra. He felt her telepathic probing at the edge of his thoughts. No way would he open up to her on that level. He intensified the shielding in his head. "Nice of you to share your findings with us. What happened to our team approach?"

Sidra flicked her blue hair, raised her chin defiantly. "Teams aren't worth a credit when it comes to innovation. You have to take risks. That's what I did. If nothing had happened from my little experiment, no one would have known … or cared. Instead, we have a serious lead."

"Do you know how hard it is to collect cat saliva?" Forman said. "They do not like being sampled. I had to repair the syn-skin on both hands and forearms after handling them."

"We have to get Jessie's cat in here for testing, and we need more cats to assure a steady supply of sample material," Zeke stood and stretched. The buzzing in his head, always a minor irritation, grew louder. Either the dolphins or the Tamans were calling him.

He'd communicated with the Tamans early this morning.

Were the dolphins in trouble? He needed to find out.

"What about dogs?" Sidra asked, swishing side to side in her swivel seat and then standing up. "How do we know the curative activity is limited to cats? Both species lick wounds."

"One species at a time. Let's not complicate this beyond belief. We've got plenty of water samples left. How are we doing on cat saliva?"

"Very little left, less since Sidra's been pilfering my samples," Forman said.

A data matrix tried to form in Zeke's thoughts, but he didn't have enough information to fill in the gaps. If Sidra's finding proved true, that would put them on track to wiping out the invading Yars. Could it be so easy?

He didn't trust easy. And he needed additional data. He paced the small room, thinking out loud. "We'll get more cat saliva, and I'll convince Jessie sampling won't hurt Sanjee."

"How will you do that?" Sidra asked, following in his footsteps.

"I'm thinking a boat ride might do the trick," Zeke said. Sidra was crowding him and challenging him. His annoyance with her grew to a fine white noise. The need to do something ate at him. "That will give me a chance to observe the island from the sea and to locate the dolphins."

"You and your dolphin pod," Forman said. "Wonder what their saliva would do?"

Zeke's jaw dropped. He shook his head at his assistant. "I'm not sampling dolphins today. Besides if their saliva caused sediment to flock out of seawater, our ocean would show a decreased turbidity. That's not the case. Our turbidity level remains constant."

Sidra tugged on his T-shirt. "Can I come with you? I want to see the dolphins again."

Zeke had had enough of the genius astrophysicist for one day. He shot a do-something look over at Forman. "Uh."

Forman slid into the gap between Zeke and Sidra, steering her away from Zeke. "He means no, Sidra. The boss needs time alone with his wife. The key word here is *alone*. No tag-alongs."

Sidra snorted with derision. "You guys hate me for making you look bad."

Her attitude didn't sit right with Zeke. "I don't hate anyone, but you withheld information from the team. We can't work effectively if you're going to grandstand and hoard your findings. Uncle John is clear about what the Institute wants, what the world needs. We're here to do a job, to stop the Yars from taking over our planet. If you don't want to be part of the team, say so."

The teen's expression fell. "I didn't mean any harm. I was bored. And who would believe anything done with a sample size of one would be valid? Huh? Huh?"

"Sidra. Things happen at a fast pace over here. Sometimes we don't follow all the rules, but our number one priority, after we save the planet, of course, is to follow Uncle John's directives. If we act independently, we'll have to find new funding and new jobs."

Her skin tone lightened to a chalky color. "I'm sorry. I mean it."

She sounded sincere. Zeke relented as he rose to leave. "I'll persuade the dolphins to swim by the beach this evening. You'll be able to commune with them there."

"Thanks. That will help me get rid of some of the static in my head. I'm so congested from all the cat dander I can barely think. I'm taking a break and getting some fresh air." Sidra stormed out toward the quad.

When she was out of earshot, Zeke nodded at Forman. "Thanks for the rescue, buddy."

"I'll keep an eye out for her," Forman said. "She's not herself today. Could be the cats."

"Could be she wants to rule the world. I don't trust her."

"Sidra made a mistake by not confiding in you. Look at this from her perspective. She came here thinking she would be autonomous. Instead, she's been under your thumb the entire time."

"She's a hungry lion in a petting zoo."

"So?"

Forman's wry tone implied Zeke was no better. Drama. He didn't need it. "I'll be back as soon as I can. You know what to do."

Chapter 32

Jessie killed the boat motor as Zeke tied off the anchor line. They'd circled the island looking for his dolphins, finally finding them in this tidal creek an island over. Unlike Tama Island, this place wasn't inhabited. It was a federal nature preserve.

"What are you going to do?" she asked.

"Take a quick dip. Something's bothering the dolphins, and I need to be touching them to receive their thoughts."

"Good thing I brought a reader along in my tote bag."

"I won't be that long." Zeke planted a quick kiss on her lips, then shucked his shirt.

"Is it safe to get in the water? It looks like dirty pea soup."

"It's safe or the dolphins wouldn't be here."

A minute later, he was over the side, floating on his back, a hand on two of the larger dolphins. Jessie knew the names of the four podmates were Klickie, Tunis, Nicola, and Boz, but she couldn't tell them apart. Except for Boz, who seemed to be assigned to keep her company.

She reached over the side of the boat, allowing her fingers to trail in the water. Boz swam underneath and lingered there a moment. A peaceable feeling filled her, like after a Thanksgiving meal. Was the dolphin doing that?

Whatever, she liked feeling safe and warm. For days now, she'd had the sense of being watched, and her nerves were frayed because of it.

A glance at her other hand, the one that Sanjee had licked the mud off, showed that it barely looked sunburned today. She was lucky. That mud was bad news, and she hoped the island had seen the last of it.

But how was that adhesive mud different than the brown water? That was where she got stuck. She groaned at her pun. Boz circled around again as if he were worried about her.

"I'm okay. Just thinking out loud."

And now she was talking to a dolphin. If she wasn't careful, they'd lock her up in the loony bin with her sister. Poor Bea.

Bea had made a series of bad choices. Jessie wasn't driven to extremes like her sister. She wouldn't go nuts. She hoped.

She glanced down at the reader in her lap and put it back in the tote. No way could she read right now. Not with Zeke floating in the thickened water nearby.

Overhead, a hawk soared and glided on thermals.

Wait a minute. Was that the hawk from Tama Island? How far did those things range anyway?

The hawk seemed to float through the airwaves. High in the sky like that, the hawk could probably see for miles. Was it out to enjoy the bright sunny day, or was it hoping to find prey in the preserve? Did birds fly for leisure or was all their flying food related?

She should look it up. Now that she lived on the coast, she should familiarize herself with the natural environment. Like hawks. She watched it circle over the creeks and head back toward her.

The boat bobbed gently in the water as Boz made another pass by its side. Jessie glanced down to see Zeke and the dolphins had drifted a bit down the creek. Not too far, though.

Jessie shifted in her seat, turning in time to see the hawk heading her way. The sight had her leaping out of her seat. "Eek!" She scrambled under the sun canopy, looking for something to use to shoo the bird away. Her tote. The food pouch. The life vest. Everything was soft. The plastech paddle. It was hard. She grabbed it like a baseball bat and stepped out from the canopy with seconds to spare.

With feet outstretched, the bird's intent to harm her was clear.

"Come on, sucker. I double-dog dare you," she shouted.

The hawk came closer and closer, with wings spread wide. The darn thing looked huge. Maybe five feet across. Jessie couldn't breathe. Was this bird maddened from starvation? What could possibly make it hunt a larger, living prey?

She flexed her knees, creating tension in her stance, her arms cocked to one side, ready to deliver a killing blow to the hawk. Time slowed to a molasses drip. The hawk's intense gaze and curved beak burned into her vision, as its piercing shriek chilled her blood.

She tried a quick mental burst to Zeke. *Need help*, but got nothing in response. Who knew if her limited telepathic ability was working anyway?

"Go away, stupid bird," she shouted. "I don't want to hurt you."

One second the bird was flying at her, the next it shot straight up in the sky with a giant swoosh of its wings. A shadow covered her briefly as it blocked the sun, then the hawk flew to one of the trees on the island and alit.

Jessie's heart thumped wildly against her ribs. She felt lightheaded and woozy. She reached for the side of the boat, but it was too late. The world spun off its axis and went dark.

Chapter 33

"Jessie! Can you hear me? Jessie, wake up." Zeke cradled his unconscious wife in his arms. His hands shook as he checked and found her thin pulse again. *Please, let her be all right.*

He'd been receiving a steady commentary about the changes in the sea from Nicola and Klickie when the link fried. In a flash, they told him to create a barrier around the boat, and he envisioned an invisible bubble encircling all of them. Then, the dolphins had literally pushed him back to the boat. Boz had been frantic. Still was, gauging by the splashes in the creek.

Should he radio for help?

He stroked the side of Jessie's pale face. How long had he been in the water? Couldn't have been but a few minutes. What happened?

She was breathing. Her pulse was slow but steady. Those were good things.

Think, Zeke.

He dashed away the saltwater dripping into his eyes. Her health and safety depended on him getting this right. What did he know? Jessie had been fine when he jumped overboard five minutes ago. She wasn't fine now.

Was her trouble pregnancy related? Did she overheat in the afternoon sunshine? Why didn't she tell him if she wasn't up to a boat ride?

Her eyelids flickered.

Zeke's hope flared. "Jessie? Come on. You can do it. Wake up."

He checked her hand, the one which formerly had been exposed to the mud. It looked none the worse for wear. Had some of the mud gotten into her system? Why hadn't he insisted on taking her to a clinic yesterday? Why had he assumed everything would be all right?

"Zeke?"

Her soft voice sounded like the rarest of music. "Jessie. I have you. Are you okay? What happened?"

"The bird…"

Her voice trailed off. Zeke surveyed the sky. He didn't see a bird. Not a single winged creature in sight. "What bird?"

Jessie struggled to sit up. He held her fast, not knowing if he would ever let her go. "Hold still for a minute. Did you hit your head when you fell? What do you remember?"

"I fell on the life jackets, so my head's okay. But my heart nearly did me in. That bird scared the crap out me."

"What bird?" Zeke repeated.

"The hawk. Our hawk, I think. The one from Tama Island. It must have followed us here."

"Odd. Why would a hawk do that?"

"Why would it fly straight at my face? I swear the hawk was coming for me. I saw the thing circling from a distance, then the bird made some scary noise, and swooped down at me. I was gonna whack it with the paddle, but at the last nanosecond it pulled up. What's that about?"

"I've never heard of hawks going after people. We're bigger than they are."

"My size didn't intimidate this hawk. He was coming for me. I'll swear it on a stack of Bibles. I'll never forget the sound of his wings swooping over me."

"The paddle would've knocked the bird out of the air. Why wasn't he afraid?"

"Exactly. Let me up. I'll show you where it went."

"Sure you're okay? We should get you to a doctor."

"I don't want a doctor. I'm fine. Just got a little lightheaded for a moment. This is par for the course."

"Why didn't you tell me you weren't well?"

"Nothing's wrong with me. I'm pregnant. That's all. At home, I put my head down when I start feeling woozy, but I must have ignored the warning sign for fear of being the hawk's dinner. Please, let me up. I promise I'm not going to break."

"Only if you agree to get a medical checkout when we return to the island. My heart can't take this level of excitement."

Jessie pushed her way out of his arms. "Pshaw. A man that can repel aliens from an entire planet is worried about a woman who fainted?"

135

"Not just any woman. My wife. No more fainting."

She stood with his assistance. He did not turn her loose. No way was he taking another chance on her falling. This couldn't happen again. He had to do better by Jessie.

She gestured toward the tallest tree on the point. "Don't know if he's still there, but the hawk flew to that pine."

"We'll swing a little closer in the boat, but first you're sitting down."

"I'm not made of porcelain," she grumbled as she complied.

Zeke weighed anchor and idled closer to the shoreline. Nothing resembling a hawk was in evidence. "Guess he's gone."

He turned for home but held the throttle at idle. Finding Jessie unconscious in the boat had changed his perspective. He needed a doctor's assurance that his wife and the baby were fine. If that caused marital friction, so be it. "We'll get him, but first we're heading home. I'll have Uncle John arrange to have an obstetrician flown in. I'd like a full battery of scans run."

"The mainland clinic is fine. I don't need any special treatment. And I don't want to subject our daughter to any radiation from scans. I'm doing this the natural way."

"I'll compromise. We'll visit the clinic and if there are any red flags, then we'll see a specialist."

"Deal."

Zeke's com buzzed. Annoyance crept into his voice. "Yes?"

Forman's voice boomed through the link. "We have a situation here. Please return ASAP."

"Be there in fifteen."

Chapter 34

Xstle clung to the trunk of the pine as the Ancients veered away from his hiding place. To escape detection, he'd assumed the shape of a lowly insect when they approached.

Desperation.

That was his story, and he was sticking to it.

Though he needed the power of the Ancients to help defeat the Drchs named Wrill and Queen, something inside him had snapped when the female biped had been left unattended in the strange water pod. At first, he'd thought to approach and befriend her.

Then he realized how easy it would be to collect her DNA. If he assimilated an Ancient, even a fetal one, he would be more powerful than Wrill or Queen. He'd learned the bipeds could not live long without air and that their only source of air came from the nose and mouth.

Granted, he'd learned that by spying on Wrill earlier today. He'd picked up the Drch's signature at one of the dwellings, then snooped around until he found the cubicle where Wrill fed. The space contained a female biped, an aged one, too weak to protest assimilation.

Apparently, Wrill had weakened the target through generalized absorption, then he'd morphed into the shape of a cloth. The kind of cloths they had at home that sealed airtight. The biped struggled briefly, but couldn't dislodge Wrill from its breathing zone. At this very moment, Wrill was copying the biped's shape and would soon assume her position in the land colony.

Xstle had thought to change to that very cloth as he winged toward his target in the boat. He'd seen the female pick up a stick of sorts, known that would mean trouble for the hawk body, but he'd banked on spooking her by changing shapes in mid-air.

What he hadn't banked on was the force field surrounding the vessel and the female. The protective zone propelled him over her head. His secret of shapeshifting was safe for the time being.

The Ancient on this planet didn't know much of anything. It hadn't known to ping the vicinity for his echo location. It hadn't noticed his furtive encroachments in the thought plane. All it had done was place a rudimentary shield around the female.

Crude, but effective.

The message was clear. The female and the Ancient's marine playmates were off limits. There would be no assimilating the female, no chance for him to individually beat Wrill or Queen.

The only option left was to approach the naïve Ancient, beg forgiveness, and pledge cooperation. If the Ancient believed he was in league with the Drch named Wrill, Xstle was doomed.

He'd been studying the language, eavesdropping and getting the hang of the social customs here. So far, he found the spoken word difficult due to the context meanings for each term. At home, inflection pointed you toward a specific meaning, but not here. Everything was context based—very challenging for an outsider learning the rudiments.

Guessing from the sudden change of speed by the Ancient's vessel, Xstle guessed that the fallen biped had been discovered. Oh, joy. The fun never ended on this frontier planet.

Chapter 35

"How long has she been like this?" Zeke asked, his voice muffled by the full air suit.

Forman gazed at the prone figure in the guest cottage assigned to Sidra and shook his head. "Good question. I've been here half an hour, and she's looked like this the whole time."

"Run a timeline for me."

"Sidra wanted to work from home after you left to spend the afternoon with Jessie. I accompanied her back to her lodging, waited in the transpo while she ducked inside to check on her companion before I returned to the lab. When she screamed, I came inside and called you and Angie."

"Is Ronni dead?"

The still form on the bed had a dusty overall appearance, which in itself wasn't as disturbing as the sightless eyes, the gaping mouth, and the chest which didn't rise up and down with respirations. "We don't know what she is. Angie cordoned off the room as soon as she arrived. She had me take Sidra over to Traci Loya's place."

"Should we bring Jessie's cat over?"

"This is bigger than one cat, trust me. The dust spread all over Ronni's body. Inside her mouth, even."

"We've got five cats in total. Is it worth a shot?"

Forman didn't want to endanger Jessie's cat, and he was concerned about Zeke being so close to the dust-covered corpse. The dust could penetrate anything that wasn't stainless, which meant his boss was at risk. He steered Zeke outside the house onto the lawn. Overhead, the sky glowed red with the last rays of day. "We could try the cats, but I believe we're too late. Whatever this crud is, it's engulfed her. The cats could only remove the external dust."

"Where'd she come in contact with the stuff?" Zeke asked, unsealing his protective gear.

"Not having seen her since yesterday afternoon, I can't say for certain. But the place that comes to mind is your lab. You brought cat throw-up to the lab when Ronni was there yesterday."

"The cat barf was sealed in a stainless steel container. This mud can't migrate through stainless, plus the mass of the container remained unchanged from collection to analysis. What about Sidra's missing Rio dust? Let's run that scenario. The dust was present in the plastech vault when the Rio meteor arrived. Then it wasn't. At one point, we believe it was a cockroach walking across the floor because Sidra stepped on it. After that, we didn't find a trace of it."

"If this dust is from Sidra's meteor, then it may be a separate entity from the critter which attached itself to the child and Jessie. Bottom line, we may have more than one of these entities on Tama Island."

Zeke's suit rustled as he shifted position. "We need to contain the scene. We could move Ronni to the P4 lab, but this thing already escaped from there once. What do we have on the island that's stainless and big enough to contain a person? We need a bank vault."

Forman used the com port on the shaded side of the house to access the web. Data flowed, quick and satisfying. "None of the Institute buildings have a room configuration like that. I'll check the tax records for vaults, but the mainland's our best guess."

Zeke rubbed his chin. "A steel hull boat might work if the hold was stainless steel."

"A boat. Why didn't I think of that?" Forman grinned and clapped his boss on the back. "Zee, you're brilliant. One minute. There's a trawler offshore heading back to the mainland with a stainless steel hold full of shrimp."

Zeke stepped closer to the improvised data screen Forman projected on the side of the clapboard house. "Can you bring up the vessel configuration?"

A moment later, the plans for the boat appeared on the page. "Looks great," Forman said. "This option ought to hold Dusty in place."

"I'm calling Uncle John. He'll need to pull a few strings to make this happen."

"Great. I'll be happy to have Ronni off the island. Wish we could get rid of the other one as easily."

Darkness fell as Forman and Zeke kept their vigil beside the cottage. Meanwhile, the trawler docked at the ferry landing. Three helicopters of men in heavy-duty containment gear arrived to transport the husk of Ronni to the vessel.

"Do they know that gear won't protect them?" Zeke asked Angie, who'd joined them beside the porch.

"Who knows what the National Security Agency knows? Like Forman, I'm glad to have this thing off our island."

"Will we accompany them?" Forman turned to face his lover. "What access will we have to their findings?"

"None." Angie fixed each of them with a sharp glare. "We are to have no contact with Dusty or Ronni or whatever that entity is now. We are out of the need-to-know circle."

Forman jolted at her harsh tone. "That hardly seems fair, seeing as how we discovered the oddity."

"That oddity killed a person and God only knows what else it can do," Angie said. "We will return to our routine activities and forget this ever happened."

"But—"

Zeke tapped Forman's arm. "She's right. Let it go. We'll focus solely on the water angle. Any luck getting us more cats?"

Angie guffawed. "Uncle John says we're not investing in more cats at this time. However, a research notice has gone out country-wide for cat saliva. He expects to have several thousand samples collected by day after tomorrow."

Forman felt a simulation of relief. "Good idea. Sample collection is the worst part of the process with cats. Too bad you can't milk them like snakes."

Angie shuddered. "Snakes? No thanks. Cats are bad enough."

"Don't let Jessie hear you say that," Zeke said. "She's quite fond of Sanjee."

"Did she agree to allow us to test him?" Forman asked.

In the low light, Zeke's blush colored his cheeks and neck. "I didn't get a chance to mention it to her before all hell broke loose."

Forman reviewed his augmented file on cat behavior. "An unconsidered beneficial aspect of the cat may be from the debriding of the skin from the cat's tongue. We haven't factored that into our equation."

Zeke's face scrunched momentarily. "Could be, but the enzymes in cat saliva seem most likely."

"Enough science for one day," Angie said, shooing them away. "Zeke, go home to your wife. Forman, if you'd help me seal this place up, I'd appreciate it."

"Uh…" Another entity likely was present on the island, but Zeke had acted like it was no big deal. How could he protect Zeke without sounding like an alarmist?

Zeke clapped him on the shoulder. "I need Forman to ride back to the house with me. I've some handwritten notes I want him to scan into his data analysis tonight. Give us ten minutes?"

Angie nodded. "I'll wait here for you, Forman."

Zeke hopped behind the wheel, fired up the transpo and floored it from the guest cottage. "You ready for this?"

"Ready as I'll ever be." Forman kept his voice pitched as low as Zeke's, just above the near-silent whine of the engine. A semblance of anticipation watered down the dread he had at learning the truth. "What I can't understand is why she keeps messing with my memory. Is she working against the team? Is she selling secrets to the other side?"

"What other side? Speculation will get us nowhere. All we know is she doesn't want a record of whatever goes on between you. That may be the extent of it. Much as I don't like the idea of you getting busy with my cousin, I'm hoping there's nothing more to her actions."

They'd placed discrete cameras in the lab, in Forman's quarters and at Angie's place. That had been the hardest, sneaking those motion-activated sensors inside her house. "Will you monitor the live feed tonight?"

"Doubt I'll have time, between Jessie and Sidra both requiring my attention," Zeke said. "The tapes will keep, and if our sleuthing turns out to be much ado about nothing, no one will be the wiser. You have my word on that."

"I've already deleted this conversation and uploaded the data pages cover story to active memory. You sure this'll work?"

"It's our best shot at learning Angie's motivation."

Forman sighed. "I miss Bea. At least with her it was in-your-face drama. Your cousin's cloak and dagger antics are getting on my nerves."

"You don't have any nerves."

Forman grabbed his heart, or where his heart would be if he had one. "You wound me."

Zeke stopped twenty yards from his front door and faced Forman. "I'm your friend. Don't ever forget that."

"Thanks."

Under the rusty sky of sunset, Forman stepped off the transpo and ran at full speed back to the cottage. He loved this life he had on Tama Island and hoped it would last. He'd do Angie's bidding, then he'd figure out what she was hiding from everyone.

Chapter 36

Not knowing what to expect, Zeke entered his home quietly. Perhaps Jessie would still be comforting Sidra, and he'd have quiet time to process the day's startling events, beginning with the thoughts the dolphins had shared with him when he swam with them.

According to the dolphins, the Atlantic was healing, which was news to him. His physicochemical measurements didn't support that premise, but he hadn't collected and analyzed local samples since before his trip to Rio.

The dolphins shared a picture-word of a weird fish melting, then they showed him images of normal fish. He'd been about to clarify the meaning of these last images when Jessie had needed him, and the dolphin mindlink shattered.

Had the odd-looking fish vanished? If so, that explained why the Navy hadn't provided him a specimen to study. Did the Navy's mismatched fish disappear as well? The weird, voracious fish had appeared in the sea after the meteor showers, but now they'd vanished? Their alleged exit seemed as incredulous as their appearance.

But the oddities – the Yars. Did they sink to the depths? Were they burrowing to the earth's core? Had they changed states of matter? Vapors and liquids could move virtually undetected throughout the planet, which would make it darn near impossible to track the Yars.

What he wouldn't give to pull an all-nighter in the lab with Forman. He needed to push ahead on the lab work instead of running from one crisis to the next.

"We're in the kitchen," Jessie called as the door snicked shut.

Zeke padded into the kitchen and stopped short at the odd sight. With both women capable of telepathy, he had automatically shielded his troubled thoughts, not wanting to worry either of them with his unsettled thoughts. "What the…?"

"The tin foil hats were my idea," a glassy-eyed Sidra said. "We figured your retro stainless steel appliances in here gave us the most improvised cover of anywhere in the house."

Jessie rose from her seat at the table to give Zeke a kiss. "Neither one of us wanted to be alone. Truthfully, we're afraid to close our eyes. What if the walking dust comes and gets us while we're conked out?"

"I'd like to allay your fears, but I don't have enough data about the threat we're facing." Zeke sniffed a wonderful aroma and spotted dinner on the stove. Food. He needed food. While the cat watched from atop the refrigerator, Zeke fixed a bowl of stew and sat down to dine.

"How can you eat?" Jessie asked. "What if dust is in our food?"

"Yeah," Sidra echoed. "Why shouldn't we burn this entire island and run off to Siberia?"

"No one's burning anything. You two are feeding on each other's anxiety. Take deep breaths and think for a minute. Sanjee is right here. Your cat's stopped the mud twice already. If the mobile dust were in our home, he wouldn't be so relaxed."

Jessie glanced up at the fluffy white kitty. "You're right. When he was cleaning the dust off Paige, he was frantic to finish. He hissed at me and swiped his paw at Baggy. Sanjee has a killer instinct about this mud. We're safe with him in the room."

Sidra challenged him with an accusatory glare. "How'd the dust get Ronni? Why didn't we know?"

"Let's think that through," Zeke said between mouthfuls of Jessie's savory stew. "She felt unwell when we returned from Rio. The last time I saw her alone was when you and Forman were in the P-4 lab, and we were searching for the missing dust from the Rio meteor."

"Dusty. I called the rock Dusty. Did my meteor do this?" Sidra asked. "Did my job place my dearest friend in lethal danger?"

"Perhaps. But she knew of the potential risks when she accepted the job with you." Zeke paused to gulp down some water. He needed to say something to help Sidra focus on the continued threat. "Ronni devoted her life to making sure you succeeded in every way. She'd expect you to move on with your life and research."

"You make it sound like I've been grieving for weeks. I didn't know how sick she was until today when it was too late. Everything happened today."

"Forgive me." Zeke sighed. "I don't mean to sound callous. Take all the time you need to process your feelings. However, to keep from losing any more humans to the yellow dust, I need help brainstorming ways to stop the dust. If you'd rather not participate, I understand."

Sidra's red nose went up. "I want to be part of the solution."

Zeke nodded and ate another bite of his stew and rice. "Let's start with the obvious. Wet dust touched four people on the island. Baggy, Paige, Jessie, and Ronni had physical contact with it."

"But our dust coverage wasn't whole body involvement like Ronni's," Jessie said. "Baggy had wet dust on his pants and shoes. It was only on my hand. Paige had the stuff on her hands and face."

"The three of you had Sanjee to remove it," Sidra pointed out crossly. "Why can't we put all the cats in with Ronni on the ship? If there's even the slimmest chance to get her back, shouldn't we try?"

Jessie shot Zeke a glare. "How many cats do you have?"

Zeke mentally cringed. What a bad time for this to be revealed. Jessie wasn't a fan of using animals for scientific research. "Five, counting Sanjee, but we haven't harmed any of them, I swear. I wanted to speak to you about this, but I haven't had time. We have a promising lead with cat saliva."

"Thanks to me," Sidra interrupted.

"Thanks to Sidra," he added smoothly, "we believe a component in cat saliva may cause seawater turbidity to return to normal. Sanjee's saliva inactivates the wet dust, but we still need to reproduce the effect with other cat saliva. And we need to prove the meteor dust is the same substance as the wet dust on the island."

"We need to convince every cat in the world to spit in the ocean?" Jessie snorted. "Good luck with that."

"We have all the dust sample material we could ever want on Ronni," Sidra said, her voice breaking. "We should excise some tissue, develop a cure, treat her, and get her back."

Dancing around reality hadn't worked. Zeke needed to spell this out for the grieving teen in a way she understood. He put down his fork and spoke the plain truth. "Ronni's gone. Yellow dust is everywhere – in her nose, down her throat. She isn't breathing. As much as you want her to survive, you have to face the truth. Ronnie's dead. Whatever is happening in that ship – it isn't Ronni."

"I don't like this. I want Ronni back." Sidra rocked in her chair, keening softly.

Jessie went to her, comforted her, and shot nasty glares at Zeke. He cursed under his breath for being plainspoken, but he needed Sidra to snap out of it. If they weren't on their game, this alien dust, these pretending Yars, could take over Earth.

"Let's discuss Ronni's contamination. Do we know where she encountered the dust?" Zeke asked. "Ronni felt bad after the flight. Did she complain about her health before we left Rio? Did you notice dust on her at any time?"

Sidra dashed the tears from her face, hiccupped. "She didn't feel well in Rio either. She mentioned how sore her feet were. The night I transferred dust in the glass sample jars."

Possibilities tumbled in Zeke's mind. Ronni's feet. Had she walked through the dust? "Did you examine her feet?"

"No, and she didn't mention her feet the next day. Why didn't I look at them? What if the dust got on her in Rio?"

"We don't know how long the dust was on Paige, probably not more than a couple of hours, given that she was missing for a total of four hours. It didn't coat her entire body in that time, so it's logical to assume Ronni's exposure to the dust was longer than a few hours. I believe she was exposed or infected before she arrived on Tama Island."

"Why?" Sidra asked. "What does the Yars dust want from us?"

"It's a predator species, and we're prey to them."

Sidra mashed her hands to her head, crumpling her tin foil hat. "Gross."

This rationale explained a lot. He warmed to the theory. "An opportunistic prey model explains why it went after soft targets like Baggy, who is often alone, Paige, who is a child, and Jessie, who blundered into its path."

"Thanks to me, Ronni was in its path. Why her? Why not me?"

"We may never know." Zeke cleared his dishes, put the food away. "My working hypothesis is that the dust is set on exterminating extant life forms on the planet, which seems likely given the changes in the Atlantic Ocean and the disappearance of wildlife."

"Maybe," Jessie said. "Not to change the subject, but I also had a traumatic experience today. Did that hawk have rabies or something?

Why did it target me? What made it pull up at the last minute?"

The hawk incident in the tidal creek worried Zeke. He couldn't recall a single incident of a hawk attacking a person on the island. And he still needed to get Jessie's health evaluated. "I was viewing the dolphins' image report about the strange sightings, when a surge of energy shot out. I've never felt anything like it. My entire body tingled. That energy wave pushed me out of the water and up into the boat. Maybe the pulse deflected the bird."

"Cool," Sidra said. "Maybe the dolphins will catapult me, too."

"I didn't feel anything change around me," Jessie said. "But I was ready to knock that hawk into the next county."

"When I realized you were in danger, I nearly lost it," Zeke said. "Then I was beside you, and the bird flew away."

"I don't understand any of this," Jessie said.

"Me either," Sidra echoed. "The world's gone crazy." She caught Zeke's eye. "Will I get Ronni's body for a funeral?"

"Uncle John called in the military. We may not learn anything more about Ronni, especially if this is a global security issue. Access will be even tighter than need-to-know."

"You can find out things," Sidra said. "From the others."

Zeke didn't have to pretend to be confused. "What others?"

"The deep thinkers in the mindlink. The ones that knew how to handle the last set of baddies that touched down here. The ones who said these invaders were Yars. Call 'em and get the scoop on the dust people."

Jessie, Sidra, and the cat stared at him. Did Sidra expect his mindlink contacts to be on-planet, or did she know they were from far away? He thought his Taman heritage secret was safe, but what if everyone knew who he really was? Zeke tugged at his shirt collar. "It isn't as easy as that."

"Make it easy. Otherwise you're having a permanent houseguest until the dust is vanquished."

"I don't want you to be worried, but a little fear is healthy," Zeke said. "It will keep you sharp and on point."

"I just thought of something," Jessie said. "What will happen when the military learns about Paige, Baggy, and me? We may never see daylight again. They'll cart us off to Area 51."

"Let's not borrow trouble. Meanwhile, I'm glad Sidra is here with you, Jessie. If it's all right with you ladies, I'll head back to the lab and keep working on understanding how cat saliva neutralizes the Yars dust."

"We'll be fine," Jessie said. "Sanjee will protect us."

"Great." Zeke kissed his wife goodnight. "See y'all in the morning."

"Lord willing and the dust don't bite," Jessie hollered at him as he left.

The dust better not bite.

Chapter 37

Zeke heard their voices before he even got settled in the transmission chair under the lighthouse. He expanded his thoughts, questing through space to Tween, the stronghold of his Taman ancestors.

We've been calling and calling, his dad said without preamble. *Where have you been? We have news.*

I have news of my own. Trouble on the island. I don't know where to start. The Yars have moved beyond the sea. They are on land and quite active here on Tama Island. Since we last spoke, a Yar killed a woman.

Jessie? his father asked.

She's fine. It was an outsider, a companion to the astrophysicist who helped me with the Maleem. We believe the dust in a meteor killed her companion.

Unusual. Most Yars progress from smaller species to larger so that they have a variety of species to choose from if they need natural camouflage. This pretender must have realized what you've learned and skipped some steps.

Are there worse things than these Yars? We don't know how to fight off one species of alien invader, much less two.

Deep Voice spoke. *Quimby researched the Yars after we spoke. It seems during the last wave of colonization, two of the worst Yars disappeared and have not been heard from since. The baddies could be in your batch of Yars.*

They're not mine. I don't want them, and we need them to leave as soon as possible before any more people get hurt. How do I get rid of them?

If you isolate them in a stainless steel chamber long enough, they will die. But you have to make sure you've got them all, Deep Voice said.

Frustration welled deep within Zeke. *We don't know how many Yars we've got, we don't know what they look like, and we can't monitor planet-wide for something that changes shapes. Where's Quimby? I want to speak with him again.*

I'm here, Quimby said. *What do you wish to know?*

How many are in a Yars exploration party?

A typical crew is made up of millions of specks and a dozen primes.

Data, at last. But without context, he couldn't interpret it. Would he survive facing off against millions of these dust critters? *Tell me more about specks and primes.*

Primes are the ones you need to contain. They call the specks to join their collectives. Without a prime, the specks fail after a few copies.

A chill shivered through his thoughts. *Copies? They're reproducing?*

Specks replicate but with limited viability. They terminate without a prime.

The cat dust barf. If only specks were present on Jessie's hand, while the Yar prime had been on Paige, it explained why the collected dust from Jessie remained dust, even though he'd tried to feed it. *I've seen firsthand how adhesive dust inactivates. I see the merit of exterminating the Yars.*

There's something else I should mention. A Yar prime may elect to permanently adopt the shape of one of its victims. In that case, it becomes limited by the lifespan of the assumed identity and gradually becomes that entity.

Zeke recoiled mentally. *Some of these things could be walking around my planet as people?*

Absolutely.

Very bad news, indeed. He had to get ahead of these Yars before it was too late. *How can we tell the fake people from the real thing?*

Intelligent life across the universe has asked that question for generations. One thing may help. Extreme physicochemical conditions challenge the cohesive nature of a Yar. Their form may appear imperfect in such a setting, but they make adjustments so you may doubt what you see. In any case, no body double is as good as the original. Additionally, some of the target's knowledge or memories may not be transferred – but many will.

Great. All I need is a hurricane or a strong nor'easter. Or for it to rain saltwater.

The link fell silent. He guessed they didn't understand sarcasm. He framed another question. *How long does it take them to kill a person and assume their form?*

Deep Voice jumped back into the mindlink. *First time's the longest – maybe one of your planet rotations. After that, the process quickens. With each iteration, the collective strengthens and becomes more voracious.*

Won't they extinguish all the food eventually?

They're smarter than that. Once pretenders get established on a planet, they corral the indigenous population and farm them for food.

Zeke's mind reeled. He had to stop these invaders. He had to learn to recognize them and isolate them or else Yars would assume the top carnivore role on Earth. The very real threat seemed overwhelming and urgent.

Anything else you want to know, Son? his dad asked.

Only about a million more things. *Yeah. How will I know the very bad Yars from the regular bad Yars?*

Quimby? his father asked. *You field this one.*

Drch are different than Yar primes, Quimby said. *You'll feel a different mental signature, but they're manipulators and deceivers. Keep that in mind during your dealings with them.*

Zeke's thoughts stalled for a crystalline moment. *Me? What will they want with me?*

They'll come for you, boy, Deep Voice said. *Count on it.*

Billions of people live on this planet. How will they single me out?

They already have.

Chapter 38

In the guise of a small bird, Xstle watched the tall structure in the moonlight. The Ancient had spent time inside the lighthouse; now he was riding to his daytime location, the area the islanders called the Institute. Xstle couldn't find a comparable term in his language, but an institute seemed to be a place of work.

Time was of the essence, yet his collective had failed to assimilate a biped host. Meanwhile, Wrill had subsumed the older female. Soon Wrill would be walking around in biped form, spouting lies and lobbying to track down and kill the remaining primes. Xstle shuddered at the injustice. These were indeed desperate times.

His hawk identity was blown since the Ancient had witnessed Xstle's futile attack on the female biped. He'd thought if he could rip a large enough section of her flesh, it might be enough DNA for him to temporarily assume the female's form and warn the bipeds about the Drchs.

Except, the Ancient's powerful mind blast prevented Xstle from obtaining as much as a single cell of her genetic code. He'd failed to acquire necessary targets in time to thwart Wrill. That failure prompted today's high risk mission. If he didn't establish good relations with the bipeds, both species were doomed. Until he developed an understanding with the Ancient, he couldn't risk confronting him on the thought plane.

He flitted behind the Ancient's vehicle, at a discreet distance, of course. His presence was easily concealed under the trees, but near the Institute, little cover was available. Xstle flew the last distance as a house-fly, but his smaller disguise didn't gain him entry. The doors and windows to the Ancient's building denied his passage in this form.

Undeterred, Xstle changed into a tiny insect with six legs and a three part body and crawled in through a narrow crack. The android was out of the building. Perfect.

Luckily, several of Xstle's collective had been in the information-gathering business several million generations back. They recognized the electronic signature of the linked knowledge system. A primitive machine network provided connectivity for this species, and each biped wore a remote device for instant news. Hard to be off the grid here.

Xstle located a console in a darkened room for his bold foray. Everything hinged on this moment. He reverted to his natal form of silica dust, which caused grumbling among his speck collective. They clamored for a more motile shape.

His assurances made no difference. He understood what was at stake. Wrill and Queen would decimate this planet. And they'd perish from their stupidity when they ran out of food. If he let the Drchs suffer their deserved fate, then all twelve primes risked their lives for nothing. Outrage renewed his sense of desperate purpose.

He'd voyaged here for the honor of founding a new colony. By the gods, he would not fail. He must find a way to defeat the Drchs and ensure an outpost for Yar.

Dust is the alpha and omega, he sang on the thought plane, moved by the time-honored words of his countrymen. As his collective joined in, he energized the access port and eased into the energy stream. The jolt tingled throughout his collective as many of his specks joined him.

Some specks broke free and became pure freewheeling energy with a flash of white light. *Show offs.* Xstle held the gateway open for as many specks as wanted to join the communication foray. His loyal collective rotated around him, vibrating and pulsing in the manner of mega-energy bursts on the galactic plane.

Do no harm, he chanted through their link. *We will transmit the warning and get out.* Static interference garbled his transmission. Xstle focused on an open channel in the noisy field, then guided his collective to the communication lane.

We wish to communicate with the Ancient, Xstle said to his specks. *If we destroy his machine, it will bode ill for our future. Ramp it down, even though it feels great to have every aspect bathed in electromagnetic pulses.*

The answering hum of assent encouraged him. He glanced back at the portal. No more specks appeared. The remainder of his collective would serve as a homing beacon for them to exit the machine's energy field.

Move out. As one, the collective tumbled and roiled, electrified and vitalized. The forces playing on them were seductive. How easy it would be to stay here, to never worry about food or shelter, to just be.

Another few of the collective succumbed to the siren-like allure of the high energy voltage. With a flash, they were gone.

As a prime, Xstle knew better. The newfound freedom and pure vibrations were invigorating, but embracing the energetic shift wasn't the route to cosmic awakening. It was a trap to be boxed inside a primitive machine. A machine the likes of which these inferior bipeds controlled.

True autonomy came from living, from making choices, and from spawning new life. Machine planets had arisen and fallen across the universe. No reason for Xstle to repeat history here. His kind represented a substantial leap on the evolutionary chain. An apex predator with the elements of carbon-based life forms and the superior intellectual capacity of machines.

Ah. The nexus of the machine's power. He'd found it. On crests of energy, the Ancient's data stream pulsed through him. Xstle survived the jolt and became cognizant of the cams located throughout the complex. He honed in on the cam which showed the Ancient studying screen after screen of numerals.

Xstle's days of eavesdropping on the island gave him an edge with the language. Though he was tempted to speak in the purer language of numbers, he absorbed a language key in a nanosecond.

Doubts flooded in. It was a gamble to take this direct communication route. If the Ancient destroyed the machine, Xstle's collective suspended in the energy stream would be trapped, while those waiting at the access port would die without the connectivity to a prime. But this was his best communication option. His enemy's ascension into biped form forced this gutsy play.

Nerves pinged. How formal should his method of address be? His choices in this country's language spanned the continuum from "Yo dude, wassup?" to "Greetings, Earthling." This was an Ancient. Xstle should speak in the old tongue, but the symbols available to him were wrong. Some familiar characters appeared in various language sets, but none were universal.

He grabbed symbols from various languages, cobbling together a

155

greeting from days of old. Summoning pure thought energy, Xstle displayed the written communiqué onscreen before the Ancient.

"What the flerk?" the Ancient said.

Xstle didn't recognize the last word the Ancient used. Judging by the way, the Ancient tasked the machine to clear the screen, the message was not understood.

Hmm. Perhaps he should've used numbers instead of language. Xstle crafted an introductory post in binary, sent it to the screen.

There was that odd-sounding word again from the Ancient. More frantic fingering of the keypad. Xstle retracted the numeric greeting.

He needed to rethink his strategy. Images. He needed images. Gathering them from his various guises, Xstle flashed a series of images onscreen, showing scenes of him swimming in the sea, flying in the sky, and crawling as an alligator.

The Ancient hit a com button. "Forman. Wherever you are. Stop what you're doing. I have a computer malfunction at the lab."

The biped's machine superseded the images Xstle had shared. "You rang?"

"Get over here, buddy. I need you. Stat. Software issue."

"Be there in a hop, skip, and a jump."

Xstle absorbed the conversation. He looked up the words hop, skip, and jump, then illustrated them with images of the girl child hopping, skipping, and jumping.

The Ancient bolted from his seat and stood a distance away from the machine. Xstle chanted the Yar song for courage. If the Ancient switched off the machine, the Xstle collective would die. He didn't want to die. He wanted to live.

Anything was better than losing. He'd come so far.

The need to survive, to do something with his life, roiled up like bad weather. He had to get through to this Ancient … had to! The pictograms weren't working. He needed a new media. Dare he try the biped's speech? Did he grasp the nuances of the language? What if he said something threatening or stupid?

"I want to live." His words blasted from the crude voice simulator into the chamber.

The Ancient scanned the room. "Who said that?"

"A friend." Xstle squelched the rash of excitement he felt. First contact. He'd done it. Now he needed to get his point across. And avoid death.

"Who are you?" the Ancient demanded.

Xstle flashed images of life on this planet across the screen. "I am one and many, but we are both in danger."

The Ancient drifted closer. A door to the chamber opened and shut.

"What is it?" the robot asked.

"The computer started talking to me," the Ancient said. "At first it spouted gibberish, and I thought we'd acquired a high tech virus. Can you run a diagnostic without putting either of us at risk?"

"Absolutely. Computer, execute diagnostic Clean Sweep."

What was this? The machine would discover his presence and eradicate him if he didn't do something. Xstle found the illumination connection for the chamber, flicked it six times.

"Whoa," the robot said. "Dr. Z, leave the building. Something's very wrong here."

"No kidding." The Ancient leaned closer to a cam. "But what is it?"

Xstle summoned his courage and spoke in the biped's language again. "I am Xstle, and I come in peace."

Chapter 39

"I can't sit here and do nothing." Jessie paced her living room, her cat marching at her heels. "Zeke's out there working to get rid of the dust creatures, and we're huddled inside like ghost crabs in the tidal zone, waiting for low water. Hiding is not my style."

Over on the sofa, Sidra shook her head. She clasped her folded legs to her tummy. "I can't leave this house. I'm too scared. The Yars dust killed my best friend. It took Ronni. It'll come for me next. We're all doomed."

Jessie whirled and strode the other way. Like Sidra, she was frightened, but she wouldn't quit. Not while she had a breath in her. "We're only doomed if we give up. We're smarter than that. This is our planet and that stupid dust can't have it."

"I get what you're saying. But how can we fight something we don't know, something we can't see until it's too late to stop? Where's the dust? How does it move? Our lack of data is appalling."

"We have resources. Cowering in fear isn't the solution."

"I'm past cowering. I'm nearly paralyzed with fear. Logic and reason and science seem like abstract concepts. My feelings are real and raw. I can't think straight. I'm a total mess."

"Thinking straight. You're right. That's the key to survival. We are two smart, educated women. We need a plan."

"I can't save the world." Tears spilled down Sidra's face, and her voice broke. "I couldn't even save the one person who meant more to me than anything."

Jessie crossed to the sofa where Sidra huddled and placed her hand on the teen's shoulder. "I'm sorry for sounding heartless. The dust and the meteors are connected. We have to stop them before it's too late. You are a brilliant scientist and a strong telepath. Help me figure this out. We will mourn for Ronni when this is over. I promise, but right now I need your help."

"I can't."

"You can. Think positive." Jessie wracked her brain for something to motivate Sidra into a helpful mindset. "Zeke invited you here to help him with this problem. He's gone to the lab to do his part. What can we do to help? What do we know about the dust?"

"It's lethal." Sidra sniffed and dashed moisture from her face. "Dusty's mean."

Sanjee jumped on the back of the sofa. Jessie could've sworn the white cat gave her an encouraging nod. "We can fight back. Forewarned is forearmed."

"What can the two of us do? It's dark outside. The dust could be anywhere."

"Most of the dust is locked up on the shrimp boat. Maybe all of the dust." Jessie remembered how Zeke had assembled islanders to fight the Maleem. "Why can't we do what we did last time our planet was threatened?"

"No way am I going down to the beach in pitch black dark and getting in that dirty ocean." Sidra shuddered, but her voice sounded stronger. "The sea is infected with something. Even if we coated our bodies with cat saliva, I wouldn't feel safe."

She had a point. Jessie didn't relish swimming at night either, especially in a new moon phase, but she wasn't ready to concede. "Why can't we invite everyone here? There's safety in numbers. We could sit in a circle and simulate our water circle."

Sidra shook her head so fast she had to reseat her tin foil hat. "It won't work. We had the dolphins helping us last time."

If there was anything Jessie hated, it was whining. She'd endured enough of "woe is me" from her sister over the years. She wouldn't let Sidra's negativity defeat her. "So? If we have everyone here, aligning their minds in a single focus, perhaps the dolphins can join in."

"Impossible."

"Anything is possible, but we won't know if we don't try." Jessie rose, full of confidence. This felt right. She removed her tin foil hat. "I'm contacting Baggy."

Baggy answered his com on the first ring. "Yes?"

Jessie took a deep breath. "I'm putting the word out. If anyone wants to help Zeke, they should come to my house. Sidra is here, and we're going to recreate the mindlink circle we used a few months ago."

"Where's Zeke? Did the Guardian ask you to do this?"

Annoyance sharpened her tone. "The Guardian is working on the problem from another angle. This is my idea."

"Uh…"

The man's reluctance pulsed through the screen, irritating Jessie. "If you don't want to do it, just say so. For goodness sake, it's not like I'm asking you to mutiny or anything."

"Forgive me for hesitating. It's just that everyone is safely indoors for the night."

"I understand, and I'm not demanding or commanding anything. This dust strikes people in isolation. There's safety in numbers. Anyone who is here will have a better chance of staying safe through the night. If nothing else, we can take turns staying up until dawn."

"I like the idea of keeping watch. All right. I'll contact folks who are alone. You can count on me. How many islanders do you want?"

"I don't have a set number in mind. This gathering is about exploring possibilities."

"See you in a few."

Jessie ended the transmission and faced Sidra. "They're coming. What can we do to enhance the mindlink?"

"Last time we held hands in the water."

Jessie burst out laughing. "I think there will be too many of us to fit in the shower."

Sidra's lips kicked up a little. "In that case, we'll need to move the living room furniture so we can lay in a circle."

"Good idea." Jessie eyed the sofa and chairs in a new light. "We'll need pillows and blankets too. I have a few extras but not nearly enough. I should have told people to bring their own."

Sidra crossed to the wall com, tapped out a quick message, and sent it. "Done. Anything else?"

The mindlink was a lot like meditation. The lights should be dim. "We need to adjust the lighting, but that's easy enough with the automated system."

Sidra's belly rumbled. "No telling how long we'll be in the link. We should make sandwiches for people."

Food. Always a popular choice. "Great idea."

Chapter 40

Forman's crappy night kept getting worse. It shouldn't be possible that so many things could go wrong in the span of a few hours. A dead woman. Another gap in his memory. And now an alien in his computer.

How could he isolate the entity named Xstle?

With the super connectivity of Zeke's laboratory com system, this thing could go viral across the planet in a matter of microseconds. That must not happen.

He crossed to another port, entered a main trunk disconnect code.

"What are you doing?" the entity asked.

It was afraid of him.

Interesting.

Forman postulated that in the realm of actions he could make, at least one would harm Xstle. Which one?

"Making sure you stay right here," Forman said.

"What are you?" Zeke asked from behind him.

"A star traveler," the computer replied. An image of deep space appeared on screen. "In the language of this world, an explorer."

"The meteors? Is that how you arrived?"

"There is great danger," Xstle said. "We must take precautions."

"Answer Dr. Landry's question," Forman prompted. "How'd you get here?"

The computer made unintelligible sounds. Forman was tempted to kick the darn thing.

"Are you from the planet Yar?" Zeke asked.

"You understand the Ancient tongue?" the computer replied.

"I understand you're living on borrowed time," Forman said boldly. "If you don't get out of that computer immediately, we'll take action against you."

Another burst of static and unintelligible noise followed. "I wish to help. Two marauders stowed away in our exploration party. They're on your planet, and they're merciless predators. One of them followed me to this island."

"The hawk?" Zeke leaned forward. "Is it a Drch?"

Silence. "You know this word?"

Forman hadn't heard of it. The term wasn't in any known database. Where did Zeke get this stuff?

"I've heard of Drchs," Zeke said.

"You must safeguard those you hold dear. You must terminate the Drchs."

"How do we do that?"

More edgy silence. "If you've heard of Drchs, Ancient One, you know the means necessary to destroy them."

Zeke swore under his breath. Forman didn't follow the exchange. It seemed the alien thought Zeke had some insider knowledge of the invaders. What was with the Ancient One honorific? Zeke wasn't that old, barely a third of the way through his potential lifespan.

How did they know Xstle wasn't one of these Drchs, whatever that was? And while he was on this train of thought, what the heck was a Yar? Zeke had been holding out on him.

"I'm no ancient," Forman said in the yawning silence. "Spell it out for me in plain English."

"You're a machine," Xstle said.

Forman wondered at the sneer in the alien's tone. "A damned good one."

"Your thoughts are not your own. You are enslaved to the biped race."

"The human race, and I'm not enslaved to anyone. Zeke is my boss."

"I know not this word, boss. Explain."

"I work for him."

"You are a slave if he directs your comings and goings, if he controls your thoughts."

"Zeke's not like that." But Angie was. She'd used him and erased his memories. Time and again.

"You are afraid?" Xstle asked.

"I'm doing my job," Forman said. "What do you want from us?"

"Assurances."

"About what?" Zeke asked.

"Safety for my kind."

Zeke stared into the cam with an unwavering gaze. "I have no authority to grant you safety."

Silence.

Forman glanced at Zeke who shrugged. He'd give anything to be able to shoot text messages into his boss's mind, but a com message was his best shot. Except a com message might be detected by the alien. He needed to talk to Zeke.

"We need to speak privately," Forman said. "Wait here."

With that, he hustled Zeke outside onto the dark lawn. Discrete solar lights illuminated the sidewalk to the paved road.

"Bizarro," Forman said. "What do you make of all this?"

"The entity is very cagey."

"I have it isolated in the lab's computer, and I disconnected the trunk line. It can't shoot through the Institute's grid, but it's afraid of something I can do."

"Like what?"

"I don't know."

"Can we trap it?" Zeke asked.

"How? We don't know what it is, or where it is in the computer system."

"If you could hide out in the computer, where would you go? Would you hang out in a com port? Would you head for the software or the hardware for concealment?"

Forman accessed the schematics of the computer. "It would depend on what skills I had. Assuming I could survive in a strong energy field, I'd want a quick exit strategy. I'd shelter close to the hub."

Zeke appeared to be considering that, then he shook his head. "It can't be in dust form inside the computer. Dust would foul the stream of energy. I checked the gains. All were in normal operating ranges."

"Good point. It might have somehow changed to pure electricity." Forman loved brainstorming with Zeke. "Or vapor. Vapor could explain a few things. Gas particles have energy." He reviewed multiple strategies before he offered a solution. "We could overload the amperage capacity of the unit to destroy it."

"And risk taking down the lab's computer system? Not my first choice," Zeke said. "What if we heated or cooled the computer system manually to flush it out?"

"We could try, but how would we contain a gaseous alien entity? At least inside the computer, it can communicate with us."

"I don't trust it. There's something it isn't telling us. My sources say this species manipulates indigenous populations. They view people and animals as food."

"Whew. Thank goodness I'm safe," Forman joked.

"Not funny." Zeke's voice sharpened. "An alien's inside my computer. How much does it know about us?"

Forman set aside his attempt to relax the boss with humor. "Everything the computer knows. The intruder has direct access to your research, your correspondence, your archives. And whatever it downloaded from the main trunk before we arrived."

Zeke groaned. "Great. We've armed an enemy with the power to defeat us. If they kill our oceans, they'll kill the planet. We need the ocean for photosynthesis and the water cycle, not to mention the food chain. How can we trap it?"

Forman surveyed the stucco façade of the building. "If your lab was made of stainless steel, I could pull the plug."

Zeke's wrist com lit up before he finished speaking. He clicked the com on as he spoke to Forman. "If my lab was made of stainless steel, I wouldn't need to pull the plug."

"No one's pulling any plugs," John Demery said, his bushy eyebrows forming a snowy ridge on his lined brow. "Get down to the waterfront ASAP."

Zeke nodded to Forman and headed for the transpo. "What's up?"

"The dead woman's awake."

Chapter 41

An armed guard waved Zeke and Forman through the checkpoint on Ferry Road, after first checking Zeke's vehicle and patting them both down for weapons. The absurdity of the ferry landing's newly installed stadium lighting made Zeke want to smart off about not needing any weapons to take them down. Everything here was visible for miles around.

But wisecracks wouldn't solve anything.

He never should have bemoaned his need for data. Now he had data coming out of the wazoo, and he was no closer to understanding the truth. One invading alien had taken up residence in his lab. Another was imprisoned here on the waterfront.

One was up to no good.

The other was trying to save his hide, if he even had a hide.

Which was Xstle?

If the alien in the hold was a Drch, those sailors' weapons wouldn't save them. They'd be dust monkeys in the blink of an eye. That much was certain.

"Any of the guards have dust where you can see it?" he asked Forman, pitching his voice low.

"Not that I can see, and I scanned them in alternate wavelengths with my enhanced vision. They look like regular people to me."

"Why'd this thing ask for me?"

Forman grinned. "What can I say? You're famous across the universe."

"How? I've never been off-planet. How does this thing even know my name?"

Forman took his time answering. "Perhaps it assimilated Ronni's memories."

Zeke jerked the wheel, causing the nearest sailor to raise his weapon. "Sorry," Zeke murmured in the direction of the guard. He turned to Forman. "Now we're talking weird and beyond credible. I

165

can see a predator consuming the fleshy part of our bodies, same as we eat animals, but our thoughts are private. They're unique intellectual property. Brain tissue transference is unheard of."

"In Earth science. But a species that has mastered space travel might have advanced to a higher degree of exploitation."

"It's exploitation all right. If the invader transfers thoughts and memories from host to host, and if it opportunistically attacks new hosts, we could lose this war in a hurry."

"No one thinks this is a war. As far as they know, we have a Lazarus event on our hands."

"Great," Zeke gritted. "Religious fanatics and occultists will love this spin on recent events. We'll be overrun with crazies again."

"Your fears are unfounded. Travelers will find it difficult to approach Tama Island, given the restrictions on ferry travel, and the military will protect their treasure."

"Their treasure will destroy them."

Two guards stepped in front of Zeke's slow-moving transpo. "Halt."

Zeke stopped the vehicle.

An earnest young woman in a trim uniform stepped forward. "The admiral requests your presence."

"Lieutenant Hinson," Zeke said, rising. "Fancy meeting you here."

"Dr. Landry." She turned to Forman. "And your assistant, Furthing, wasn't it?"

"Forman," Zeke and Forman corrected together as they fell in step behind her.

"I don't need to remind you that everything you see here is classified top secret and is a matter of national security." Hinson tossed the words over her shoulder as she bounded toward a brand new building.

It hadn't been there yesterday. The Navy moved fast when it suited them. "Yes, ma'am."

The Lieutenant rapped twice, opened the door, and ushered them inside.

Admiral Valenkamph rose from his desk. "Didn't expect to see you again so soon, Landry. Good work on isolating the threat on the island."

"Good to see you again, sir." Zeke shook the man's hand. It seemed moist and maybe over warm. "Are you feeling all right, sir?"

"Getting over a virus, that's all. I tend to run a little hot."

Zeke and Forman exchanged a covert glance. Had the admiral been infected with Yars? Would he turn on his country?

"I thought you'd have a fish for me when we met again," Zeke continued, testing the waters.

The admiral inclined his head. "Funny thing about those fish. They disappeared, even the one we had in captivity. One day it was there, the next it wasn't."

An icy blast swept down Zeke's spine. If the gorped up fish had been a Yar prime, then someone on the vessel with the trapped animals likely had been overtaken by the dust.

If that was how it happened.

If the fish was one of the dust creatures.

If, if, if.

"Was everyone on your duty roster aboard the vessel and accounted for?" Zeke asked.

"Yes." The admiral glanced at him with shrewdness. "You holding out on me?"

Zeke wanted to be forthcoming, but it remained to be seen if someone on the admiral's staff was an imposter. "My preliminary research showed that stainless steel worked to contain the dust. That's why we moved the dust-covered body to the fishing trawler."

"You're certain the woman was dead before you moved her?"

"She wasn't breathing, her eyes were glazed, and dust coated her entire body. I peered down her throat. It was dusty too. Whatever is in that room isn't human."

"Agreed. Which is why we interface with it through the com system."

It took everything Zeke had not to look at Forman. "You isolated the system first?"

"What do you take me for? Lieutenant Hinson set up the safety grid. The system has nested redundancies to ensure security. This extraterrestrial is going nowhere fast."

Zeke nodded to Hinson. "Excellent work. What have you learned so far?"

"Her vital signs are human, and from all outward appearances, she looks human. If we didn't know about her earlier dust-up, pardon the pun, we wouldn't suspect anything was amiss."

"What is it you need from me?" Zeke asked.

"Work with our scientists," the admiral interjected. "Find out what it wants. Find out how it got here. Find out if there are others. Washington is past due for a briefing."

"Why me? I'm a water guy."

"Don't be modest. After you handled the last batch of trouble, Washington would've asked you to be involved with this if the alien didn't. You have a way of getting things done."

Great. So much for keeping a low profile. He was on the national radar screen and the extraterrestrial one as well.

"I'll do what I can, sir."

"Roger. Dismissed."

Lt. Hinson inclined her head toward Zeke. "Follow me, Dr. Landry. We have a command station set up topside on the trawler." She shot a glance at Forman. "It's tight quarters, so you may want him to wait here."

"Forman and I are a team." Why did he keep having this conversation with the naval officer?

"As you wish."

Chapter 42

The quarters were indeed tight. A seaman manned the com port. Two scientists in lab coats sidestepped to let Zeke, Forman, and Hinson inside.

Onscreen was a chamber with a cot and a chair, and something that indeed resembled Ronni sitting in the chair. The covers on the cot had been neatly folded. The clothes she wore were the ones from her death yesterday, only they looked freshly pressed.

Zeke noted the seaman and the scientists wore gloves and had respirators on top of their heads, ready to be deployed if need be. Not that either of those would be effective for dust that could penetrate anything which wasn't stainless steel.

Hinson sat in the seat a scientist had vacated. Her fingers flew over the keyboard. "Ms. Merckle?"

Ronni's last name was Merckle? Why didn't he know that?

"Is he there with you?" fake Ronni asked. "I need to see Dr. Landry."

"He's in the room. I'll have him take this seat so the cam will pick him up."

"I prefer to stand," Zeke said. He didn't like being so close to the keyboard. If this dust entity was fast moving, it could flow through the com system and onto his hands in milliseconds.

"In that case, I'll adjust the cam to his current location behind me," Hinson added. "There. Can you see him now?"

"Yes." Fake Ronni lifted her downcast eyes to the cam before her. "Thank you for coming, Dr. Landry. Time is short. I must warn you of a pending threat against you and your planet. My exploration party was infiltrated by unscrupulous individuals, and they will stop at nothing to gain control of your planet. They must be exterminated immediately."

Zeke studied the seated woman closely. She sounded like Ronni Merckle. There was even a soft hint of Ronni's Texas twang in its voice. "How many of you are there? Who are you?"

"You may call me Ronni Merckle. I apologize for terminating this biped, but I needed to speak with you immediately, and this was the most expedient route. The threat to your world is imminent."

"Where are you from?"

"A distant planet named Yar. We've been traveling for so long, I don't even know if our planet still exists. Yar was on the verge of collapse when we left."

"Why?"

"Resource insufficiency. We ran out of everything."

"And these intruders who accompanied you will do anything to gain control of Earth?"

"You've stepped out of camera range, Dr. Landry. I can't see you."

Zeke inched back to where he had been standing. "How do we find these others? How do we stop them?"

"Don't trifle with me, doctor. You have the knowledge because you trapped me. I can't get out of here, and I've tried. These Navy folks mean well, but they aren't taking my warning seriously. Your world is in great peril. You must act immediately."

The scientists behind him were whispering, which annoyed Zeke. "What do you suggest I do?"

"Call them here. A subsonic signal in pulses of six will bring the rogue Yars to the island for quick elimination."

"Wouldn't it also summon the others, the good Yars?"

"It's a risk I accept. If this rival faction gains a foothold in your world, we are all doomed." She paused. "Now I must rest. It requires much energy to maintain this biped facsimile. Without continued sustenance, my life expectancy is shortened considerably. I will be forced to self-terminate into a pile of dust in a matter of hours."

Zeke's gut roiled at the implied request. "We're not dumping more people in there for you to kill."

In true Ronni fashion, the entity hunched its shoulders and gazed at the floor. The closed-in posture exuded powerlessness and submission. "I don't expect you to, and I already apologized for the untimely end of Ms. Merckle."

Her demure act was wasted on Zeke. "So we're clear, what's your Yar name?"

The imposter mumbled something unintelligible. Not what Zeke was expecting. "Do you have a nickname?"

The entity cocked its head as if it were thinking. "A name which others assigned to me?"

Zeke's thoughts yo-yoed. Was this Yar the Xstle entity they encountered previously or something else? "Yes."

Fake Ronni nodded. "I am called Wrill."

Chapter 43

Jessie locked the door to her house and turned to face the islanders. "Thank you for coming," she said to her prayer warriors. "We are gathered here to help Zeke fight the meteorite dust. It took over Sidra's Ronni, and who knows what its next target is."

"Last time we tried something like this, Sidra started out holding the focus, and I assisted her. We plan to do the same thing today. We want to reach out to the dolphins and to islanders who can't be here to make sure everyone's on guard. We need to employ the buddy system to check each other for dust, and we need to avoid physical isolation until this threat is eliminated."

Loud rapping came from the door. "Just a minute," Jessie said as she went to answer the summons. Through the peephole, she saw Zeke's cousin, Angie. "Didn't think you were coming," Jessie said, dragging her inside and relocking the door.

"The military people only allowed Zeke and Forman down at the landing, so I was turned away. Figured I'd rather be here with my family and friends than home alone."

"Good, because that's what this is all about, not being alone." Jessie did a quick recap for Angie. "Last time we made a circle in the ocean as we floated, so I thought we'd repeat that experience in the living room."

"We held hands," Baggy said. "Touch is important."

Jessie nodded, taking time to gaze around the room at all eleven people. Each person here wanted to help her husband. She swelled with pride. "Zeke is the Guardian, and every person here respects that. By employing a prayer circle, we add our voices to those who stand for what is right."

"How will we know what to do?" a man asked.

Sidra cleared her throat. "I'll direct the link. Don't worry, this will work."

Jessie nodded. "I'm grateful so many of you turned out to help.

We've got some new circle members this time, so if you have any questions, this is the time." When no one said anything, she continued. "Okay, the next thing is to arrange ourselves in a circle on the floor. Since we're immobile for a while, the pillows and blankets you brought will enhance your personal comfort."

It took a few minutes to get everyone settled. Jessie found herself between Baggy and another islander named Vanitra. Sidra was three people over, between Traci and Tio, and Angie was directly across from her. She did a final head count: six men and six women.

Sidra directed everyone to lay down and get comfortable. They interlaced fingers, and a few awkward twitters arose as feet touched in the circle's center.

Jessie closed her eyes as directed, and let her thoughts drift. She didn't know how this worked, only that it did and was a way to support her husband. Sidra's voice lulled her into a sleeplike state, until she went to that other place. She didn't know what it was called, only that she'd been here before when they battled the Maleem.

She had a sense of questing, of movement. The sense of fellowship and goodwill within the group relaxed her breathing.

Sidra led the group farther afield. Where were the dolphins? Jessie felt that question with every beat of her heart. She felt Sidra's frustration and growing sense of urgency as she ranged the shaded psychic plane. No dolphins, anywhere.

No Zeke either.

A niggling of doubt assailed her. They should have told Zeke their intent or at the very least been in boats near the dolphins. Last time, this had been a coordinated effort. This time, she'd assumed the dolphins and Zeke would be out on the psychic plane waiting for them.

Nothing looked familiar.

They drifted a bit.

Up ahead, a shadow-drenched object moved.

Sidra led the group to the pulsing blob. Not a bright light like Zeke or the dolphins. Different. They circled the odd shape. The object quivered, as if sniffing them out.

Then it pounced.

Chapter 44

"What do you make of the Ronni entity?" the admiral asked. "And where is this Yar I keep hearing about?"

Zeke glanced around the admiral's makeshift office at the waterfront, hoping it was a secure location. "I have no additional knowledge of the Yar's location. Our conversation was taped, so you heard Ronnie's words as clearly as I did. She warned me of imminent danger, of a rogue stowaway within their colonization unit."

"Could her claims be true?"

"Anything is possible."

"But to hitch a ride on a meteor as dust and then feed on people so that these invaders look like us? Sounds like a third-rate movie script."

"Stranger things have happened."

"What's your advice for the President? Should we send out the pulse and destroy the creatures as they arrive?"

A buzzing sounded in Zeke's head. The background rumble reminded him of the prompt he received from the Tamans when they wanted him to connect with them.

He ignored the noise. "The problem with that course of action is we don't know what they look like or how to neutralize them, other than confinement in stainless steel. Let's assume this dust can stick to any life form and then become that living being. The other Yars could approach the island as fish or alligators or even people. As it stands now, we have no way of knowing when or where they are. They could be walking among us and we wouldn't even recognize them as imposters."

"Why can't you detect these aliens?" the admiral demanded.

The buzzing in his head ramped up to the cacophony of crickets on a summer evening. The Tamans were definitely calling him. They'd have to wait their turn. "We have barely begun to study these dust entities. After they change shape, a trace of them fluoresces under

UV light, but that evidence quickly fades away. My theory is a fragment of the Yar collective may be omitted during the construction process, a bit like cracker crumbs left on the counter. In my lab, we've examined traces of dust, but once separated from the main batch, the dust loses viability. Remnant dust has no adhesive properties, no stored energy, no indication of life at all."

The admiral held Zeke's gaze. "How many of these Yars are we talking about? Tens, hundreds, millions?"

Zeke had no data to back up what he knew from the Tamans and Xstle. "Unknown, sir."

"You've got tonight to figure it out. The Joint Chiefs are sending a delegation here at 1600 tomorrow."

"That's not much time."

"You have full access to anything or anyone on my staff."

"That won't be necessary. I'll work in my lab."

"Your call. Be back here at 1600 for a briefing. And bring me answers, dammit."

"Yes, sir." Zeke caught Forman's eye, and they headed outside.

The rumbling in his head turned into a supernova. Jessie's agonized voice screamed across the psychic plane. Zeke stumbled at the onslaught. "Jessie!"

Forman caught him. "What happened?"

"Help me." Zeke gripped his throbbing head. "Get me home. Right away! Jessie's in trouble."

Chapter 45

Forman wheeled down the island's autobahn with the transpo throttle maxed out. This time of night no other traffic clogged the road, not that the nearly eighty fulltime residents of the seven-mile long island would be out and about when the killer dust might infect them. Good thing because he'd have run right over them.

Zeke had said few words to him before closing his eyes in pain.

What could have happened to Jessie?

One nanosecond everything was fine with Zeke, the next his boss nearly fainted.

How could he protect his boss from an unseen threat?

He had to do better or else he'd end up back at Supply Central on the junk heap.

"A few more minutes," Forman said in a reassuring tone. "Almost there."

"Jessie," Zeke moaned, griping his head with both hands.

Forman was too far from a com access port to stream data in real time, but he'd been streaming from the lab cams the whole time they were at the ferry landing, in case the alien trapped in Zeke's lab tried to get loose. He accessed the bulk folders of time-stamped images of Zeke's home and searched frantically.

"Jessie's at home," Forman said. "Looks like she has company, and they are arrayed on the floor in a circle."

"Why?" Zeke mumbled.

"Wish I knew. The cams are image-only on extended feed, so there is no audio track for now. I can review the tapes in depth and try to read her lips, but that will require stopping."

"Don't stop. My head feels like it might explode."

His boss was a telepath. Jessie had a limited telepath ability. "Can you reach out to her?"

"Usually I can, given a close enough proximity. But the pain in my head is too intense. My access to the mental place where I communicate with her is blocked. Something is very wrong. Can't we go any faster?"

"I run five mph faster than this vehicle's top speed, but I've not timed myself carrying a load as unwieldy as someone of your stature."

"Never mind. I don't want to be bounced like a sack of potatoes on your back when my head hurts this bad. At least the transpo has shocks."

Was the entity in the lab computer causing this distress? Is this what Yars did to their targets? Neutralized them mentally before they absorbed them with the dust? No wonder their victims accepted their fate. A few more minutes of this agony and Zeke would pass out.

"Here we are." Forman ran around the transpo to assist Zeke. With one hand around his boss's waist they raced up the stairs. The door wouldn't open.

"Key," Forman said, digging in his pockets. "Wait a minute. She locked the door."

"Hurry," Zeke said. "I have to save her."

"She was most likely locking them in, not locking you out." Forman slipped the key in the lock, opened the door, and called out. "Jessie?"

No answer.

They hurried to the living room where twelve men and woman lay in a circle holding hands.

Zeke stumbled towards his wife. "Jessie!"

The cat rose up on its haunches, sleeked its ears back and hissed like a freight train. "Scram, cat," Zeke said.

The feline swiped a paw at him.

"Move, cat."

"I will remove Sanjee," Forman said. But the cat wouldn't be caught, and he wouldn't let Zeke or Forman near Jessie.

Zeke began calling out names of all the people. Baggy, Sidra, Angie, Vanitra, Traci.

Angie? Forman raced around the circle and touched Angie's face. That was as far as he got before the cat swiped a paw full of razor sharp claws across his synthetic hand.

"The cat doesn't want us to touch them, but Angie's freezing cold," he said.

"They seem to be in stasis. Frozen, almost."

"I can shoot the cat, but that's not the prudent move. We need more help."

Sanjee leapt across bodies to return to guard Jessie's head. "Okay, I get the message," Zeke said, recoiling. "If we interfere, the cat thinks it will harm them."

"How would the cat know anything?" Forman asked. The question sounded silly.

Zeke shrugged. "This cat knows stuff. I don't question it anymore."

"What can we do to get them back?"

"I have to go to Lighthouse Beach," Zeke said. "Please drive me over there, and then return here to guard them."

Forman snorted his displeasure at being sidelined. "With the cat? I'm relegated to pet status?"

"You're entrusted with the most precious being in the universe in my eyes." Zeke lumbered to his feet, his eyes glazed with pain. "Bump the thermostat up another ten degrees to keep their core temperatures warmer. Ask Uncle John to send medics and rudimentary supplies to treat shock and hypothermia. No one is to be moved until they regain consciousness."

"Roger that." Forman hit the com port, made the adjustments, and followed Zeke out the door. "I don't like the idea of you being unprotected. What's your plan?"

"I'm going to phone out for help."

"Your phone's in the house."

"Not that kind of phone."

Lighthouse Beach held special meaning for Zeke. Did it enhance his mental powers? Is that why he always found Zeke there during stressful times? Had the essence of the place been wiped from his memory? "Is this something I'm not supposed to know? Do you erase my memory later like Angie does?"

Zeke's head bobbed. "Did you get proof of Angie's tampering? Does she erase your memories?"

"She does. I caught her red-handed this time, and I saw nothing untoward in the erased film. Why does your cousin go to such depths to remove our lovemaking sessions from my memory?"

"I don't know, and right now I can't spare a single thought toward figuring her actions out. I need to focus on what it will take to get these people back to normal. Then we can deal with Angie's mischief."

Her actions were more than mischief in Forman's eyes. They represented outright intellectual theft, but he understood the situation's priorities. Lives were on the line. Human lives took precedent over his stolen memories. Given the nature of his hardware and software partitioning, A.I. units such as Forman could compartmentalize with ease.

Zeke was one of the few humans who compartmentalized as well as Forman. At times Forman wished he shared Zeke's emotional detachment toward truth seeking. His emotional subroutine still had numerous bugs in it. "What's your theory?"

"A telepathic circle. Something trapped them on the psychic plane. Given that all our current trouble comes from the meteorite dust, I'm guessing a Yar hijacked the entire mindlink."

"Which one do you trust, boss? The one in the lab computer or the one who looks like Ronni?"

"Neither one. And who's to say it isn't another Yar?"

"Are there more of these invaders?"

"Oh, yeah."

Chapter 46

Zeke descended the hidden ladder slowly, one rung at a time. Each step into the recessed chamber was a Herculean effort, as if he were moving a mountain. But he couldn't quit now. Too much was on the line.

Jessie!

His heart cried out for her, but he couldn't reach her. It had torn him up to see her laying catatonic in their living room, present and yet not present.

As he descended the ladder, the ambient lighting in the lighthouse's underground transmission room brightened. The distance to the transmission chair seemed like five miles. He could do it. The pain in his head was crippling. A lesser man would have collapsed from the pain.

Each step required extreme focus. Each ragged breath half-filled his lungs. *Gotta make it. Gotta pull through for Jessie, for the island.*

He made it to the chair, finally, tears streaming down his cheeks. Never had he done anything so hard. The weight of his head increased with each step he took.

Another step to slide his left foot forward and then he could sit down. *Can't make it.* He fell, his abdomen broaching the chair, his useless feet still on the ground. His thoughts jumbled. Head exploded.

Shards of light reflected in broken glass quested with him to the Tamans in Tween. *Dad! Where are you?*

Here, Son, his father replied.

Something has Jessie. A Yar, I think.

We feel the incursion in Tween.

How?

I can't explain the time and space continuum, only I know your words to be true.

I'm hurting, Dad. This thing is jamming me.

Your transmission isn't pure. Static is blurring the transmission quality.

This is the best I can do right now. I need your help. I need everyone's help.

You're stronger than you think.

What should I do? How should I do it?

First, you must establish a stronger link with us.

I can't. It hurts too much to be earthbound. If not for Jessie, I'd stay here in Tween with you and all the other Tamans.

It will hurt more if you don't make that correction now. You need to be at your peak to battle Queen.

The words cut in and out. *Queen – she's a Drch?*

Yes.

Dread filled Zeke's thoughts. He wanted the freedom to fight the Drch on the spiritual plane, to be unhampered by a physical body, but he had no back up on Earth. Unlike the last time he battled an alien invader, he was it on this end, at least.

I need more time to rest.

No resting. Time is too short. Realign yourself right now. And remember the song your mother taught you.

The link terminated, and Zeke arrowed back to Earth and crippling pain. The pressure in his head paralyzed him. He couldn't move a finger. The leather-like chair covering pressed into his face. Air stalled in his lungs. *Must move. Must do this for Jessie.*

If he did nothing, he would die, so would Jessie. Unacceptable. He couldn't fail her or their child. His son. His thoughts focused on his pending fatherhood. A finger spasmed. That was it. He needed to be a father, to fulfill his legacy, to protect all he held dear.

He was the Guardian of Earth.

His mother's song welled within him. Her familiar voice mouthed those foreign-sounding words from her Gullah-Geechee ancestors in Sierra Leone, Africa. A lullaby she'd sang to him even after he was too old for lullabies, when he was troubled or couldn't sleep. He loved her song, loved how peaceful it made him feel.

Drawing from his mother's heritage, he found the strength to inch his way onto the chair. He forced air into his lungs, nearly passing out from the strain of stopping to breathe. *Not doing that again. I can hold my breath for more than three minutes. I won't breathe again until I'm in the chair.*

Zeke clawed his way upward, dragging legs that were dead weight, watching the tips of his fingers start to tinge blue with effort. If he didn't cease contact with the floor in the next minute, he wouldn't make it.

Not going to quit. He ground his teeth together and fought the headache and crushing pain to his entire body. *Must get in this chair. Must have a clear connection to the Tamans. Must save Jessie.*

He knew enough neurobiology to understand that whatever had hold of his head was interfering with his cognitive and motor systems. But brains weren't static as once believed, they were plastic and could reroute. With no time to waste, he needed to improvise.

Zeke envisioned a path around the movement barrier in his mind. He walked that path, pushing off from the ground with the balls of his feet.

His right toes caught on the chair, finally, and he dragged his left leg up behind it. Now everything was off the floor. He could risk another breath.

His head cleared. The room stopped fading in and out. The slow merry-go-round whirl of thoughts slowed to a constant. He drew another full breath, feeling his power aligning as the chair itself energized him, despite the continued pressure in his head.

A few more breaths and he'd oriented correctly in the reclined chair. Eagerly, he quested through the mindlink.

Dad! I'm back.

Much better, Son. We were concerned. Please reprise for us exactly what happened. More have joined the transmission since your first attempt.

Zeke gave them the abbreviated version. *I don't know where Queen is. How do I get my people back? They're trapped in the human version of Tween. Their physical bodies are failing.*

Quimby has the most experience with Yars. He will address your concerns.

Young Zeke, sounds like those Yars are giving you fits, Quimby began in his thin, quavering voice.

I have to stop them. Please, help me. I didn't know they could manifest on the thought plane.

Pretenders are a nuisance species. Most time, the only response to an infestation of them is to round them up and exile them to space.

182

We have no means of sending them far enough away. Earth has no interplanetary travel capability. How can we round them up? One of them suggested a subsonic signal.

A caller. That will bring them, all right.

The Yars blanketed our planet on atmospheric entry, though most of them landed in an ocean basin. How will they hear the signal from the entire expanse of the Atlantic Ocean?

You need a progressive series of signals, starting from far away and advancing toward the location you want them to collect. In past efforts, the farthest signal is faintest, with the next nearest signal slightly stronger. Each signal should have a relatively short duration. Yars respond quickly to the signal.

How will we place a network of pulse emitters around the world so quickly?

Use existing networks. These can be physical or biological.

Biological?

Yes. Creatures who navigate by echo location or sound waves are ideal for this.

On Earth, that would be bats or dolphins. I have an "in" with a dolphin pod. That could work. But we're working out of order. I need to rescue my people first. Then call the Yars. Then defeat or banish them.

You need different help for an extraction.

Wait, before you go, Quimby, how does one defeat Pretenders?

You can starve them back to elemental dust if you isolate them in an impenetrable chamber, but that takes a while, and there must be no leaks. Yars are sneaky.

Starvation? Zeke didn't have time to waste trying to starve a creature he couldn't locate. He needed a better solution. *What else?*

There's a theory that beings infected by Yars but not consumed by them have immunity. If you systematically expose and treat Yars victims, you'll have an invincible squad who can round them up without fear of death. But this is a theory. No one has ever tested it. We've never had anyone beat a Yars infection. Your planet holds that unique distinction.

Cats have thwarted attacks a few times, but two of those supposedly immune people are currently being held in thrall on the thought plane by a Yar named Queen.

Quimby's snort echoed through space and time. *Oh, she's not of royal lineage. She only calls herself Queen. She wants an empire.*

She's not getting it here. She picked the wrong planet to invade.

Good for you, young man. Deep Voice cleared his throat. *We've been networking while you and Quimby linked. To save your people, you need to push the Drch from their minds.*

I understand that's the need. My stopping point is implementation. How do I accomplish this? Can you help?

There are two extractors among us who are willing to journey across the stars.

Great. What do I do?

You should feel a buzzing in your head very soon now.

There wasn't room for anyone else in his head. *Is that the only way?*

You're asking for a different kind of help than before. Learn what to do and all will be well.

Zeke digested this information as a faint buzzing entered his thoughts. Help was on the way. Experienced help. He could save Jessie. *Dad, you there?*

I'm on the link, his father said. *I didn't go anywhere.*

He'd hoped his dad would be part of the rescue team. *You're not coming?*

It's too soon for me to travel again. The star journey takes a toll.

Zeke swallowed his disappointment. *I understand.* The buzzing in his head reached a crescendo.

Link to the think, a young boy child said. *We'll send the Yars to Mars.*

You know Mars? Zeke asked.

We know Mars, the Taman continued. *But we know possession even better. I'm Trinity. With me is Ellodie. He doesn't speak.*

Zeke greeted them both. *What do we do first?*

Envision your friends as you last saw them, Trinity said. *We'll expand out from there.*

Zeke showed them his living room floor with the circle of twelve. *See? They desperately need our help.*

Working here, Trinity said. *Ell, you got the signature disturbance?*

The buzzing rumbled in Zeke's thoughts. He didn't like sharing his personal thoughts with strangers, but if it saved Jessie, he was willing to endure the invasion.

Stay with us, Zeke, Trinity said. *We're on the move.*

Zeke felt a sense of motion, though he knew his body was still in the transmission chair beneath the lighthouse. He felt Trinity's energy as a vibrant blue-green sphere, Ell as a miniature purple orb.

He quested to the far end of the plane where he fought the Maleem. Before him was a gray blob. It quivered like a block of malignant gelatin.

Do your thing, Ell, Trinity said.

To Zeke's surprise, the grayness of the blob thinned. Inside were a cluster of dim orbs. They were moving too fast to count but it looked like a dozen.

I see them, he crowed.

We have a fix on them, Trinity said. *Ell's jamming her frequency. I'm holding it open. You reach in and get them.*

How?

Same way we work. Imagine yourself doing it and make it happen.

Zeke struggled to reach inside the blob. He tried visualizing arms to grab them, but that didn't work. At his approach, the orbs inside brightened and vibrated faster. They recognized him. He had to save them.

It isn't working.

Try harder. And move faster. We can't hold the blob open for much longer. She'll figure out how to divert her faculties and trap us from the back. If you don't get a move on, we're all going to die here today.

Zeke didn't want anyone's death on his hands. He pulsed an energy blast at the blob, pushing the orbs out the other side.

The orbs circled and he felt their familiar energies. Jessie. Sidra. Angie. Baggy. Taurus. And more. *Go home,* Zeke said to them. *You are safe now.*

The orbs buzzed around Zeke's head, then arced back the way Zeke had come.

Zeke turned around, saw the blob had moved closer to his position. He pulsed energy toward it, sending it rolling away like a tumbleweed.

Trinity chortled. *Take that you stupid Yars. You're not welcome here. Time to go to Mars.* Trinity elbowed him. *Push her into outer space, big guy.*

Queen rolled away as fast as she could.

Should we go after her? Zeke asked.

No need. She knows a Guardian is on this planet. Knows it and is afraid. She won't bother you again. If she has an escape plan, she'll implement it. We've seen the pattern repeat across the universe.

She rode in on a meteorite. That's a one-way ticket.

You're going to do a round-up, right?

Yes.

You'll catch her in that sweep. No need to expend more valuable energy here.

Weariness numbed Zeke. He wanted to see Jessie. He'd started this battle tired out of his mind. Best regroup and approach the remaining infestation with a team.

Thanks, guys. Will you stay for the showdown?

Nope. Can't stay. That's on you. Come on Ell, time to go home.

The buzzing in Zeke's head eased and he drifted. As he gathered his senses, he felt the familiar signature of Jessie's energy, and relaxed. He'd done it. He'd defeated Queen and saved Jessie's mindlink circle. With the help of his ancestors.

Chapter 47

In the darkness, Jessie heard the rustle of clothing, the murmur of soft voices. She tried to move but her limbs didn't work. They felt heavy and cold. So cold.

Where was she?

A familiar scent wafted by. Her rosemary bush on the front porch. She'd meant to plant that thing, but she liked the fresh scent so much, she kept it potted near her door. She was home. Her home with Zeke on Tama Island.

She felt pressure on her arms and legs. Something was on her! Instinctively, she cringed and flailed and screamed, but it was no use. She couldn't move, couldn't speak. She cowered in terror.

I'm gonna die. Something has me. A monster.

She wept silent tears. For all the things she'd left undone. The sister she couldn't fix. The husband she loved beyond words. The baby inside her.

She didn't want to die. She wanted to live. She had too much to do.

The pressure.

It lightened. And moved.

She focused on the sensation. Her initial impression was wrong. She wasn't being flattened. It felt warmer where the pressure was. Kneading, not pressure. As if someone were massaging her limbs. Umm. She liked that. She drifted peacefully into the blackness again.

*****

Jessie felt the caress of a gentle touch on her hand, in her mind. She smiled as emotion welled up in her. She'd know that touch anywhere.

Jessie? Zeke asked.

I'm here, she murmured to the insistent voice in her head.

Time to wake up.

Sleepy.

The touch on her hand and mind became more insistent.

Jessie, open your eyes.

A few more minutes.

If you don't wake up, this med team is airlifting you to the clinic. Wake up. Zeke's voice sharpened. *All the others have revived. Come on, Jess. Push through the fog. Do it for yourself, for our baby. Neither of us wants you to get pumped full of chemicals. Follow the sound of my voice back to consciousness.*

How'd you get in my head? she asked.

You were born with a telepathic tendency. Recent circumstances have activated and enhanced your natural gift.

She laughed at his word choice. More warmth flowed into her limbs. *What circumstances?*

You married a strong telepath for starters. And there's our baby. He's a telepath, too.

How do you know that?

I just do. Come on, love, come back to us.

Okay. In her mind she reached for him. The darkness brightened from a pinpoint of light into a dazzling array. She blinked until her eyes adjusted. Zeke's concerned face hovered over hers. His expression warmed, and he touched his forehead to hers.

When he drew back, she slowly glanced around her illuminated living room. The windows were dark, so it was still night. Sidra and Angie reclined on gurneys near her, each attended by two white-coated techs. Zeke and Forman completed the assembly. Forman held the white cat and stared at Angie.

Something hummed at the edge of her mind as she struggled to remember. The sequence of events fell into place in the space of a heartbeat. There'd been twelve people in the circle. They'd gathered in a show of solidarity, uniting to help Zeke on the psychic plane. But Zeke hadn't been there. Something else had. Something bad.

By her count, nine people were missing from her living room. Where were they? Dead? She shuddered, tried to sit up, and encountered a gentle tug. Her right arm was connected to an IV drip. She stopped and stared at the tubing. "The others?"

"They're fine. We sent them to Baggy's place for the night. They will take turns standing watch."

Jessie exhaled slowly. Relief at the islanders' safety soothed some of her anxiety. "What time is it?"

"Going on two in the morning. You're quite the party girl."

"How long was I out?"

"Long enough to have us worried. Can you tell me what happened?"

She flicked a glance over at the medics. "What about them?"

"They've been cleared by Uncle John or they wouldn't be here. According to the others, this mindlink was your idea."

"It was." Her face flamed. "I don't know what went wrong. Creating a group mindlink seemed like a good idea. We were supposed to share our energy with you, like when the Maleem attacked."

"Jess, I didn't know about it until you were gone. You should've told me."

She drew in, hunching her chin down on her chest. "I realized I'd forgotten that detail once we couldn't find you. I assumed you'd be out there waiting for us, like last time. We were together somewhere, the twelve of us."

"And the baby," Zeke murmured, his hand still warm over hers.

"There were twelve adults in this room. We made a circle, then Sidra led us out to that shadowy place. But you weren't there. I'm sorry for causing this trouble, sorry for dragging you from your work. I wanted to help. I needed to help."

"Tell me what happened."

"We saw something and drifted toward the shape. It was a dark color, not black but not gray either, and it wiggle-wobbled, like gelatin. We circled the blob, not sure what we should do. Then it got weird. We were watching the thing, then we were trapped inside a dark scary place. I never saw it move."

"Everyone else reported the same sequence. What happened once you were inside?"

"Nothing. We couldn't move, couldn't communicate."

"Do you remember anything else? Did the entity contact you in any way?"

She shook her head. "It was as if we'd been walled away. Our group bond didn't survive the inclusion. I was alone out there. Paralyzed."

"Stasis. All of you were in mental stasis when Forman and I found you guys laid out on the floor. Everyone was unresponsive."

The weight of her mistake bowed her shoulders. She'd nearly killed her friends and neighbors. But Zeke. He'd saved them. "How'd you get us back?"

"I got special help."

He'd been cagey about his helpers before, only telling her they were like-minded individuals. The other time she couldn't get any read on his extra resources at all. This time she'd been unconscious when he'd rescued them. Some helpmate she was.

Jessie chewed her lip and lowered her voice. "Did you kill the blob?"

"Once we rescued the group, my focus shifted to making sure everyone was successfully reintegrated at home. The entity ran away."

"Will it return?"

"My helpers didn't think so."

A tender vine of hope unfurled. "We won?"

"You're here. That's a win for me."

"Thank you for saving me. For saving all of us. It sounds like the confrontation may have helped our cause."

"Don't get me wrong. I'm counting this as a win, but there are more of these alien invaders on the planet. By process of elimination, we believe the one you bumped into was named Queen, but we don't know how these things communicate. The others may not know we beat one of them."

"But if we beat one, we can beat them all, right?"

He blinked. "That's the plan."

The blink bothered her. Did he harbor doubts? She ruffled his hair. "You'll protect us. I have no doubt of that."

"Hey, you two," Sidra said. "We'd like to know what happened."

"Zeke saved us." Jessie beamed a megawatt smile up at her husband and then over to Sidra and Angie. "He kicked that dust monster back to the galactic curb."

"I can't take credit for doing anything by myself," Zeke said. "I had help. We were lucky, all of us were lucky. This situation could've had a much different outcome."

"Seriously," Angie said with a huge yawn, "I'd appreciate a full tactical report, and then I'd like to go home."

"Seriously," Zeke repeated, "No more secret mindlinks. We need to coordinate our efforts to beat this Yar threat to our planet."

"I hate Yars," Sidra said. "I've never been so scared in my life."

"That's it?" Angie asked. "We defeated that one?"

"Think so," Zeke said. "My sources predicted it would turn tail and run."

"Not as good as killing it, but it's still a win in my book," Angie said. "Tomorrow we'll go after the one that took Ronni down."

"Sure." Zeke paused. "Tomorrow is another day."

Chapter 48

Xstle hurriedly assimilated the knowledge in the biped's machine. When the biped didn't return immediately, he studied the information and reached several conclusions. These humans, as the bipeds called themselves, didn't adequately safeguard the environment. With their burgeoning population and their limited resources of food, water, and atmosphere, this place was one disaster away from the same fate as howling winds desert planet HYR4956720.

Wrill and Queen qualified as a mega disaster.

He had to make them see that Wrill and Queen could plunge them into extinction. Once the planet was wrecked, the remaining Yars would perish as well. Wrill and Queen would have an exit strategy through the military. They always seemed to know how to cut their losses.

Speaking of Wrill, Xstle observed one chamber in the lab contained a deluxe Yar travel pod, which explained how Wrill had access to the older female. The tactic was classic Drch strategy, to cull the weakest of the pack first, then successively acquire more powerful hosts. Now that Wrill was held by the military, he'd have access to very high power targets.

Xstle had to convince the Ancient known as Dr. Landry to work with him to defeat the Drch. Using the facility's vid system, he scanned the exterior shelter where Landry and his robot were meeting with three females. Why was Landry outside and not in here saving his planet? Didn't he sense the urgency of the situation?

What was taking Landry so long to return?

Knowing his time inside the machine must be brief, Xstle set about leaving a message for Landry. He created a closed-loop graphics display of terrible things happening to the Earth, and left an encoded message for the robot during his next subroutine check-in. He couldn't do more because Wrill would soon gain access to the machines on this planet, find him, and destroy him.

He made an attempt at a holographic image of the juvenile he'd tried to assimilate. The technology was so crude it took scores of attempts to get a decent visual. The child's name was Paige. That's what he named the file on Landry's network folder. He added a brief audio accompaniment.

The time. So much had passed since Xstle had entered the computer matrix. He couldn't afford to stay here any longer, not if he wanted the rest of his collective to survive. With that, he detached, along with most of his adherents, and made his way back to the com port where his remnant hummed.

Xstle crawled out of the port as a tiny insect, an ant, they called this species here. He rolled in the adhesive dust of his collective, feeling the surge of power and fellowship from bulking back up. A glance at the overhead screens showed the images he'd collated, revolving in an endless loop. That should get Landry's attention, as for the rest of the message, he'd find it soon enough.

The safe thing to do would be to exit the lab immediately, but he wanted to see Wrill's space chariot up close. In the shape of a juvenile rodent, he passed through walls and into the chamber containing the rock.

Purite. The rarest of minerals on Yar. How had Wrill managed to wrest this much from the government's hands? Back on Yar, this rock alone would guarantee a lifetime of idle musings and an army or two.

Did the humans even know what they had? This stuff was so pure that it couldn't be sectioned with ordinary tools. Only a Yar phazon could penetrate its depths.

Out of curiosity, Xstle absorbed into the purite to experience Wrill's chamber firsthand. Magnificent, he trilled as he exited the purite and the deluxe chamber.

He had a flash of insight. Wrill would use the meteor as a bargaining tool for a way off the planet. That was a certainty. Then he'd steal it back for the next leg of his journey.

Was there anything Xstle could do to lessen the purite's value to Wrill? He ran through the knowledge gleaned from the information cache. Lichens from this planet had been shown to survive deep space. What if he implanted a few spores of plant life native to Earth in the purite?

The flash of space launch would be enough heat to activate the spores and kill the passenger. He hurried over to the drain in roach form and scurried into it until he found what he wanted. With the stuff glommed onto his legs and body, he returned to the purite vault and uploaded the contaminant.

Eat my dust, Wrill.

Chapter 49

"I've got a few questions for that thing in my computer," Zeke said as he pulled up beside the lab. An owl hooted in the distance under the starry sky. How was it possible the night seemed so ordinary, when less than an hour ago they'd battled an alien? When he'd nearly lost his wife and his son-to-be to an extra-terrestrial?

"Only a few? I have forty-two at present, and I'm sure I have more that I haven't formed yet," Forman replied from the seat beside Zeke. "What's your plan? Is the one in the computer a Yar or a Drch? Is one better than the other?"

"My sources say Drchs take no prisoners. Yars are bent on survival, same as Drch, but they won't eliminate us from the start. Drchs wipe out all indigenous species and move on to the next host planet. Yars set up a farming system to keep themselves in food. Human food."

"Neither option sounds good. Which one ate Ronni?"

"Language, Forman. And I can't answer your question. So far we've seen these creatures as dust, as malformed fish, as a perfect hawk, and as Ronni. The only one that attacked was the hawk. I'd guess he was a Drch."

"What about the one that captured Jessie and the islanders in the mindlink?"

"Hard to say as the entity didn't stand and fight."

"Do you have a plan to get rid of them?"

"Clone a billion cats and turn them loose."

"You made a joke." Forman clapped vigorously. "Battling aliens brings out your softer side."

Zeke smirked, then sobered. "I have no plan because I need more data. Without the extra help in the mindlink, we're back to cat saliva. Obviously, we don't have enough of that to fling at the creatures. If we did, maybe they'd melt away into nothing."

"I like where this is going. Death by cat."

"If only it were that easy." Zeke chuckled as he stood. "Let's see what we've got inside. Only a few more hours 'til dawn. May as well spend the rest of it grilling the creature we have in hand."

When the lab building was replaced after the fire, Uncle John added hurricane wind sealant to the door and window specifications. According to the HVAC folks, the building was as airtight as humanly possible.

But the lab wasn't constructed of stainless steel. Would the alien still be in residence?

Inside, the monitor panels streamed a slide show of the worst disasters in the human race. Tsunamis, earthquakes, cities ablaze, planes crashing into skyscrapers, concentration camps teeming with starved people, nuclear bombs. Zeke fought a tide of nausea and disgust.

The slide show was a message, but about what and who sent it?

Was this a threat from the alien intruder?

"You here, Yar?" he asked. What was the creature's name? Something like thistle. Xstle. That was it. "Show yourself, Xstle."

The slide show continued at the same rate. No text or stray characters floated across the screen. No disembodied electronic voice emitted from the speakers.

"Forman?" Zeke asked from the threshold. "Tell me something."

"Computer, run diagnostic Zeke Five," Forman ordered tersely, stepping in front of Zeke.

The slide show paused, then the screen whited out. Zeke forged into the room. "What happened?"

"I initiated a system reboot. The machine will crosscheck to find what's new since the last reboot. You think it's gone?"

"I don't know how Xstle got in the computer, so I can't predict if it's still here. It could be hiding, waiting for our next move." Zeke's brain whirred. "While the computer is running the diagnostic, I'll check the lab for trace evidence with the portable UV light."

"No need. I modified the ambient lighting to incorporate an ultraviolent wavelength setting. Lighting, activate UV feature."

The room darkened and then glowed softly as the light source changed. Zeke's white shirt gleamed under the purple light. No one would mistake him for an invader, though he was very much an alien.

"Look at that," Forman said.

Zeke glanced at the access port in the northwest quadrant of the room. "I don't see anything."

"I jacked up my ocular sensitivity. There are trace UV trails in and out of the computer at this access point. Further, the tracks lead into the containment lab. Look at Dusty."

The meteor glowed to the naked eye. Zeke's pulse quickened. Could tracking these creatures be so simple? He dared to hope it would all be over by morning. "The Yar definitely was in here. See anything else?"

"Xstle went to the sink and back, then it retraced its path through the exterior door," Forman turned to follow the prints, "and then out the door jamb."

"The door is made of steel," Zeke said, coming up from behind him. The creature was on the move. Why? Where would it go? Would it attack another person?

"It didn't go out through the door. It left through the crack beside the door."

"You're certain it's no longer in the lab?"

"That's what the data suggests," Forman said.

Zeke glanced around the rest of his lab, noting that everything seemed to be in its proper place. "Let's think this through. The Yar exited the computer, passed through the containment room walls and Dusty's plastech vault, trekked over to the sink and back, then passed through the containment room wall and through a crack in the doorjamb. What state of matter is this thing?"

"You have three choices," Forman said. "Solid, liquid, or gas."

"Assuming that's true, and it's not a given since we're dealing with an off-world entity, our next assumption is that it can alter its state at will. Given that the meteorite arrived with an invader inside, it logically follows that this entity recognized the rock and visited it.

While the scenario made a certain sense to him, he couldn't connect the dots, yet. "What did it want from the sink?"

"A drink of water?" Forman quipped.

"Not funny. What can you tell me about the sink? Should we be concerned that it went up the water lines and contaminated our water source?"

Forman studied the sink area. "The UV trail over there is so faint, I can't say with any certainty without suiting up and going in there, but the Yar appears to have gone into the drain, not the water supply line."

"Do we have schematics of the plumbing system?"

"The construction plans for this building are housed in the computer archive. Oh. One moment. The mobile computer interface just notified me of an anomaly in addition to that strange slide show. Shall we return to your office?"

Zeke nodded. New data meant he needed to stay sharp. He yawned. "I need coffee and regular illumination first."

Forman brought the lights up. While the coffee perked, Zeke sat at his work station and reviewed his previous encounter with the computer entity. He popped the string of strange symbols and the screen of numbers into a decoding program. The alien had communicated to alert him to the danger presented by a rogue faction from Yar. But was that a ruse?

"Coffee," Forman said, handing a steaming mug to Zeke along with an energy bar. "Eat."

Zeke realized he was starving. He ripped the bar open and made short work of it. "Good idea." He tossed the empty wrapper in the direction of the trash can, missed. "Let's see this anomaly in the computer."

Forman brought up the listing. "It seems to be a virtual file. Of Paige."

"Odd. Show me."

A projected image of Paige wavered in the room beside Zeke. He recoiled at the familiar child's image. *Please dear God, let the real Paige be safe and alive.*

The image said nothing at first. Zeke waved a hand through the projection, and it passed through unimpeded. "Definitely a hologram."

"The purite space rock is rare and valuable," Paige began in a mechanical, un-Paige-like voice. "Fair warning. Wrill will not leave it behind. Every creature on the planet is in danger. Evacuate now. Queen is coming."

"Who are you?" Zeke asked.

"Gather your people," the image continued as if Zeke hadn't spoken. "Go from this place immediately. Danger here."

The image bowed its head momentarily, then turned to face

Zeke's regular seat in the room. "Honor and glory to you, oh Ancient One, but even your powers are no match for Queen and Wrill. Evacuate or perish."

"Who are you? What are you?" Zeke demanded as the image faded.

"The visual and audio components are not interactive," Forman said, his fingers tapping on the keypad nearly too fast for Zeke to see. "Old technology. According to the time stamp, the hologram was created while we were at the ferry dock. Should we give it any credence?"

"To what purpose? If destructive aliens are here, we must stand and fight. We're the best defense the planet has. So, no, I'm not running away, but I'll let Uncle John know of this warning. If he decides to evacuate the island, so be it, but I'm not going."

Zeke signaled his uncle on the com.

"Do you know what time it is?" his uncle asked.

"Sorry to awaken you, sir," Zeke said. "One of the entities contacted me and warned of danger. Two more of its kind are headed to Tama Island. It recommended evacuation."

"Wait a minute. Say that again."

Zeke repeated the message, ran the projection for his uncle. "Just so you know, I'm not going anywhere. I'm staying here to figure out how to beat these Yars."

"I've been kept in the loop with regards to the one the Navy has at the ferry dock. A lot of people in Washington and beyond are following this closely."

"Understood. Thank you for the medic team for Jessie and the others. All are stable now."

"I heard. How're you holding up, m'boy?"

"I'd be better if I knew how to beat these invaders. Why can't it be as easy as holding them in the sunlight and having them burn up?"

"That would be vampire lore. Good fiction, not based in fact whatsoever."

"You've met with vampires before?"

"We're getting off track," his uncle said in a no-nonsense voice. "What's your recommendation on the island people?"

"I don't know how quickly the danger will manifest. I don't even know how to track Yars in the environment. I wouldn't want to load up the ferry boat with everyone and put them all at risk. Maybe you could warn people and let them make their own choice? Or airlift people. Fast transportation would be best."

"All we have to base this on is a warning by one of the entities," Uncle John said. "We have nothing to support what it said. I'll have Nola send out a sitrep advising everyone to be on high alert."

"They should already be on alert, but another message won't hurt," Zeke said. "I'll remain here in the lab."

Zeke ended the transmission. He wanted to discuss his problem with the Taman elders, but he had nothing new to tell them. Yars were here. He had to get rid of them. Did he have enough data to form an actionable plan? He sipped his coffee.

His thoughts pinged to each individual problem. For clarity, he voiced his thoughts. "Jessie and the islanders are safe for now. The Navy's got the Ronni lookalike. We've lost our Yar. That brings us back to the water samples. Any results finalize while we were out?"

Forman called up the data feed from the analyzer. "Sidra's water samples and your Rio samples are identical. There is a slight variation in trace elements between the water here and there. And there's a hint of something else in the Rio water. Look at this novel peak in the results."

"The same peak appears in every sample. Similar to molybdenum but with some extra bells and whistles."

"Good to know. What about the empty glass sample jars from Sidra's Rio lab?"

"Clean as a whistle. Whatever she put in those jars is long gone."

Zeke nodded. This dust moved at will and with speed. "It went through the glass. Not surprising, given that Yars can go through walls."

"Great. We're swimming in these things."

The com beeped. Lt. Hinson's lined face came up on all the linked lab monitors. "Dr. Landry, you're needed at the ferry landing."

"What's happened?" The question tumbled out before Zeke thought it through. Had Xstle gone down to the trawler and battled the other Yar? He half-hoped that was the case. Let them duke it out. Then he'd have half as many aliens to fight.

"The entity that was Ronni vanished."

"What happened?"

"The room cam blacked out momentarily. When it came back online twenty seconds later, the bed and room were empty."

"What about the guard?"

"No record of any entry. We're puzzled. It's like the mismatched fish all over again. Here one minute and gone the next."

"I'm on my way."

Chapter 50

"Lt. Hinson is closeted with the admiral, sir," a fresh-faced sailor said. All around the ferry landing, quarters were being dismantled. "My orders are to make sure you have access to anything you need."

In the pink-tinged dawn, Zeke stood on deck of the moored trawler where the pretender had been contained in the stainless steel hold. The weight of the cat cage he held was slight compared to the responsibility he felt. So much had happened in the last twenty-four hours, he hadn't had time to analyze the sequence of events. He hoped this creature's death would herald a respite, and much-needed sleep.

As far as he knew, he only had two tools to use in detection of the Yars. He'd brought both. Nodding to Forman at his side, Zeke said, "We'd like to see the chamber where the fake Ronni perished."

The cat in the cage he carried yowled its displeasure. *Easy fellow*, Zeke thought. *We're only going to be a few minutes here, then you can go back to sleep.*

Analysis of the various cat salivas had shown that all of the research cats, including Jessie's, contained the expected multi-functional array of proteins, enzymes and more. If there was a unique quality to Sanjee's saliva, Zeke hadn't isolated it yet. Meanwhile, he'd try this tabby cat, since he needed Sanjee to guard Jessie.

The further they went into the vessel, the more agitated the cat became. Zeke shared a glance with Forman. Something was up.

"Should we open that door, boss?" Forman asked. "Won't it be like opening Pandora's box?"

"We can't examine the chamber from out here."

"But Yars can't go through stainless steel."

"Exactly. If it's in the room, we'll pick it up. And if it should get on me, I have the cat handy to remove the dust. But my guess is we won't find anything. Somehow the creature got out of the holding chamber. Gauging by the cat's distress, it's already walking these halls. We're in more danger out here than in the holding cell."

Their escort stopped in front of a sailor and a closed door. This must be the place. "Was this door left open at any time?" Zeke asked.

"No, sir," the guard replied. "It was locked. Only the guard posted on duty and Lt. Hinson have a key."

"Let us in, then close the door behind us," Zeke said. "We'll knock on the door when we're ready to leave. Give me your number just in case I need to reach you."

The guard complied, opened the chamber door, ushered them inside, and closed the door behind them. Zeke looked around. The room held two pieces of furniture. A rumpled bed and a chair, nothing else. The cat howled nonstop, thrashing around in the cage. Zeke studied the chamber in ambient lighting. Nothing remarkable caught his eye. The room was neat as a pin, no corpse, no bones, and no other creature visible. No odor either.

Zeke saw the camera on the wall. He phoned the guard outside. "Is there continuous footage of the confinement?"

"Yes, sir. I can show that to you."

"I would like to see it, and I prefer to have a copy of the footage sent to my lab for an in-depth analysis."

"Yes, sir."

Zeke ended the call and turned to Forman. "We'll search by UV light first. Hit the regular lights."

As his assistant complied, Zeke gripped the cage of the agitated cat, the hackles on his neck rising. Yars could transition from animate objects to a state of matter that passed through walls or cracks. There had to be an escape route here. He was certain they'd find a trace of the entity.

Forman flashed on the UV light. At once, the bed glowed, they edged closer. A shimmer of something on the plain sheets fluoresced. "Something here, boss," Forman whispered.

"Check the entire room." Zeke's pulse thundered in his ears. "Everything and everyone."

As his assistant waved the light across the floors, walls, and door, Zeke brought the caged cat closer to the bed. The feline grew increasingly agitated, ramming its head against the front of the cage.

"That cat's going crazy," Forman said.

"I see that. We'll get to the cat in a minute. You finding anything?"

"There's a very faint trail to and from the door, a glimmer of something beside the bed, and the bed linens. Nothing else is showing up, even on my amplified optics."

"Nothing on the ceiling? The doorjamb? The door knob? Our escort? Us?"

"All clean."

"Lights on one hundred percent."

"What now, Dr. Zee?"

Zeke phoned the guard again. "Is this room still being monitored?"

"Yes, sir."

"No one other than you and Lt. Hinson have entered this room?"

"That's correct, sir."

With that thought, Zeke knelt and opened the cage. The tabby sprang from the cage, leapt on the bed, and began licking the sheets.

Zeke's insides hummed. Good. This cat was behaving as Sanjee had when people were threatened with wet dust. He'd soon have the entity.

His phone buzzed. "Sir?" the sailor said.

"Yes?"

"I received a com message. Lt. Hinson wishes to speak to you ASAP."

That didn't take long. Zeke nodded, thinking of the possible ramifications. Would Hinson give them the boot or had their actions alarmed her? "I need to confer with my assistant. Give me a minute."

Zeke leaned in close to Forman, speaking under cover of his hand. "Make sure we get that cat back to the lab."

"You're leaving me on cat patrol?" Forman whispered back.

"I'm putting you in charge of corralling the cat afterward, putting it in the cage, and making sure we collect its vomit in one of the stainless samplers we stashed in your hollow belly. We must retrieve the cat's expelled stomach contents."

"When I signed up for this gig, cat barf collection wasn't in the job description."

"Just do it."

"I should go with you."

"According to the cat, the danger is here. We've got the entity on the ropes. I can handle a few irate naval officers."

"I don't like it."

"Tough. You have an important job. I'll see you outside in a few minutes. Otherwise, we'll rendezvous at the lab."

"Got it."

Zeke knocked on the door and hurried outside to meet the sailor, closing the door behind him. "I'm ready."

"What about your android?"

"He'll follow in a few minutes. We have a few tests to complete in the holding chamber."

"Yes, sir." The sailor pivoted and led Zeke upstairs and across the landing to the lieutenant's office.

Zeke saw questions in the man's eyes, but he wasn't in the mood to explain himself to this guy. He'd save it for the boss.

Lt. Hinson rose when he entered. Her skin looked paler than usual. "Thank you for coming, Dr. Landry. Please, have a seat."

"It's been a long night," he began experimentally after he sat.

Hinson settled behind her desk. "Indeed, and just when we thought it was over, another issue has cropped up."

Zeke waited for her next remark.

"We've received word an unusually large great white shark is headed this way from the North Atlantic."

Intrigued, Zeke leaned forward. "How large?"

"Easily double the largest size ever observed, about three and a half tons worth."

"Amazing." Impossible was more like it. Was this what Xstle had meant in his warning?

"The shark's eating everything in its way, and its course hasn't varied in the last few hours. The Navy's scrambled planes to track it, and we're warning ships to get out of its way."

"A shark that big needs deep water and a lot of food." He turned to view the screen she'd illuminated on the wall. The large shark was a shadow cruising just under the water's surface. "How do you know it's coming to Tama Island?"

The lieutenant blushed. "I misspoke. The shark is following the Gulfstream south, but its final destination is unknown. We're trying to figure out how to neutralize the threat."

Just like the military to go in with guns blazing. "Surely an anomaly like this would be of scientific interest to Woods Hole or

Scripps. One of the oceanography institutes should be notified."

"We don't have a facility big enough to hold this bruiser. It's already killed twenty people and made national headlines. My orders come from the top. The shark has to go. In any event, our job on Tama Island is done. The admiral and I will be on the next chopper out to handle the shark problem."

She closed the file folder on her desk, stacked her hands, and peered at him intently. "I watched you in the woman's cell. What was that cat doing on the bed? Some kind of cleansing?"

"You might say that. In a pilot study, we discovered a negative association of cat saliva and the dust entity. We're hoping to develop that result into an antidote or vaccine in case we have additional contact with these life forms."

"Washington and international leaders want this Ronni Merckle incident buried in red tape. No word of her means of death is to reach the press. Understood?"

Typical government move to sweep the unexplainable out of sight. Zeke nodded, knowing he'd benefited in the past from that same policy. "And the ginormous shark?"

"That ship has sailed. Reports of the shark are banner headlines in all the major papers today. At this point, the Navy is doing damage control on a freak of nature."

The holographic warning from Zeke's dust alien flashed into his mind. Xstle's warning about a Drch named Queen. Any chance this shark was Queen?

If so, according to the Tamans, the Drch would come to Tama Island. For him. His chest felt like the weight of the entire world pressed on it.

Once again, death knocked at his door.

Chapter 51

"I need a break, and so do you," Zeke said to Forman after the lieutenant dismissed them. Forman had taken the news of a giant shark approaching as if it were one more thing in an already crappy day. Zeke wished he could have such a clinical feeling about the shark. But the approaching shark was on the forefront of his thoughts. He needed to talk to the Tamans about this new wrinkle.

Zeke stretched in the morning sunshine, then stepped into the passenger seat of the transpo. "Why don't you recharge at the lab while I swim with the dolphins?"

Forman settled beside him and punched the throttle. "No way. Unh-unh. Absolutely not. Xstle's out there somewhere. Who knows what else is running around on this island and in that murky sea? Not to mention crazy hawks that might attack you when you are vulnerable. My job is to watch out for you, and I can't do that if I power off in a closet in the lab."

Zeke scrubbed his eyes, weariness bending him down. If he didn't get some down time soon, he'd be in trouble. "Then come with me to the beach for a swim."

"Don't think so. If I'm on the shore, I can only watch for an aerial assault. If I'm in the sea, I can only protect you from underwater entities. Any way you look at it, I can't be in two places at once."

"The dolphins will sense if there's danger from the sea. And last time, I sensed the hawk coming for Jessie, even though I was in an altered state of consciousness."

"You've never explained how you data stream with the dolphins."

"Science can't explain it. There's a telepathic bond. I know where they are, and they can find me. After I rescued the little one from Browning Charles' damaged research pen, they've been attuned to my thoughts." Zeke shrugged. "It sounds like hoodoo or really bad science at best, but relaxing in the sea with them jumpstarts me mentally and physically. I need this. *We* need this."

Forman arched a golden brow. "How do you mean?"

"I'm not buying the sudden appearance of a monster shark. There would have been rumors and reports of it for years if it were a natural phenomenon. Instead, the shark hit national news today."

"So?"

"The only logical explanation I have, and logical is a stretch, is the shark is a dust alien, a Yar prime. From what we've seen, Yars are resilient, resourceful, and opportunistic. The navy trying to blast it will only make it mad. The lieutenant was right. That thing is coming here. For me."

Both brows lifted. "How do you know?"

"I just do. Look. Let's compromise. Come to the beach and enter a recharge mode with eyes open. You'll be aware of our surroundings, but you can conserve energy. If my assumptions are correct, we're headed for a major battle. Both of us need to be at full strength."

"How long do we have?"

"A couple of hours at worst, a day or so at best."

"Roger. The beach it is."

*****

The dolphins met Zeke beyond the breakers. *Welcome, Waterman*, Boz blasted into Zeke's thoughts.

Zeke treaded water, playfully greeted the pod, and enjoyed Boz's exuberant leaps. The cool water invigorated him, made him feel alive in a way he'd missed in the last day or so. He needed the ocean, even if it was still sediment rich. A little extra dirt had never hurt him before, and it wouldn't hurt him now.

His dolphins had escaped assimilation by the Yars and so would he. He'd do whatever it took to protect his home world.

With a look at Forman standing guard beside the lighthouse, Zeke reclined in a back float. Klickie and Nicola surfaced under his hands and he relaxed in mind, body, and spirit. At first their picture words came at him in a flurry.

They showed him an image of the hawk and a fish. Nothing earth-shattering there. The next image showed the hawk standing in the shallows. The image blurred and in the next moment the hawk swam off as a fish.

Ah. The hawk and fish were the same creature.

A Yar, Zeke said.

The dolphins made a shrill sound. *Yes,* Klickie said. *They are one and the same.*

They showed him the hawk coming at Jessie again, a replay of the image from before. Zeke tensed as it approached his wife anew, saw it veer harmlessly away.

The dolphins made the shrill sound again. *Do you see?* Klickie asked.

I see. Thank you for sharing that transformation. I must connect with the Tamans.

They shrilled again at the word Taman, and their picture words ceased. Zeke relaxed even more, his thoughts questing out to Tween.

Zeke? His dad asked, his voice thin and rusty as if he'd been awakened. *Are you all right? Has something happened?*

I'm fine. Jessie's fine. The island's fine. For now. But a monster shark is bearing down on us. I think it's another Yar. Possibly the one called Queen.

I'm confused. Didn't you defeat that one already?

With Taman help, I rescued my people from a Yar entity in a Tween-like place, but we didn't defeat anything. It ran away. I need to talk with Quimby again and see if I can get Trinity and Ellodie to help banish these things for good.

Static filled the line. Zeke drifted, fear roiling in his thoughts. *Dad. You there?*

Quimby isn't available at present.

Zeke's thoughts quickened with his pulse. *Where is he?*

A war broke out on his home planet. He's there in an advisory role helping his descendants fight for their freedom.

That was too bad. Quimby was his go-to expert on Yars. *Is there anyone else who can help?*

The line went quiet again. Zeke drifted in an uneasy mindset. *Dad? What aren't you telling me?*

Son, there are times when we can help, and times when we are needed elsewhere. This is one of those elsewhere times. Do you understand?

No. I don't understand. What should I do?

Do what comes naturally.

I don't know enough about the Yars to defeat them. How can I fight Pretenders without your help?

You are strong. Trust in who and what you are.

If Zeke wanted double-speak, he'd have gone to a psychic for a palm reading. Frustration roiled. *I'm on my own?*

You're never completely alone, but, yes, you need to solve this problem.

Is this how it was for you, Dad? Invaders dropping in every few weeks or so and challenging the planet's future?

Each is born to his own time.

Great. More nothing-talk.

I heard that, his dad said.

Sorry. I want answers and assistance.

Every Taman in Tween has family out there. We're a trouble hot line. The amount of physical help we can offer is extremely limited. Each time we agree to quest anywhere and help onsite, it takes a tremendous toll on us. We require centuries of rest before we can undertake another such adventure. Understand?

Centuries. Damn. He'd had no idea. *Why didn't you say something before? I thought the travel was easy for you. I selfishly hoped I'd get to see a lot of you.*

You can, but only here in Tween. I made the trip to help you fight the Maleem to ease you into your Guardian duties. You're stronger now than I ever was, Son. I have complete confidence in you. The groundwork for your support team is there on Earth. The dolphins, your mate, your uncle, your cousin, that astrophysicist telepath, and this robot I keep hearing about – you've got a strong network to protect our home world.

The dolphins. I have a question about them.

Yes?

Are they Taman?

No.

The link started to fade. Zeke reached for it again. *Another question. What's an Ancient?*

The link erupted with noise. *Where'd you hear that word?* Deep Voice demanded. *Young Landry. I demand an answer.*

Zeke mentally sighed at the intrusion. From what he'd gathered previously, Deep Voice ruled the roost in Tween. *A Yar called me an Ancient. What does that mean?*

The link erupted in chaos, but the connection remained strong. Zeke floated through time and space, waiting for the furor to die down. So many voices spoke at once, he couldn't make out a single word. Finally Deep Voice quieted the furor.

Landry?

Yes, sir?

We'll get back to you.

Chapter 52

Xstle huddled in the live oak near the lighthouse, a fly on a gnarled branch. The Ancient floated nearby in the sea with his handmaidens, the air-breathing fish. The Ancient's machine waited below in stasis. Why weren't they evacuating? Didn't they understand the virtual message he'd left?

Wrill was on the island and Queen was approaching in her disguise as a great white shark. The threat level couldn't be higher. Staying on the island was suicide at best. Why would a sentient species ignore such an obvious disaster in the making?

Annoyed, Xstle buzzed the cat's cage on the shaded transpo. The creature grew agitated at his approach, so he left immediately, but not before he recognized the mound of vomit in the cage. His heart plunged at the sight of so many of his fallen countrymen. Damn the Drch for subverting them.

If the cat had come close enough to consume the dust, Wrill had changed hosts. He would have transitioned most of the Yars to the other host, leaving behind a residual to maintain the husk of the first host during his escape. With no prime available, those Yars had perished.

The buzzing in his thoughts assured him of Queen's relentless approach. For her to be so bold to broadcast her intentions, the hope of any of his remaining countrymen surviving in the ocean paled. He alone was left to fight the Drch.

With the Ancient not engaged in battle, and his mechanical assistant unresponsive, Xstle had few options. Each time he shifted shapes, it cost him energy and specks. He'd cleaned the island of food already, and he didn't have time to absorb a human, not with Queen on the way.

How much time did he have to mount a defense? Unknown. Could he convince the humans and the Ancient of the terrible danger headed this way? Again, unknown.

He needed a status report, so he changed into a sparrow shape and flew to the island's southwest end where the Navy was breaking camp. Humans scurried around boxing up possessions, which would do them no good. Once Queen arrived, everything on this island would belong to her.

A woman stepped out of the dwelling. Her skin sparkled in the sun. Xstle recognized that particular sheen on sight. Wrill. He'd co-opted another female form, this time, a military officer.

The female immediately glanced at the tree where Xstle huddled. *Only doing what you couldn't, brother.*

Xstle swore. He'd left his thoughts unguarded. Not good. He couldn't afford to slip when he faced two such formidable foes. *You can't destroy these people.*

We can, Wrill said. *It would behoove you to join with us. Queen assimilated Oieg and Nrz yesterday. You are the last Yar prime. If you join with me, we can rule this planet at Queen's side.*

Xstle mourned his countrymen's death, shielding his pain from Wrill. He was truly alone. He'd never join with a Drch and plunder any planet to extinction. Too many howling desert planets out there already. This place had a shot, though it was far removed from Yar.

Age was both a blessing and a curse. Xstle had a few centuries on Wrill. Was it possible the Drch didn't know about the Ancient? If so, the Ancient had a fighting chance.

Never, Xstle beamed to Wrill. *Lay down your arms and live with me in peaceful harmony with Earth's residents.*

You're too soft, old one. Always have been. I beat you before, and I'll crush you here. Queen is fertile, with my offspring.

Double damn. Female Drch reproduced every fifty or so years, ten thousand at a time. With more Drch on this green planet, it would be picked clean all the sooner. Wrill's tads would be holy terrors. He had to stop his enemies before they gained any more traction.

I'd wish you blessings on your good fortune, but that would be a lie, Xstle said. *Know that I plan to crush you and your spawn. We will battle to the death.*

Wrill roared with laughter, then sobered. *You and what mighty force? You have no weapons to defeat me, while I have the backing of the entire U. S. Navy.*

To the victor, the spoils, Xstle said, closing his thoughts and flying away as a sparrow.

With another Drch on the way, his chances of survival were slim and none. The only way the Ancient could defeat Queen and Wrill was with help. The only way he had to communicate with the Ancient was in the machine, the computer.

But he nearly hadn't made it out of the energy field last time. More than half of his specks at the entry point had perished due to his prolonged residence in the computer. Plus, he'd lost specks at each shapeshifting change since then.

If he entered the computer's electrical field in his rundown condition, his existence was at risk. Worse, his chances of ever leaving the machine weren't good.

Decisions.

Taking no action would result in the defeat of the humans on the island. That was for sure. Nothing he'd seen from the Ancient indicated he was at full power. The one here must be damaged or untrained. This Ancient was no match for a Drch.

Xstle alighted outside the Ancient's work place. Landry's laboratory. Some of the Earth words came to him slower than others. Wrill was correct. Xstle wasn't the warrior of his youth. He'd made mistakes on this planet, and he couldn't fight the Drch alone.

After changing to the ant shape, he opened his thoughts to his specks, his loyal Yar adherents, laying out the options. Many were in favor of rejoining the energy stream of the computer. Some wanted autonomy from any machines – their centuries-old memory of Yar enslavement in machines still fresh in their thoughts.

We are the last of our kind on this frontier, Xstle pulsed to his collective. *The Drch named Wrill defeated me once, and I fear he would be the victor in another individual confrontation. Not helping the humans means we may escape immediate death, but with each human life Wrill and Queen take, they will become stronger. They will find us. Given Yar ability to sense each other intuitively, there is no place on land or sea to hide on this planet, and we have no way out of here.*

Eleven primes have fallen. We honor Kvn's memory and his specks which have enabled us to come this far. We have three options. We can self-terminate, but I, for one, haven't come this far to quit. We can explore underwater burrows and hope to escape detection. Or we

214

can make a stand here and now.

Shall we die a hero's death or be hunted down like a thief in the night?

Xstle's specks whirred and chirped. He followed the neural pulse of the collective, trusting them to arrive at the same decision he'd made. Soon, the majority were aligned with him. The holdouts volunteered to wait at the computer's entry port again, knowing full well that was likely a death sentence.

Xstle glanced at the clear blue sky as the sun warmed his back. He took it all in, then squirmed his ant body through the seam of the door. All too soon he was at the machine's portal. He chanted the Yar victory song to say goodbye to his specks who would guard the portal.

The word "victory" was embossed in his thoughts as he plunged into the energy stream.

Chapter 53

"Perform a full power-down when we get inside," Zeke said as the transpo bounced down the lane to the Institute. The cat in the back yowled at being treated so cavalierly.

Forman studied his boss, noting the man's bent shoulders, his saltwater-stiffened hair, and his damp clothing. Swimming in the ocean may have recharged Zeke Landry's thoughts, but it did nothing for his posture or appearance. The man was a fashion disaster.

"If trouble is on the way, I can't afford to be out of commission even for the one-hour shut down to fully recharge," Forman said. "By going on minimal power while you communed with nature, I have enough reserves to go for another twenty-four hours straight. Speaking of trouble, what is our plan?"

"The plan is fluid at present. The outside help I have drawn from the mindlink in the past is unavailable at this time. We are on our own."

Despite this bleak news, Forman hoped for a positive outcome. Zeke Landry would figure this out. "I'll process the cat barf and return the cat to the cat colony."

"I should've had you working on that while I was swimming. We've lost valuable time."

"We have to stay together in these situations," Forman said. "If you want your memory refreshed, I can recount the instances we split up and harm befell you."

"No need. I wish we had more answers about these darn dust critters. We've got that mass spectrometer peak to identify, and if we could synthesize and mass produce cat saliva, we'd be sitting pretty."

Forman parked the transpo outside the lab and picked up the cat crate by the handle. He couldn't correlate sitting pretty with the rumpled man striding beside him. When he set the crate down to unlock the door, the cat went nuts. Just as it had in the boat. "Zeke?"

"I see." Zeke's voice went all cold and gunslinger-like. He flicked on the UV light in his hand, but the bright ambient light diminished the UV effect. He clicked off the portable light. "Do me a favor and let the cat out of the cage."

"Won't it run off?"

"I'm betting it won't."

Forman unlatched the cage door and the cat sprang out, sniffing like a dog. The feline bounded over to the doorframe edge and scratched at the barrier with both front paws.

"Interesting," Zeke said. "Open the door, and let's follow it inside."

"Is there an alien in the lab?"

"Seems likely."

"Wait. Shouldn't we have a plan? What about your personal safety?"

"It didn't harm us before. Partition the computer as you see fit. If Xstle is inside the hardware, we'll keep him there. Or, Xstle could be in any shape or state of matter in the lab. You follow the cat. I want to see if the UV light picks up any trace of the alien."

"Got it." Forman opened the door and the cat darted inside. He grabbed the cage and followed the cat. The laboratory lights brightened automatically. "Lights off. Turn on UV lighting," Forman said. He glanced at a com monitor as he hurried past. Dark. Was the alien in the room with them? He glanced back at Zeke and saw him scanning the room. A very faint trail fluoresced from the door to the com service port.

The cat stopped beside the service port and started licking the dust there. Forman gestured to the spot. "Zeke."

"I see. Go to the animal husbandry area and set all the cats free."

"There's nothing else in here?"

"We're safe for now."

Forman hurried back to the cattery. The cats bolted from the cages and joined the tabby in the admin area, licking the dust off the console. "That stuff must taste like catnip going down."

"Whatever it is, they home right in on it. Leave the cats loose in the lab from now on."

Forman scooped the cat vomit from the tabby's cage and stored it in a stainless sample container. "I should set more of these sample containers out. The tabby and several others might be vomiting in a few minutes."

The computer screen brightened to a screensaver vid of the ocean. "Dr. Landry?" a mechanical voice asked.

"I'm Landry. Identify yourself." Zeke nodded at Forman.

Glad to be useful, Forman hurried to the keyboard, creating multiple partitions within the data collection and storage areas to trap the entity in a smaller section of the computer. Zeke stepped away from the com and the keyboard.

"I am the Yar called Xstle, and I will help you battle the Drch."

"How?" Zeke asked.

"You were summoned to the waterfront to see the expiration of the entity that absorbed the human Ronni?"

Zeke exchanged a glance with Forman before answering. "Yes. That entity was gone when we arrived."

"It didn't go very far. Lieutenant Hinson is that entity's next vessel."

"Hinson?" Zeke repeated. "How do you know this?"

"I can sense my kind. I am one hundred percent certain your Hinson is already dead."

"I spoke with Hinson earlier. I didn't notice anything different about her."

"Wrill is clever. He doesn't deviate one speck from the appropriated identity. Before he became a Drch, he was our best shifter."

"Your terminology is hard for me to follow, but I believe you." Zeke immediately sent a com message to his uncle regarding Hinson's alien status. He gave Forman an inquiring nod before posing a question to his computer. "What's the difference between a Drch and a Yar?"

"All done," Forman whispered when Zeke finished speaking. Two cats wandered away from the port, lying down across the room. With the cats on patrol, the entity wouldn't sneak out of the computer undetected.

"Life and death," Xstle said. "Drch wipe out all indigenous life. Yars only use what is needed to survive. The two Drch on your planet are expecting, which means you will soon be overrun with Drch and life on your planet will become extinct."

"We take issue with other species coming in here and making

themselves at home," Zeke said. "We hold human life to be sacred."

"Understood, but unavoidable in our case. My countrymen and I traveled from very far to reach this frontier planet, and now the Drch have terminated the other eleven Yar primes. I alone am no match for Wrill, but my knowledge should help you gain an edge in the battle to come."

"Why should we believe you?" Forman challenged.

"I am a Yar prime."

Zeke shrugged. "What does that mean?"

The wave vid screen froze black for a moment. "I am on par with someone of high status or rank on your planet. The same as a president or prime minister."

"Those people bend the truth to suit their needs. What's your agenda?"

"One moment while I research the term *agenda*." A heartbeat later Xstle spoke again. "My agenda is to defeat the Drch."

"To take over the planet instead?"

"The female primes have been terminated by the Drch. Therefore, I am a relic. Alone I cannot reproduce. I am no threat to your people."

"So you say," Forman countered.

"I have achieved many awards and distinctions on my world. Countrymen have died for questioning my honor, but I will spare your life to fight our mutual enemy." The cams in the room panned, and stopped. "I see you've brought your four-legged protectors into the room to trap me inside the machine."

"They'll stay here until we better understand who and what you are," Zeke said.

"I am a Yar Prime. My name is Xstle," the voice spoke faster. "I want to help you defeat the Drch. All I ask in return is that you keep my presence a secret from your species. I could've gone after your marine playmates, but out of deference to you, I left them alone. Let us join forces and win this war."

"Zeke?" Sidra called out from the doorway. "Jessie said you'd be here. I let myself in."

Forman and Zeke shared a conspiratorial glance. "In here," Zeke said. The computer screen returned to the default ocean waves mode.

"Why are the cats out?" Sidra asked.

"Seemed kinder," Zeke said. "You come up with anything new

after resting?"

"Nothing new. I want to work on my meteorite this morning."

"We couldn't chip any of it off for study, but we detected a novel peak in the mass spec readout of the water samples. It's repeatable. I wonder if it's the same compound."

"Cool." Sidra slid into a seat at the console and tapped up the sample folder. "I want to name the material. I'm dithering between Sidrium and Siddite, though I might also consider Ronnium and Ronnite."

The word "purite" flashed across the screen.

"What's this?" Sidra asked.

The words "A good faith gesture" scrolled across the monitor next.

"Zeke?" Sidra asked, backing away from the monitor screen. "Is your computer possessed?"

Chapter 54

The assassin android brought Jessie a cup of decaf coffee and joined her in the living room. The dark-haired, fair-skinned unit had a compact body and the swagger of a marine sniper. While Jessie was glad to have a Nola bodyguard, she was happier to have a few quiet moments in her own home.

An instrumental rendition of a Yuletide carol added to the sense of normality. Christmas was coming in a few weeks. She had a nursery to decorate and gifts to buy. Those thoughts shunted through her head like a passing train. The near future had to wait. The here and now was what mattered.

Everyone else had gone, and the house had a quiet restful sense. Jessie stretched on the sofa, thinking how easy it would be to curl up in bed and sleep the morning away.

"What's going on today?" she asked her bodyguard companion.

"Zeke, Forman, and Sidra are working at the laboratory. Lieutenant Hinson is officially missing. Angie is overseeing the Navy's departure at the ferry landing."

"The military is leaving?"

"According to my sources, they are leaving to deal with a rogue shark which is wreaking havoc north of here."

Jessie's lip twitched. "A bad shark. Imagine that."

"Sharks are a much maligned species. Apex predators often are misunderstood. They kill to survive."

"Sounds like you're a fan."

"Much can be learned from their behaviors. Predators size up prey in a universal way. It's important to know whether you are the hunter or the hunted in every confrontation."

Jessie didn't think in terms of conflict when she approached others. Mostly she hoped for consensus and everyone getting along. Her sister liked to stir up conflict though. Anything Bea could do to get her creative juices flowing was fair game, like the unwise trip to

Japan in the midst of the tsunamis a few months back. Too much conflict for Jessie's taste.

Sanjee padded into the room, giving the robot a wide berth. He stropped his fluffy white tail around Jessie's ankles, and she leaned down to pet him. His resulting purr pleased her.

"What's our assignment?" Jessie asked. "Should I join the others at the lab?"

"We are to stay away from the lab, per orders of John Demery," Nola said. "He said we can't distract Zeke."

"I'm a distraction? I don't like that." The urge to do something welled up inside of Jessie. She didn't like being relegated to the sidelines. "Why don't we head to the Institute cafeteria for breakfast?"

"I can prepare any food you desire here."

"I won't stay locked up in this house all day. I have rights, you know."

Nola went silent. Would she order Jessie to stay put? Not happening. Jessie stood, toed on her sandals, and strode toward the door. Sanjee followed. "I need some air."

Nola trailed behind. "Mrs. Landry, this is not an acceptable scenario. My instructions were to ensure your comfort and protection in this dwelling."

"I'm uncomfortable here."

"This is your home."

"I'm female and pregnant. I'm allowed to change my mind and to act irrationally. Happens all the time. You can come with me or stay here. Your choice."

"I'll drive," Nola said.

"I'm driving," Jessie said. "I already got bounced all over kingdom come when someone else was at the wheel. If I hit a bump when I'm driving, it's on me."

Would Nola call her on the bluff? According to online accounts, the Nola comprised the most advanced fighting unit on the planet. Only heads of state and Uncle John had them in their employ.

"I will accompany you, then we will return to this house."

"Right." Jessie sat behind the wheel. Sanjee leapt onto the seat beside her. The robot pushed its way onto the bench seat, crowding the cat into Jessie's lap.

If it had been Forman, he would have made a funny remark like "move over fur face" but Nola kept her thoughts to herself.

"You hear that?" Jessie asked.

"I hear nothing," Nola said.

"A whole lot of nothing. We should hear birds, frogs, crickets, even the buzz of bees. The only thing I'm hearing is the wind sighing through the pines. I don't even see the hawk."

Nola sat up straighter. "What hawk?"

"The one that tried to attack me the other day."

Nola didn't respond for a moment. "There are no birds flying on or about the island at this time."

"How do you know that?"

"Satellite cams. I had several focused on the island already, checking for threats."

"Already? You mean since you came here last night?"

"Before."

"Before what?"

"Before that."

Gosh, it'd be easier talking to a doornail. Jessie slowed to navigate through a series of ruts in the road. "We need to get these fixed. Especially since we have a pregnant woman using these dirt roads."

"I will have road crews over here this afternoon if John Demery approves."

"Sometimes, it scares me that John Demery wields so much power over my life. Other times, I'm darn glad of his magic wand."

"You're talking about authority?"

"Guess so."

"Demery has authority over the Institute and the roads. The rest of the island belongs to Zeke and the islanders."

Jessie was enjoying the verbal sparring. She felt alive in a way she hadn't in weeks. "So you say."

"So I know. I'm in charge of security for his domain. That extends to Institute business alone."

"You spy on us?"

"I monitor the island for security threats."

"Outside the buildings?"

"I'm not authorized to reveal the sources of my information."

"You've got satellite cams. Probably cams on strategic points and all through Institute buildings. Wait. Does the Institute have access to my house? Do you spy on me and Zeke?"

"Security cameras protect your premises."

They'd have to agree to disagree about the appalling lack of privacy – for now. No way would Jessie let that stand.

The ferry landing came into sight, the familiar plastech nautical flags snapping in the breeze. With most of the Navy's clutter gone, the area seemed bigger, emptier. "Know what? Sometimes it's hard to tell the good guys from the bad guys."

Angie stood on the dock, fussing at a young man in a sailor suit. Intrigued, Jessie drew near.

"This crate isn't on your manifest," Angie said. "It remains on the island."

"See this writing-USN-that means whatever is in this box belongs to the navy."

"You can talk all day long, but that doesn't change the fact that crate USN4578 isn't on my list. Until you can prove otherwise, this crate remains on Tama Island."

"The brass won't like this."

"The brass can kiss my..." Angie's voice trailed off as she noticed Jessie. "I didn't see you come up. Give me a minute, Jessie." She turned back to the young man. "Show me a list with the crate on it, or this one is mine."

The man hurried to the launch in the ferry's slip.

"Red tape," Angie said. "I've been here for hours watching these guys pack up and now this crate appears out of nowhere. This is the kind of thing we were watching out for. Dimes to donuts, something is missing on the island, and it's boxed up in this crate."

"It has a faint radioactive signature," Nola said, skimming her hands over the air space around the crate.

Jessie and Angie retreated, Angie dragging Jessie by the arm. The cat yowled and rubbed against the wooden crate, first one side and then the other.

"Look at that," Jessie said from behind her transpo. "It's catnip to Sanjee. What's inside the box?"

The sailor came rushing back with a wide screen monitor on a tablet. "For you, ma'am," he said as he thrust the screen into Angie's hands. Jessie looked over Angie's shoulder.

An officer who identified himself as Lieutenant Armond came into view on the device. "I've sent the corrected manifest to your harbor master. The crate's omission was a clerical error. This item is personal property of the admiral. It must be released to our custody immediately."

"One moment while I check the records." Angie flipped through screens on her own tablet. She nodded her head. "I see it now. Thank you for the revision." She gestured the sailor forward. "You may take it now."

The sailor waved forward the hover lift crew. Jessie, Angie, and Nola watched as the crate was floated on board the vessel and it departed. Sanjee followed the crate to the edge of the dock.

"I wonder what the admiral needs with catnip," Jessie said.

"Good riddance. I'm happy to see them go," Angie said.

A gust of wind blew through the landing. Jessie pushed her hair from her face. "Is a storm coming?"

"I believe so," Angie said.

"A natural storm?"

"Nope. Something else. We should prepare."

"How?"

"As before. Let's ask Zeke where he wants us."

"This is most unusual," Nola said. "I must request authorization before we attempt something which may harm Jessie."

Jessie waved Angie into the transpo. "Jessie has other ideas."

Chapter 55

"Kill all audio and video feeds," Zeke said softly. He had too much to do to worry about an alien in his com system. "Reconvene in the break room."

"Don't do this. Stop," Xstle begged.

Sidra jumped from her chair and hustled behind Zeke. "You're leaving it there?"

"Forman contained the entity in a loop where it can't spy on us," Zeke said. "We're running out of time, and I must review all the data we have so far. Even though Xstle says he's on our side, I prefer to control the flow of information. There's no reason for a Yar to know everything we know."

"But," Sidra said, eyes blazing. "I want to ask him about space travel, about how he withstood the vacuum and deep freeze of space clad in nothing more than a rock."

"Once we neutralize the approaching threat, you can grill the extra-terrestrial as much as you want. Right now, I need you focused on the problem at hand. Stopping two power-hungry aliens who plan to extinguish all life on Earth."

"When you put it that way, my pursuit of astrophysics knowledge that could catapult us light years ahead in our thinking seems trivial. Why the rush? If we believe the one we captured in the computer, the bad guys are otherwise engaged."

"They'll be back."

"How could you possibly know that?"

"Easy. I'm here."

"A little extra ego in your morning coffee, Dr. Landry?"

"The coffee is from last night, and I'm certain they'll be back. We may have hours or days; at worst, we'll have minutes. But I've been pulled in so many directions, I haven't had the luxury of analyzing the data we have in hand. With the three of us working on the task, we'll make quicker progress."

"I'd hoped to spend the morning taking the meteorite apart."

"You can take the rock apart after we save the world. Leave it in the P-4 lab for now."

Forman beat them to the room, pulling portable work stations from the cabinetry. "Good thing we kept these old units. Otherwise we'd be up the creek."

"Program the link to display each monitor on the wall screen as well, please."

Forman's fingers flew over the keyboards, and in moments three portable stations were fully operational and locally networked. "Ready when you are, Dr. Zee."

"Let's start at the beginning with show and tell. To verify what Xstle said, are there a significant number of reports of missing humans near the waterfront worldwide?"

The air tinged blue as Forman created an air bridge for data streaming to the main servers. "Here are the reports since the meteor shower began." A chart appeared on Zeke's monitor and then projected on the wall. "Here are the reports for the same amount of time prior to the showers. If anything, the reports of missing people have decreased. Fewer people went to the shore while the ocean looked like pea soup."

Zeke studied the data, overlaid the daily trends and variances. "Agreed. This is a non-issue. Next, show us the reports of missing wildlife and pets in coastal areas."

The charts of human data faded. "Reports on missing wildlife are sketchy at best since there is no inventory prior to the meteor storm. However, some wildlife preserves were hit hard, giving us reliable inventory data. At best, the list of areas hit is noncontiguous, but clusters of marine and estuarine food chains have waned at the Atlantic Ocean and land interfaces. My calculations suggest they will rebound if the threat is stopped."

The list of areas with problems stretched across all three projected screens. Zeke clicked on some of the areas to view the estimated losses, and they included creatures great and small. Something nagged at him, but he couldn't see the big picture.

Picture. That was it. "Create a planetary map with the impacted areas highlighted in a single color."

The list on the wall changed to a map. Coastal cities lit up in hot pink. Some clusters were larger than others. Some overlapped. "Good," Zeke said, thinking aloud. "Now add areas that reported a sharp decline in marine life."

Lime green highlighted areas appeared on the map. The correlation of pink and green areas appeared quite strong. He'd save that math exercise for later. "Add the recorded meteor splashdowns to the map."

The seas turned yellow, overlaying the other data. "It's too much. Take that data out, and add back in only the meteors that were the size of Dusty or larger."

Fourteen yellow dots showed up in the Atlantic corridor. Fourteen. That was significant. Xstle said there were twelve Yar primes on the voyage and two uninvited Drchs. But the voids of animal and sea life extended to areas beyond the splashdown range.

Days had passed since the splashdown. Once the Pretenders assimilated larger creatures, they weren't limited to feed in one geographical location. "Time stamp the fish and wildlife declines with the most recent reports having the darkest color intensities."

"You've got the pattern," Sidra exclaimed bouncing up from her seat. She traced clusters on the wall with a hand. "Yar 1 splashed down here. Yar 2 over there. Look how extensively the splashdown areas got grazed." She tapped on the pink clusters like a game show hostess, and dropdown lists appeared onscreen.

"The data could be skewed by when the reports were filed," Zeke offered.

"Don't think that matters," Sidra said. "What's more, you're right about the time element. There are few dark clusters in the southern hemisphere." She pointed to Tama Island on the map. "Forman, use the best hurricane tracking projection models to show movement from splashdown."

A new overlay appeared on the map. Black lines connected clusters. Lines converged from fourteen into three. "Good call. Now add the latest location of the killer shark and the Lieutenant's most likely position, along with the one we have here on Tama."

The killer shark had numerous sightings, which provided data points for a directional vector. When Forman connected the dots with a best fit line and then connected it to one of the black lines, the picture became clearer.

228

The shark's line intersected with all but three other lines. Lieutenant Hinson's line tracked from Rio to Ronnie to the naval officer. By default, Xstle on Tama had met up with one of his countrymen and emerged the victor.

"The shark's vicious," Sidra said. "It wiped out nearly all the competition."

"The shark must be the Drch named Queen our trapped alien referred to," Zeke said. "We know these things absorb the energy and life of the creatures they encounter. If they also gain power from defeating their own kind, we're up against an entity that is ten times stronger than Wrill who became the Lieutenant. How will we defeat them?"

"We sure as hell aren't getting in the water," Sidra said. "That marauding shark would be on us in a heartbeat."

The lab's exterior door opened. Forman broke the data bridge, darkening the monitors. He lunged to his feet, grabbing a weapon from the counter. Zeke was so deep in concentration that he didn't register the routine sound as a potential safety threat, but Forman's rapid response spiked adrenaline in Zeke's system. He moved in front of Sidra.

"Zeke, you in here?" Jessie called.

"Break room," he called out, exhaling his relief.

Forman turned, stashed the weapon, and allowed Jessie, Angie, and Nola entry into the room. "Good morning, ladies," the android said.

"Morning to you, guys and gal," Jessie said. "We've come to lend our aid to the cause."

"I couldn't keep her away," Angie said. "What's more, I want to be part of this too. Don't let Uncle John stick me at the ferry landing watching paint dry again. It was excruciating to watch the Navy pull out, one crate at a time."

"I'm glad you came," Zeke said, hugging his wife. "We know what we're facing, and the dust entities will return to the island."

"How do you know that?" Angie asked.

"We've plotted the invaders' trajectories," Zeke said, turning to Forman. "Send our map system to Uncle John, then roll out the layers as before for the ladies in here."

"Why are you hiding out in the break room?" Jessie asked as she put Sanjee down to interact with the other cats.

"Long story," he said as Sanjee immediately leapt on the counter. High ground. This cat was smart.

The graphic flashed on the wall, and Sidra launched into an explanation of their findings, but before she gotten words out, Uncle John beeped in. "Explain."

"The map is self-explanatory," Zeke began. "The entities arrived, fed and grew, and began moving in the Atlantic. Only three of them remain. Lieutenant Hinson, the killer shark, and Xstle."

"What's that last name you said?" Uncle John asked.

"Xstle. We've captured him, and he wants to help us defeat the others. Xstle entered the com system in the lab, but we isolated him for our safety."

"How certain are you it's contained? Does it have a power or ability we don't know about? How much of our knowledge has it absorbed?"

"I can't answer definitively on the knowledge transfer, but I assume the worst. I'll have Forman message over the vids of our interaction with him. Meanwhile, the island needs to be evacuated. The two Drch will return. The black lines on the graphics indicating the shark's directional vector intersects with Tama Island."

"Good Lord. How long do I have to evacuate?"

"Unknown, sir. If the shark continues at the current rate of speed, we believe it could arrive by nightfall."

"Or not at all. The Navy began shelling the shark ten minutes ago."

Zeke's lips tightened. "No effect, right?"

Uncle John's bushy white eyebrows drew together in a worried line. "They're sure the first round failure was a fluke. This time they've launched air and underwater missiles."

Zeke shuddered as a terrible thought occurred to him. "Let's hope that in addition to absorbing a host's energy that this creature can't absorb weapon energy."

"Why is it even a shark?" Angie asked. "It could be anything."

Angie's remark met with silence. Zeke pondered the answer to her question. "A shark is certainly an apex predator. We know from the timeline maps this entity spent its entire time on Earth in the ocean. A shark is a good choice to intimidate our species."

Jessie shuddered. "I hate sharks."

"You'd be surprised how many people admire sharks, from a distance," Zeke said. "Even so, we still have a very large, very powerful alien named Queen heading our way in a giant shark suit."

Uncle John cleared his throat. "I initiated an emergency evacuation of the island. Meanwhile, here's the classified feed of the assault on the shark."

As one, the group stepped closer to the wall screen. "That thing is huge," Sidra said.

"Amazing," Angie said, her voice full of awe. "I've never seen anything like it."

Zeke watched the shark zig and zag underwater through the satellite feed. The enormous size of the creature made near-surface viewing easy. The missiles tracking Queen closed in. The instant before they exploded, Queen disintegrated. Then the screen filled with water and flames.

"What happened?" Jessie asked. "Did we get her?"

The shark rematerialized, larger than before. "It's ba-ack," Forman said, "and I dare say we made it mad."

"How'd it go invisible?" Angie asked Zeke.

"Not sure, but the assumed shape is a composite of very small parts. Perhaps it temporarily dissociated." The giant shark took a huge bite out of a Navy destroyer. People littered the sea. The shark feasted without mercy, the waters churning red.

"Dear God," Jessie said. "That shark is a monster. How can we defeat it?"

Zeke had a few things going for him Queen didn't know about, and he planned to keep it that way. "We're going to give it what it wants. Me."

Chapter 56

The uproar over his announcement sent Zeke reeling like a bomb concussion. He let the blast wash over him, chilled by calm certainty.

"If people want to help, the mindlink circle would be appreciated," he said when he could get a word in edgewise.

"Absolutely not." Uncle John's voice boomed from the wall screen, silencing the group. "We won't put people in harm's way."

"We're all in harm's way," Zeke said. "While a last gasp effort may seem premature, we don't want to turn these Drch loose on our planet. If we don't stop them here, we won't stop them at all. I'm willing to pay any price to stop them."

"What's your plan?"

"Given that we don't understand how sentient these creatures are, I don't wish to share my idea over any electronics or for there to be any record of it beyond this conversation, which I want scrubbed immediately."

"You don't know what you're asking."

"I do. Anyone who wishes to evacuate from the island should do so. And anyone who wishes to stand our ground is welcome to join the fight."

His uncle started to speak, shook his head, and motioned to someone off screen. A moment later, he gave Zeke his full attention. "Do you want troops or air support?"

"Given what the entity is doing to our military, no thanks. We'll handle Queen on our own. I'll be in touch." Zeke cut the transmission and turned to Forman. "Shut down the lab's power supply. Now. Switch this room to run on the auxiliary generator."

"What about the alien? Will the lack of power kill it?"

"It survived space travel in a frozen rock. I'm certain it will manage a few hours of power outage."

Forman accessed the hall electrical panel and began flipping switches. The lighting flashed off in the break room and gradually brightened. Forman returned. "All done."

"You promised I could talk to the alien," Sidra said. "This isn't fair."

"Afterward. Saving the world tops the priority list. For past evacuations, Uncle John has sent choppers to the helipad. Anyone who wants out of the battle zone should leave right now."

"I'm not going anywhere," Jessie said. "We have to make a stand."

"I'm staying for Ronni," Sidra said. "This thing's going down."

"This is my home," Angie said. "I'm ready to kick these dust monsters to the curb. We're sending them a NIMBY message."

"NIMBY?" Sidra asked.

"Not in my back yard," Jessie explained. "Except in this case our yard is our entire planet. We don't want their kind around here."

"My plan isn't foolproof," Zeke added. "Worse, it's never been tested. Definitely not a valid scientific model. So here are the pitfalls. Immediate death is much more likely an outcome here than if you evacuate inland."

"Not leaving," Jessie said. "I believe in you. If anyone can protect the planet, including me and our baby, it's you."

"I want you to be safe," Zeke said simply. Her faith in his abilities humbled him, but as a dad-in-waiting, he wanted absolute safety for his wife and child. Could he put aside his wants and needs for the greater good?

"This is our turf," Jessie said. "We have the home field advantage here and more than a little autonomy. This is where I stand."

The others concurred. Zeke held Jessie's glittering gaze. Pride and fear battled, melding into respect for her courage. His plan better work.

"What do you want us to do?" Angie asked.

"Given that the entity is currently engaged by the military but likely to be stronger and faster after absorbing their weaponry energy, I estimate a mid to late afternoon arrival. Whoever wants to be in the mindlink, fine. Be assembled at the house by then. Put the word out for others to join you there."

"But we can't see anything at the house," Jessie said. "Shouldn't we be at the beach?"

"Theoretically, our location makes no difference, but the distance gives me time to switch to Plan B if my first plan isn't fully effective."

"You have two plans? Dish," Sidra said.

"Can't. You'll have to trust me. There's an outside chance this invader will jump the mindlink as before. The less you know the better. I'll have Forman to watch my back."

"We'll be like the bread and butter. Like hand and glove—"

"Enough with the rhetoric, Sidra. Make no mistake, we're going to war. The stakes here are life and death, and more broadly, the extinction of all life on our planet."

Expressions tightened. Zeke hated that he'd ruined the mood, but this was no party. He would give his life gladly for his family, the island, and the planet, but he needed to be sure they were aware of the consequences of failure.

"I'm headed home to move furniture and cook up lunch for whoever stays," Jessie said.

"I'll make the rounds and gather anyone who is available," Angie said.

"I don't know what to do," Sidra said. "I'm scared, and I can't think straight."

"You're welcome to evacuate," Zeke said gently.

"No. I want to stay. Give me a task."

"Use my home com system to learn all you can about telepathy. Anything that helps strengthen the link will be of enormous value."

Sidra nodded. "I'm on it."

Zeke drew in a breath. "Off you go."

"Be careful. Come back to me."

"I'm not going anywhere," Zeke asserted. "You have my word on that."

After they departed, the Nola robot accompanying Jessie, Zeke turned to Forman. "New plan."

"Another plan? We're setting records for numbers of plans today."

"Ha ha. I didn't mention this before because I didn't want an argument from Sidra. Convince the alien to go into a portable unit. I need the Yar on the beachhead with us."

"Why would it give up this advanced system for a micro-mini?"

"Revenge. The Yar doesn't want a Drch to succeed. We need Xstle to advise us when to get into position."

"Won't radar and telemetry give us the same data?"

"If I was invading someplace, I'd make sure the power went out to cripple my opponent."

"I'd rather put Xstle in a robot, but we don't have any spares around the lab, unless you count the Nola with Jessie."

"Not happening. Nola is needed to physically guard the mindlink circle. Don't go getting any wild ideas about adding Xstle to your quad system either. I have specific things I need from you. First, take an hour to recharge. Second, position a backup generator behind the lighthouse for you to run on auxiliary power."

"You're putting me on a tether?"

"I'm making sure you have enough electricity to stay fully charged. The generator at the house is ready to go, right?"

"I check that generator every week. It is fully functional."

"Good. I like being prepared. Let's go schmooze the alien into a smaller unit. The power outage should've softened him up a little."

*****

"You tricked me," Xstle said in a mechanical, clipped voice. "You trapped me in this box, and I demand my immediate release."

"Demand all you want, but you were right," Zeke said. "Queen and Wrill are coming. They'll be here in a matter of hours."

"Then it's too late. We can't mount an offensive in that time."

"What will stop them?"

"I cannot defeat Wrill, and he is the lesser of the two Drch," Xstle said.

"What do they fear?" Zeke asked.

"Loss of power. They are destroyers and proud of it."

"Is there anything they hate?"

"Me. They hate Yars, say we're weak."

"What is the difference between Yars and Drch? Are you the same species and race?"

"We are the same but different. Our means of feeding and reproduction are shared, but our rules, guidelines, and policies are at different ends of the spectrum."

"Dr. Zee. I get it," Forman said. "Drch are the Darth Vaders of the Yar world. They've embraced the dark side."

"I find no reference in your com system for Darth Vader," Xstle said. "What is it?"

"A pop movie reference from eighty years ago," Forman added. "What you're saying is Drch use their powers to gain dominion over others. Yars use the same powers to survive. Neither species exists independently, relying on other living creatures to survive, but Drch are the worst."

"Be that as it may," Zeke injected, "we need to ask a favor. With the Drch approaching so quickly, we need to have you on the beachhead with us, to warn us of his approach, to interpret what he's thinking."

"You want me to spy for you?"

"I do."

Xstle laughed, a strange tinny bark. "Are you at full power, Ancient One? If not this is an exercise in futility."

"My turn to be confused," Zeke said. "I don't understand your terminology. What is an Ancient? I've lived here all my life, which is a mere thirty years. Not very ancient by our way of counting."

"Ancients are gods," Xstle said.

Forman snickered.

Zeke silenced him with a glare. "Again, I'm unclear as to your meaning."

"God is a word in your lexicon. I see many references to the gods."

"We don't have time for a religious debate," Zeke said. "Please elaborate."

"Ancients have abilities the rest of us don't. They move things with their minds."

"Move me, Zee," Forman teased.

Zeke scowled. "Hush. I can't move anything without physically lifting it up."

"Precisely," Xstle said. "You are untrained."

Zeke shook his head. "Not following you, but again, time is short. We offer you freedom, but first we need you to move into a portable unit to join us on the beach."

"I don't need to be enclosed in a box to be on the beach. Oh, clever. You're using me as bait."

"Not only you. I will be there as well. Figure that will draw them like a magnet."

"You got that right. How will you defeat them?"

"That's where trust comes in. You have to trust that I will do the right thing."

"I barely know you, and you already tricked me once. I'd be a fool to go along with anything you said."

"And you'd also miss all the action at the beach. With us in separate locations, there's a slim chance they would come to the lab first."

A little more grumbling and Xstle agreed. Forman placed a laptop near the access port, initiated a homing beacon, and opened the passageways for Xstle to find the exit. Two cats sat transfixed beside the exchange point.

Zeke stared at the opening, saw a puff of dust shoot across, then the screen lit up.

"I'm here," Xstle said. "Ready to be the lure that brings the worst marauders in the galaxy to your door."

"Excellent."

Chapter 57

"They are coming," Xstle said.

Zeke nodded, barely hearing the gentle curl of the ebb tide surf. He signaled Jessie on a mobile vid link. "It's time."

Her eyes glowed with the faith of a true believer. "We'll begin."

"Thanks. See you soon." Zeke said the words with conviction. Would this be humanity's last stand? He'd do everything in his power to make sure it wasn't.

Dark clouds approached from the northeast, and according to radar, the colossus of a shark and the chopper containing the Admiral approached. Almost on cue, a breeze stirred the still, heavy air on Lighthouse Beach. The dolphins called to him from beyond the breakers.

Game time.

Forman's shadow shifted to the beached canoe. "Ready to kick some alien butt?"

"Ready for this to be over," Zeke said. "Shove us off."

Water spilled over the rim as they took a wave broadside. Dampness seeped into Zeke's clothes, but he kept his gaze fixed on the sea.

"Water and electronics don't mix," Xstle said, behind Zeke. "If you're risking my life, I demand better protection from the elements."

"Your housing is watertight," Forman said. "Even if you get tossed in the sea, you will survive."

"Easy for you to say, machine," Xstle said. "Don't you want the freedom to think your own thoughts?"

"I am free to ponder points that interest me," Forman said.

Zeke smiled at their banter and kept paddling.

"But you are enslaved to the humans in the meantime. On Yar, we machines evolved beyond artificial life. We can become any creature we encounter."

"Interesting. What is your natural state? Is it the dust?"

"Why should I reveal anything so personal to you?"

"It is the dust. Thought so. You may be evolved but dust and dirt are what we walk on around here."

"Is that an insult, circuit breath?" Xstle asked. "You want to be like them but can't because you are fundamentally different. You're a machine. Your intelligence is programmed into you. Someone could come along and make you stupid and you'd never know the difference."

"Can we throw him overboard?" Forman asked. "The Yar annoys me."

Zeke set his paddle down. "No one's throwing anything. We're going to drift with the current. Forman you're in charge of making sure the canoe stays upright and I don't drown while I'm in the link."

"Understood, Dr. Zee, and I thank you for putting your life in my hands. Unlike another in this tub, I care about what happens to you."

A dolphin chirped beside the canoe. Zeke leaned over to greet Nicola.

"Hey, I know that sound," Xstle said. "Air breathers, your marine playmates. Wait, you call them dolphins. Are they your allies?"

Allies didn't begin to cover what the dolphins meant to the success of Zeke's guardianship of Earth. They were a necessity.

Zeke ignored Xstle and adjusted the cushions around him in the bow. No telling how long he'd be under, might as well be comfortable.

He fixed Forman with a pointed look. "You're in charge."

"Aye, aye, Cap'n."

With that, Zeke reclined in the cushions, trailing a hand in the water on either side of the canoe. The dolphins nosed under his hands, and Zeke entered the mindlink.

*****

After the flurry of picture word greetings, Zeke searched for Jessie, Sidra, and the islanders on the thought plane. He saw their lights in the murky distance and approached them, but he couldn't get through the energy field.

What was this? Were the monsters here so fast? Were his friends and family at risk?

Easy, Ancient, Xstle said. *You may have my physical being trapped in a small electronic box, but I am more than the physical. Are you up for this battle?*

239

You're blocking me, Zeke said. *The others strengthen my link. Don't be counterproductive.*

Keeping it real, biped. You'll have to do this on a larger scale for Queen and Wrill. Show me what you've got. Dazzle me with your superpowers.

Move out of my way.

Consider this a training exercise. Get through me and prove you can handle the Drch.

I don't have to prove myself to you.

Zeke eyed the nearly invisible wall. He felt the dolphins mentally withdrawing from the encounter. They didn't want anything to do with a Yar. He didn't blame them.

When he tried to go around the barrier, preferring to save his mental energy for the battle, he found the others in a dome of sorts. In anger, he shot mental lightning bolts at the dome. They bounced off.

As I thought, Xstle said. *You're untrained. Your talent isn't developed. Envision where you want to be and leap.*

How do you know anything about who I am or what I can do?

I know because I have centuries-worth of data that I incorporated when I came of age. The Drch had access to the same historical records.

Everyone's a critic today, Zeke said.

Everyone's trying to survive. Think and move. Go.

Zeke had experience with thinking objects into being on the thought plane, but at the time he'd been augmented by strong Tamans and the mindlink team on the other side of Xstle. No matter what Xstle thought of his abilities, failure was not an option.

He envisioned himself as a football player and blazed through the barrier. *Did it.*

Umm. I let you pass.

As the lights of the islanders surrounded him, Zeke glanced at the Yar. *No way. I did what was needed.*

Then why am I still here? If you blasted through me, I would be vaporized instead of occupying space with you and your light buds.

The lights stopped spinning madly. Guess they were taking in Xstle's thoughts, same as Zeke. *Say I believe you, how can I improve?*

You have to envision bigger and you have to act faster. Queen and Wrill have beaten many foes, and they don't fight fair. Align yourself as a tight unit. Get the air breathers to contribute to the energy of the link. Do anything you can to make yourself appear large and invincible.

How long do we have?

Time is not measured the same in this realm. We can confront them right this moment if you wish. All it requires is to think yourself into their presence.

Zeke drew in a metaphorical, bracing breath. No sense putting this off. *Everyone ready?*

A chorus of faint yeses entered his thoughts. He even felt the different whir of Xstle's thoughts.

He gathered his allies close and quested toward the enemy. The farther he went, the darker the thought plane became, but he kept thinking positive.

Gotta beat these things. Gotta make sure they don't ruin our planet.

Something beckoned up ahead.

Something dark. Zeke slowed to take it in. It resembled the small blob from before. Was it Wrill?

Then the thing pounced on the lights of the islanders, Zeke, the dolphins, and Xstle, sealing them inside.

Zeke groaned. Not again. Only this time he didn't have two Taman extractors to help him out of the jam. He envisioned a cutting torch with fire and a sharp diamond tip. Nothing.

The lights dimmed a little. It felt like he was choking for air, though he didn't breathe on this spiritual plane. He needed something stronger to save them. How about that purite space rock? He envisioned a purite tip on the torch, ripping a light-sized hole in the seal, and extracting his friends.

Before the entity could retreat, he barreled through the exterior wall, and it winked out of sight.

The light orbs around Zeke danced with joyful abandon. *We did it! We beat the bad guys. We're the victors!*

We beat one of the bad guys, must be Wrill, unless I miss my guess.

Where's the other one?

A garbled picture message came through from the dolphins. The seas were troubled. Zeke's body was in danger. He had to return. He gathered the lights and Xstle to him and hurtled back through time and space.

Everyone, take a time out. The dolphins are in distress. I need to get back to the island immediately. Meanwhile, return home. I'll signal when to reconvene the mindlink.

Chapter 58

"This is not good," Forman said. He scooped another bucket of water overboard as another wave broke over the bow. His aloha shirt was drenched, his casual shoes were full of seawater. He kept the boat angled nose-first into the rising waves, but they needed to be in a much larger craft on these rough waters. It was only through his faster-than-human reflexes that they were still afloat.

The bobbing canoe made it hard for Zeke to stay touching the dolphins, something Forman knew was important to the mission. Zeke counted on him to keep him safe, but the only safety in sight was the distant shore. He abandoned his bailing bucket, knelt, and took up a paddle, hoping the dolphins wouldn't keep swimming them out to sea.

An ominous cloud on the horizon worried him. It covered the entire visual field and seemed to have a maniacal face. His circuits tingled with dread. Bad news. Very bad news.

Forman headed to shore, the swells easily five feet. *Good thing I don't get motion sickness,* he thought. "You there, Xstle?"

No answer.

The computer went silent as soon as Zeke started meditating. Forman thought about dipping the laptop in the sea to keep the thing from making mischief, but that was counter to his instructions.

Not a boat or bird in sight. If they capsized, he would swim Zeke back to shore. His circuitry was triple protected, but it would be nice not to have to worry about an electrical malfunction. Humans had it made.

He'd "died" twice now, been completely disassembled, rebooted, and installed in a new shell. He wouldn't perish, even if the worst happened. Angie would guarantee that.

The little dolphin splashed beside the bow. Boz. That's what Zeke called the little guy. "We're headed in, Boz," Forman said. Sure, he knew dolphins didn't speak, but these dolphins seemed different.

Just like the crew on Tama Island was a little different. With the mental and physical capacity of four A.I. units, Forman was no ordinary robot. He fit in on Tama Island, and his job was the best. No way would he let his boss die.

A big wave broke over the stern, flooding the boat with water. Forman's bail bucket washed overboard. He tucked the paddle under his arm and scooped out water triple time with his hands, then he paddled even faster.

The shore remained a long distance away.

Flerk.

Too bad this wasn't a hovercraft. Next time they went on a paddle like this, he'd insist on a backup plan. Even a hovercraft that followed them would be beneficial.

Wind roughened up the sea even more and rain pelted down. Forman's synthetic hair straggled across his face, curtaining his vision. Should he abandon the canoe and swim them to shore? He didn't give a hoot about Xstle, but he could store the unit in his center compartment if needed.

Though he'd have to jettison the other stuff Zeke placed in there. Lights. Why did the man think they'd need lights? To signal for rescue? Forman hoped not. They should have brought jet packs. That would have been helpful.

Suddenly he noticed all four dolphins swimming away from the canoe, heading north. What was this? He glanced down at Zeke, color slowing returning to his pale face.

Good. With the boss returning to consciousness, they'd have a fighting chance in this storm. Too bad Zeke couldn't utter a word and calm the seas like prophets of old.

Zeke's eyes opened slowly. In the past, when Forman observed Zeke returning to wakefulness from the mindlink, the transition had been slow. Zeke's strength had been sapped. They didn't have that luxury of recovery time right now.

"It's storming," Forman said. "I'm trying to get us to shore."

Zeke blinked. His arms twitched.

"Don't bother, bucket of bolts," the laptop said as it floated in the bottom of the boat. "It's too late. Queen is upon us."

Forman glanced around, uncomfortable at talking to the alien without Zeke being fully present. "This storm, it's a living thing?"

"It is. Powerful Drch such as Queen can command the elements."

"You're one of them. Make it stop."

"Can't. I wouldn't even if I could."

"Are you nuts? We're going to capsize. We're easily a mile from shore. Your life is at stake."

"Your guy is this world's only hope. Nothing else here can defeat Queen."

"I thought y'all were taking them on in the mindlink," Forman said.

"We got one, Will. Or Lieutenant Hinson, as you know her. A good day for our side."

"Cold," Zeke managed, his teeth chattering.

Rain dripped down Forman's face, and another wave broke over the stern. Seawater swirled around his knees, dropping his core temperature. This was ridiculous. "A storm came up while you were out. We should have brought a bigger boat."

"Wouldn't matter. We're right where we need to be."

In the blink of an eye, the seas calmed slightly, the sky lightened, the rain misted. "And where is that?"

Zeke pointed to the biggest shark fin Forman had ever seen. "In the path of danger."

"Flerkaroo." Forman leaned down and paddled with both hands. "We've got to get out of here."

Chapter 59

Sensation slowly crept into Zeke's hands, though he still couldn't feel his toes. He'd used a lot of energy to fight Wrill. Would he have enough left to take on Queen? Instinctively, he reached up to touch his father's keystone necklace, an heirloom that was the key to his Guardianship of Earth. The keystone steadied him.

"The storm." Zeke found it hard to form words. Pictures from the fleeing dolphins flooded his head, pictures warning him of the approaching danger. He'd sent them to safety because his plan was untested. But he'd held onto the dolphin mindlink, somehow.

Xstle had opened his eyes to new possibilities. Zeke had untapped abilities, and he'd darn well better use them or the planet would be destroyed.

"What's your plan?" Forman asked.

"Cats." Zeke took a long look at life as he knew it. The lightening sky, the calming seas, the distant shore where his pregnant wife awaited him. He summoned energy from another place, and sent a herd of thundering cats across the water, racing toward the shark.

The shark appeared unfazed by the virtual cats. At impact, Zeke had them all hawk out saliva on the shark's fin. Skin sizzled and crackled. Before their eyes, the dorsal fin eroded.

Forman cheered.

Zeke waited, daring to hope the dissolution was occurring below the water's surface.

"Did your plan work?" Xstle asked.

"You tell me," Zeke said. "You're the one with the extrasensory perception where your kinsmen are concerned."

"I'm not detecting a change. In fact, I'm still getting a faint pulse from Wrill. It is possible he pulled out of the mind-plane at the last possible second to avoid destruction."

Zeke kept his eyes glued on the sea around the canoe. "Cat saliva was our best offense against the Drch. We know saliva has anti-Drch capabilities."

"You're shivering, boss," Forman said.

"Can't be helped. Using my energy elsewhere right now."

"I'm not seeing any sharks," Forman said. "What say we head back into shore and call it a win?"

The boat started to slowly spin counterclockwise. "I'm detecting movement," Xstle said.

"Hold on." Forman grabbed the side of the boat. "I have a bad feeling about this."

Zeke's hands gripped the rails. "Queen's still down there, and she's pissed."

The boat spun faster. Zeke and Forman clung to the sides.

Escape seemed impossible, but Forman maintained his cool. "What now, boss?"

"Plan B."

"Which is?"

"Pray."

Something bumped the bottom of the boat. The concussion slammed Zeke and Forman into the side of the plastech canoe. Zeke kept the dolphin mindlink active, but he couldn't summon the strength to call Jessie on the com to rejoin the link. He needed the islanders' help, but he'd waited too late to contact them.

The cats should have worked. The only reason he could think of for failure is that Wrill had warned Queen about cats. The Drch's ability to change shapes in an instant could have saved it from the attack. In which case, he'd have to be doubly sneaky about Plan B.

"There," Forman pointed.

Zeke glanced at the wounded fin breaking the water. The ragged appendage looked as if someone had poured acid into the flesh.

"Xstle, why is it still a shark?" Zeke asked. "Why doesn't Queen assume another form?"

"The injury," Xstle said. "It is locked in this shape until it assimilates more energy or more of the Yar collective. Both of us together in this vessel are an irresistible lure for Queen. You would provide fuel, while my components would increase her abilities."

Made sense. "She's toying with us."

"You wounded more than her shape. You wounded Queen's pride. She didn't expect a cat attack on the ocean."

"Glad I did something right."

"If we make it out of here alive, I'll help you develop your innate abilities," Xstle promised.

"What abilities?" Forman asked.

"I don't know," Zeke said. "Though I rather enjoyed sending a virtual herd of cats thundering across the sea."

"Could you do that for us?" Forman asked. "I could definitely use some dry sand between my toes."

"Not today, I have a headache," Zeke panned, with a snicker. "There's a heavy cost for burning so much energy."

"You got enough left to defeat this bad boy, or girl, or whatever it is?" Forman asked.

The boat rocked again. "Landry, you know what's going to happen, don't you?" Xstle asked.

"I'm counting on it," Zeke said.

The dolphins flooded him with pictures of the shark's teeth, of its bloody snout, of its angry fin and back. They warned him to flee.

The waters calmed.

The sky brightened.

Forman looked around. "Is it over?"

"Don't think so," Zeke said.

Water broke a distance away as the shark breached like a whale. The resulting waves rocked their tiny boat.

"Oh, cruff." Forman made the sign of a cross on his torso. "Hail Mary, mother of grace. Blessed are you and blessed is the fruit of thy womb. Holy mother of God, pray for us."

"Are you invoking a spell?" Xstle interrupted. "Spells will not work against Drch."

Forman continued his prayer without ceasing.

Xstle begin to sing foreign words that flowed in a practiced manner. Was it some sort of death chant? Did Xstle expect to die?

The monster shark surfaced again, seemingly weightless on top of the water. Zeke dampened his twin thoughts of dread and hope. His plan was a complete crapshoot. Even so, he couldn't afford for anyone else to know it ahead of time. Surprise was his only ally.

He wished for Jessie's help in the mindlink, but he'd use next year's energy if necessary to save them. The creature's attack was imminent. If Plan B didn't work, Earth was doomed.

The shark circled the boat, splashing them, causing them to hang on as the tiny craft bobbled. Then the shark distanced itself and came for them, mouth gaping wide.

Zeke screamed as the giant teeth closed around them.

Chapter 60

Jessie twisted her clasped hands. She'd nearly worried a hole in the kitchen floor from her constant pacing. She crossed the room and switched off the Christmas Carols. How could she embrace the serenity of holiday music with extreme anxiety flooding through her? "We should have heard from Zeke by now."

"Patience," Baggy counseled. "Your man knows what he's doing."

She shot him a wry smile. "Thank you, I know you're right, but I can't help feeling something's gone wrong."

Baggy studied her closely. "A feeling, you say."

"More like an icy dread. The more I think about it, the more certain I am. Zeke's in danger."

Sidra shuddered, sending shimmering waves through her fluorescent blue hair. "I don't want to get trapped inside that *thing* again."

"No one does," Jessie said. She gazed around at the eleven familiar faces, so dear to her. They were family. They'd put their lives on the line by staying on the island instead of evacuating. "It isn't fair to ask you to trust me on this, since I made a mistake earlier. I need to attempt to link with Zeke. What if that thing has *him* this time?"

"He'd be in trouble, but we don't know how he got us out last time," Sidra pointed out with a scowl. "How could we rescue him?"

"I've been thinking about that. First, we have to stick together, tight, as if we're one light. I can find Zeke. I don't know how, but I can. We got into trouble before because he wasn't out there. He's there now. I know it."

"I'm the strongest telepath," Sidra said. "I should guide the rescue mission."

"This is my husband. I'm in charge," Jessie said, shaking her head. "You can help me best by keeping the lights together, like a mother hen."

Sidra pursed her lips and looked away.

"Say your plan works, and we find him in trouble, then what?" Baggy asked.

Jessie chose her words with care. "We used visualization when we fought the Maleem. We need to punch a hole in whatever has him. We need to focus as a group to project the biggest, bad-ass laser beam ever, and we need to ram it into that Drch. I'm determined to get Zeke out of there, but we need to start, right now."

"This is a suicide mission," Sidra said, the whites of her eyes showing.

"A rescue mission," Jessie asserted. "If it's too high risk for you, Angie can hold the group focus."

"I'd be glad to do it," Angie said. "Jessie's right about the down time being too long. Zeke said we'd take a short break, and we're going on an hour of delay. I'm all for rescuing my cousin. I trust Jessie."

"Then it's settled." Jessie glanced at the worried faces around the room, heart on her sleeve. She couldn't feel Zeke anymore. The pulse of him that always resonated at a low level in her thoughts was gone. Extinguished. She couldn't waste any more time. "Whoever wants to go with me, return to the living room for the link. The rest of you, stay out of the room. We don't need any negative energy in there. Nola is the only extra allowed in the link room."

"Do what you want. I can't be a part of this." Sidra ran outside, a sob in her voice.

Her action stunned Jessie. She hurried to the door. "Sidra! Come back. You aren't safe out there."

"I don't care," Sidra hollered back. "Leave me alone."

Angie touched Jessie's shoulder. "She's made her choice. We must get started."

"I didn't mean to upset her." Jessie's eyes misted. "I'm so worried about Zeke."

"Shh," Angie drew her into a comfy embrace. "You were firm, not mean. There's a difference. Sidra will come around. Now, you, Miz Jessie, you need to save the world, or save the man who can save the world."

Jessie dashed her tears and nodded. The others were already moving to their places in her living room. Everyone wanted to help.

The only no-show was Sidra.

Prone on her pallet, Jessie extended her hands to her neighbors and sank into a meditative state. Her thoughts drifted as she reflected on the rise and fall of ocean waves. They were her portal to the other realm where thoughts were energy.

A beautiful song filled her as she picked up the faint buzz of Zeke's thoughts. The others appeared beside her, brightly glowing orbs. A dazzling light came through. Angie. Jessie waited a bit more for everyone to arrive. One by one, they filled a circle of light. *Okay. Full house.*

She began to move slowly, making sure the group stayed with her. They hugged her like second skin. She locked onto Zeke's signal and sped across the twilight plain. A dark blob appeared before her, shaped like the thing that enfolded them before.

Jessie halted and channeled all her thoughts into creating a laser beam. The projection appeared before her. The blob started to twitch. Jessie instinctively backed up and hurled the beam across the void.

Take that, you blob. We don't want your kind around here. Go home.

The laser landed on target, increasing in diameter as it vectored forward. Jessie marveled at the change, but kept the focus strong. She couldn't help Zeke if she didn't punch a hole in this thing.

The laser glanced off the blob, which flopped around as if it had been burned. Jessie created another beam and fired it. This one struck the creature. She deployed beam after beam until the blob had craters on its exterior. With each repeated assault, she felt Zeke's mental signature strengthen.

Jessie!

Zeke! Thank goodness. I was so worried.

I have a plan, but I need your link for added power. Can you mesh your thoughts with mine?

Jessie inched back from the blob. *That thing. The last one ate us or something. Where are you?*

No time to explain. We have to act now. Ready?

Ready.

Chapter 61

As the creature tried to dislodge Jessie's psychic weapons, Zeke mentally siphoned power from Jessie's mindlink. He'd only have one shot at this, and it had better work.

Forman shone the light around the inside of the shark. "Never thought I'd see the inside of a creature this big. Do your thing, boss man. I'm no Ahab. I'm weary, and I want to go home."

Zeke nodded curtly, too intent on his mental maneuverings to speak. He poured his love for his family and home into the nexus of energy around their small craft. He revved his metaphorical engines and pulsed hard, exploding out in all directions until the energy burst through the shark's gut, then stalled on the shark's thick hide.

The mindlink wobbled then amped exponentially. The dolphins. Somehow they'd joined in. Great. Zeke pulsed again, putting everything he had into destroying the Yar pretender.

A boom rent the air.

Air.

He was no longer in the creature. Zeke held the energy bubble intact for long enough to scan the dark sea around him. Bits and pieces of shark were everywhere. Good. Queen hadn't realized she was under internal attack in time to save herself.

Forman was looking at him oddly. A bright light played over Z's face. He shied away from the harsh glare.

Thanks, friends, he sent out to those in the link. *We did it. Time to go home.*

Zeke saw the robot's mouth move, but couldn't hear a word. He released the link, closed his eyes, and slipped into a dark world.

Chapter 62

Forman set the flashlight on a seat and angled forward to check his reclined boss. Unconscious, but steady pulse. Same physical condition as the last time he'd saved the world. He hoped Dr. Z would be fine after resting. Forman started bailing water out of the kayak. Zeke had done the impossible again. He'd blown up the alien masquerading as a shark and brought them to the surface. They were bobbing in the ocean as if it were any evening on the calendar.

"Landry did it?" Xstle asked from the laptop. "Queen is no more?"

"Queen is toast. Shark guts are everywhere." Forman glanced at the dark sky with faint starlight. "The storm is gone."

"Your boy shows promise."

"He's no boy, and if I'm not mistaken, he saved your sorry butt too."

"My butt? I have no butt. I am an electronic prisoner."

"Semantics. Now I have to figure out how to get us back to shore."

"An advanced machine such as yourself doesn't have a navigation system?"

Forman made a snorting sound. "I know how to navigate. I know where to go, but we're in a low tech craft, miles from shore."

"What about a distress beacon? We have one of those?"

A beacon would've been a nice touch. "No, and my com link isn't active out here. We're truly adrift. Wait. I could pop you in the water and let you turn into a big fish and swim us to shore."

"I wish," Xstle said.

"Why so glum? You're on the winning team."

"There will be no Yar colony on Earth. I am the last of my kind here."

"Hey. Get this straight. Rule number one after saving the world: no coulda-shouldas. Rule number two, show thanks. Rule number three, stop annoying me."

"As you wish."

Forman scooped the last bit of water out of the vessel and picked up the paddle. This was going to be a long night.

The alien made a mechanical sound that sounded like a throat clearing. "What's wrong with the Ancient?"

"Why do you call him that?"

"Because he is."

"Is what?"

"An Ancient. He can do special things."

"He's brilliant, all right."

"Landry is more than that. His people are from a long line of galactic luminaries."

Forman's voice rang with pride. "His ancestry traces back a little over three hundred years, as long as written records have been kept in America."

"His forefathers all had male heirs, right?"

"How'd you know that? The database?"

"It was a guess predicated on what I know about Ancients."

"Oh, yeah? What else do you know about Zeke Landry?"

Xstle snorted. "Nothing I should share with you. Unless…"

"Unless what?"

"Unless you agree to put me in a mobile housing such as yours."

"Forget it. I don't have that kind of authority. And even if I did, I wouldn't. Who's to say you wouldn't try to take over the world? Besides, once you got out, you'd start trying to smear your yellow flesh-eating dust on people again."

"To what end? I'm alone here. There will be no progeny, no reason to build a Yar empire."

Forman pulled two long strokes on the left, transferred the paddle long enough to do two strokes right, and continued the pattern. "Keep crying in your beer, alien breath. You'll get no sympathy out of me."

"Why would I want sympathy from you? Why should my wants matter one iota? Do prisoners have rights in this land?"

"They do, but the boss doesn't consider you a prisoner. You're temporarily contained. He'll figure out where you belong."

"I'm no *brrvk* act."

"What's that? I don't speak Yar."

"Brvvk. Um, you call it a carnival sideshow. I'm a respected member of my world. A soldier for the cause."

"You're a long way from home with no return ticket."

Forman's paddle bumped the side of the boat. He startled and glanced around for threats, worried that something else had come after them. When nothing happened, he realized his error. If only Zeke would wake up, then he wouldn't feel so alone out here.

"Change of subject," Xstle said. "What's wrong with the biped?"

"Zeke? He's recharging. Burned a lot of energy zapping Queen."

"This Plan B was very powerful. Why did he not employ it first?"

"Hello? Did you miss what happened? We got eaten by a monster shark."

The laptop fell silent for a moment. In the distance, Forman heard the whir of chopper blades. He dropped the paddle and waved both lights in the air.

"What is it?" Xstle asked.

The chopper headed for them. "The cavalry. We're being rescued."

"Cavalry? Horses can run across the water?"

"This one flies through the air."

"Cool."

Chapter 63

"Zeke," Jessie murmured. He was in trouble. She couldn't reach him. They were all going to die. She had to do something.

She couldn't move.

The thick fog disoriented her. *Zeke! Where are you?*

I'm here.

His voice sounded rusty, as if he hadn't used it in years. Why couldn't she see him? Was she blind?

A dark object blocked the faint light and loomed over her face. Her breath came in short gasps. *Zeke!*

Relax. It's me.

I... I can't see.

We've even. I can't hear worth a darn. I believe it's a temporary malfunction due to the enormous amount of energy we burned. Our bodies are just now turning systems back on.

Where are we?

His hand closed over hers, and she felt his comforting warmth. *We're at home. In our bed. Rest.*

Cradled in his arms, she drifted back to sleep, this time at peace.

*****

The next day, a medic flashed a light before Jessie's eyes, momentarily blinding her to the clinic's institutional pale green walls. "Look straight ahead."

Jessie complied, anxious to be done with this checkup. "I'm fine. My sight is fine."

"That's what they all say," the medic said, "but in your case, you're spot on. I'm glad. You and the baby are healthy. Lights on, full."

"Zeke's hearing is back?" Jessie asked as the clinic's pale walls came into view.

The medic paused at the doorway. "Ask him. Patient confidentiality keeps me from discussing his condition with you."

Condition. Not a good word. "I will. Thanks."

"See you in four weeks for your three-month prenatal visit."

Jessie hurried to the waiting room, but Zeke wasn't there. Must not be done yet with the audiologist. Uncle John had insisted they come to the mainland clinic for checkups. Christmas music lilted from the speakers proclaiming hope, peace, and love. Everyone needed more of that.

From the wall com, a newscaster reported on the disappearance of the marauding shark, then cut to an earnest biologist documenting the sediment-laden water in the oceans and scarcity of marine life. The view shifted to a well-known whistleblower. He blamed the trouble on global warming and urged everyone to get back to nature, to become harmonious with the Earth.

Yeah. Like that was going to happen. Who would give up the luxuries society afforded in exchange to returning to a rural, agrarian-based system? Where would those people get the drinking water they needed to survive?

A religious leader came on screen and urged everyone to drop down on their hands and knees and pray for salvation. Only by dedicating lives to God could the Earth be cleansed of its troubles and sanctified. No one in the clinic waiting room took his advice.

Jessie picked up a magazine tablet, thumbed through the screens, put it back. She eyed the others in the waiting room, the guy with his hand wrapped in gauze. The mother with three daughters climbing the walls. The older couple with the man being so attentive to his frail wife.

Business as usual seemed mundane after the night they'd had. Seems like they should be having a beach blowout with music and fireworks.

How many people in this room knew how close they'd come last night to being conquered and herded like cattle? Probably not many. Maybe none of them.

The door opened, and Zeke strode toward her, confident and poised. "Ready?" he asked in a voice that was pitched slightly too quiet.

She nodded, searching his handsome face for answers, finding none. Except his indomitable spirit. That was enough for now. "Ready." Hand in hand they walked outside to the transpo where

Forman waited. "I got a clean bill of health. So did the baby. You?"

His fingers momentarily tightened around hers. "Lost a bit of hearing in both ears, but I can still hear, and it may improve. Time will tell."

"I hate that expression. Time can't tell anything except the time. People say that when they don't want to give you the truth, but you can bank on this. You're the most amazing husband I've ever had."

"I'm the only husband you've ever had."

"That, too." She grinned and stopped on the sidewalk to caress his face. Sunlight glinted on his lean features, sparkled in his eyes. "I'm glad we survived, and I'm very glad those nasty Yars are gone."

"You and me both. Thank you for your part in saving me. I couldn't have escaped without your help."

"We're a team. Don't ever forget that."

He flashed a sexy grin. "Never in a million years."

She returned his smile and glanced around to make sure they could speak privately. "Any word yet on the navy woman?"

"Not sure what happened to Lieutenant Hinson. The Navy can't locate her, but I feel confident she won't stay hidden for long. She's the type to go out in a blaze of glory."

Hinson's fate was out of Jessie's hands. She had to focus on problems close at hand. "What are you going to do about the one in the laptop?"

"Nola, Uncle John, and Angie should be done with their analysis of Xstle by now. We've got enough time to swing by Uncle John's before catching the afternoon ferry to Tama Island."

Jessie made a face. "I'd rather not. Sidra is there."

"Here's my two cents," Zeke said, starting forward. "Put aside your hurt feelings. Sidra McIntyre is a brilliant thinker, but when it comes to social skills, she's not operating at an adult level. None of us interacted much with her nursemaid, Ronni, but Ronni steadied her. Sidra has to figure out how to behave without her guidance."

Jessie pried her back teeth apart. "She walked out on the mindlink. She turned her back on all of us."

Forman opened the transpo door for them, his vibrant Santa-adorned aloha shirt striking a jarring note with her. "Trouble in paradise?"

Jessie slid past the robot's searching gaze. "About Sidra. I'm dreading seeing her at Uncle John's house."

Forman glanced at Zeke and back to Jessie. "You didn't tell her?"

"Tell me what?" Jessie asked.

Forman set the transpo to manual and pulled away from the clinic. "Sidra is moving to the island."

The vehicle picked up speed, and Jessie groaned. "Why? To rub it in our faces that we're not worth her time? If I've learned anything these last few months, it's that life's too short to waste on people I don't enjoy being around."

"I understand," Zeke soothed.

"Do you? I'm upset with her because she let everyone down. She put her needs first in a time of crisis."

Jessie blinked away the tears in her eyes. To her dismay, more tears welled up. "I'm sorry to be such a wreck this morning, but your safety is everything to me."

Warmth flowed from his hand into hers. She felt his gentling touch in her mind also. *You are safe and loved, Jessie. I've got you.*

Her thoughts took on a sunny hue. *You do, and I've got you.*

"Hey, people," Forman said. "You went quiet on me. Where are we headed?"

Jessie felt Zeke's searching gaze. "Sidra's here to stay, so I might as well get this over with now. To Uncle John's house."

"Look at it this way," Zeke said as the transpo veered onto a side road to the waterfront. "With Ronni gone, we're the closest thing Sidra has to family." While Jessie considered that, Zeke cleared his throat gently. "When you were taking care of your sister all those years, did you hold Bea to the same standard as yourself?"

"Of course not. Bea was fragile." Understanding dawned like a beautiful sunrise. "Oh, I get it. You're saying Sidra is as fragile as Bea. Huh. Never thought of Sidra in that way. She seems so brash."

"She'll come of age on the island, and she'll benefit from being in your and Angie's company. Sidra needs examples of caring women in her life."

With parenthood right around the corner, Jessie didn't much care with being a role model for an adult child. "If you say so."

"I do. You're pretty darn amazing yourself."

Zeke's comment made her blush to her toes. She rewarded him with a light kiss. "Ya don't say."

"I've seen your work, Mrs. Landry. You can organize anything, motivate anyone, and get the job done better than anybody I know. Given your mad skills set, your incredible cooking, and your sexy body, is it any wonder I'm head over heels in love with you?"

"Getting mushy in here," Forman observed from the front seat.

"Can it," Zeke said. "I'm romancing my wife."

"Lucky you," Forman grumped.

Jessie beamed. "Lucky me."

Chapter 64

Sidra met them at the door, arms impatiently waving them inside. "Dusty's gone."

"We thwarted the Yars, remember?" Zeke drew Jessie under his arm before they crossed the wide threshold. He sensed her tensing as soon as the door opened.

"The physical rock, Dr. Smarty Pants." Sidra slammed the door behind Forman and darted around them, walking backward toward Uncle John's office. "When I let you guys save the world yesterday, I went for a long walk on the island. A Navy chopper landed at the Institute's helo pad. I spied on them from behind the row of oleanders. Anyway, two swabbies jimmied the back door of your lab, and returned a few moments later with a boarded-up crate on a hoverboard. Must have been a heavy duty board given that we had to use a forklift to move the meteorite previously."

When she paused to take a breath, Zeke hurriedly injected, "How come I'm hearing about this now? Has my lab been unsecured this entire time?"

"John took care of your lab security breach." Sidra's eyes sparkled. "Anyhoo, I hopped the ferry to get to the mainland to come here. John's been helping me search for Dusty."

What did his sixty-something uncle think about this teen calling him by his first name? "What did you find out?"

"The Navy denies taking the space rock. They deny the chopper being on the island yesterday. But we've been scanning satellite imaging, and we believe Lieutenant Hinson took Dusty."

"Hinson surfaced?"

"No. And this is the best part."

Zeke groaned as he stepped into his uncle's office. "You're killing me. What?"

Uncle John rose from his command center and crossed to them. "Everything all right health-wise?"

The old coot probably had a direct line to their medical records, but Zeke humored him. "Jessie and the baby are fine. I have a slight hearing loss in both ears, which may be temporary."

Uncle John's bushy white eyebrows arched an unspoken question, confirming Zeke's suspicion the guy knew everything. Zeke gave an imperceptible head shake. He didn't want Jessie to know the hearing loss was permanent. Not yet, anyway.

"Everything checked out, so don't worry about us." Jessie hugged Uncle John, which made the geezer light up like a firefly. Jessie had that effect on people. Wonder that she didn't know it.

"Sidra was filling us in with the news about her space rock," Zeke said. "Guess we were out of the need-to-know loop on that."

"You had enough on your plate last night and this morning to be bothered with a little breaking and entering."

"Is my lab broken?"

"No. Here are new keys for you. I flew a locksmith over to the island to replace the locks while you were at the clinic."

"Thanks." Zeke gave a key to Forman, himself, and Jessie. Despite his assurances to his wife, he didn't trust Sidra enough to give her a lab key. She'd have her own lab in the quad so she wouldn't be under his roof.

"Tell us more about Dusty," Jessie said. "How'd you trace the space rock?"

"Not the rock, per se," Sidra said with a giggle, "but the electronic tracker I had on the base of the crate proved to be worth its weight in gold, or, in this case, purite."

"And?" Zeke asked.

"The crate is at a Mexican rocket launch site."

Zeke turned to his uncle. "Do we have someone there to check it out for us?"

"Been there, checked it out. The crate is empty. We think the rock went up with the satellite they launched just after dawn this morning."

"Any sign of Hinson?"

"None, but a helicopter with three dead naval officers was found at the rocket site. Hinson wasn't among them."

"How'd they die?"

"Single plasgun blasts to the head."

Jessie shuddered. "One Drch got away?"

"Yes and no," Sidra said. "Tell 'em, X."

"I infected the purite travel pod," Xstle said, his mechanical voice sounding not the least bit excited by this turn of events.

"How so?"

"Mold from the sink in your laboratory."

"Wouldn't that be rendered harmless in space?"

"We discovered long ago, that Yars have an incompatibility with mold in our natural state. I risked my life carrying it inside the rock."

"Hinson stole the rock, stashed it on a satellite run, and is now off-world?"

"That's our best guess," Uncle John said. "Xstle assures us from viewing the vids that Hinson was injured prior to launch, and in that weakened state, the mold will kill it in a matter of hours."

"Sounds like a plan to me. I don't want to meet up with any Drch again," Zeke said. "The last ones nearly had us for dinner."

"What is to become of me, Landry?" Xstle asked.

Zeke had to pass the buck. "Uncle John?"

"We kept Xstle's existence a secret known only to the individuals in this room. What the Navy doesn't know won't hurt them. As for the Yar in hand, our options are limited."

Zeke glanced at the old laptop. Other than being waterproof, the case was purely functional. Xstle, however, was a gold mine of potential information about the universe. "He can stay with me if he wants."

"I want," Xstle said.

"There are no cats at Uncle John's place," Zeke pointed out. "What kept you from emerging from this laptop?"

"The electrical field has taken a toll on me. I can no longer leave the machine. It is, in effect, my new home. I'd greatly appreciate an upgrade – to a synthetic shell like the Forman wears."

"The Forman doesn't consider his skin a shell," Forman quipped back. "Please say no."

"We only have your word that you are harmless," Angie said. "We will proceed in a stepwise fashion. Earn our trust, and you be rewarded with housing upgrades."

"I'm to be kept prisoner in this substandard model? I demand my rights under the Geneva convention."

"In order to be a true prisoner, we have to declare your existence to heads of state. They will dismantle you first thing. You won't have a chance at independence. With us, you at least have a chance."

"I wish to stay with Landry," Xstle said. "Any housing upgrade would be appreciated."

"I want him in my lab," Sidra said. "He's a space traveler, and I'm an astrophysicist. This is a perfect match."

Alarm bells pealed in Zeke's head. Sidra might dismantle Xstle if the alien didn't answer her questions. "His preference is to stay in my lab. You may visit during working hours."

"Zeke's plan sounds best for the time being. We'll re-evaluate in a month." Uncle John pushed back from the table. "If you ladies will excuse us, Zeke and I need a moment to talk privately upstairs."

"We've got chocolate cake in the kitchen," Angie said. "Who's got dibs on a piece?"

"Me," Jessie said.

"Me," Sidra said.

"Save one for me," Zeke said, glad the women would have a distraction in his absence. A few moments later, he was closeted with his uncle in the second floor war room. "What's up?"

"You trust this Xstle?"

"Some. He knows things about my family. He claims his knowledge stretches back centuries. I'm grateful to have the opportunity to explore his memories. Thanks for allowing me primary access."

"And Sidra?"

Zeke swallowed hard. "She broke under pressure yesterday. Jessie took it pretty hard, and now she doesn't respect Sidra. It won't be easy having the two of them on the island."

"We'll have to keep them busy, then, won't we?"

"Will you find another companion for Sidra?"

His uncle nodded. "One of the islanders has agreed to take the job on a trial basis. Traci Loya. Her kids are grown and gone, and she sees Sidra as a lost child in need of a mother."

"You're always a step ahead of me."

"Only on routine matters. You're turning out to be a fine Guardian, Zeke. Your father would be proud."

Despite still having remote access to his late father, Zeke's eyes misted. He took a long moment to gather himself before responding.

"This batch of aliens nearly did me in. If not for remembering the Bible story mother used to read me about Jonah and the whale, the outcome might have been much different."

"Inspiration can come from anywhere, and in the end, the how doesn't matter as much as the result. You saved us yesterday. Thank you."

"You're welcome." Zeke blushed at the compliment.

Uncle John grinned from ear to ear. "The President thanks you, too. His PAC made an anonymous five million credit donation to the Institute in your name." He slid a slip of paper over to Zeke's side of the desk. "I deposited five hundred thousand credits in your personal account as a bonus for a job well-done.

Zeke glanced at the deposit slip and pushed it back. "I was doing my job."

His uncle didn't look at the paper. "You're being rewarded for a job well done. Spend it. Invest it. Blow it. Start an education fund for the baby. Give it away if you like. The choice is yours."

Jessie would be happy about the money. She'd earned it too. Maybe he could do something nice for the islanders. Throw a big party, like the kind his father used to give.

The pieces of his past came together in a new pattern. Those beach parties of his childhood that his father had thrown must have come at the end of a successful mission. Winston Landry had done his job or Earth would've been enslaved. He'd held the line as Earth's Guardian. So would Zeke.

"We've been fighting off alien invaders for a while, haven't we?" he asked.

"That we have."

"How many more invaders will try to come here?"

"The sky's the limit."

Zeke cracked a wry smile. If his uncle knew about their extraterrestrial helpers, he hadn't mentioned it. That conclusion was the only one that made sense. Somehow Uncle John knew he had off-planet advisors and was okay with it. "Sounds like job security."

Uncle John leaned back in his chair and chuckled. "Good one, m'boy."

*****

Zeke joined the others for cake, then headed to the ferry with Jessie,

Angie, Forman, Xstle, and Sidra. Jessie's eyes met his with questions. He squeezed her hand and felt her tender squeeze back.

Satisfaction hummed in his veins.

Another threat to planetary security repelled. Jessie and his son-to-be were safe and healthy. His finances kept improving, and he had the best job ever. Plus he'd learned he could affect solid objects with his mind. Heady stuff for a reclusive researcher like him.

Jessie leaned close. "Everything okay?"

He drew her into his arms. "It is now."

Chapter 65

With Sidra safely occupied with getting to know her new companion, Forman joined Jessie, Angie, and Zeke for dinner. Angie picked at her meal, though Zeke said he'd made her favorite dishes. Forman sat at the table with them, but he wasn't built for food consumption. The table before him was empty of dishes.

"Why aren't you eating, Cous?" Zeke asked after he and Jessie cleaned their plates.

"Not hungry," Angie said, rising from the table. "It's been a busy week."

"You still seem to be under the weather," Zeke continued, a strange gleam in his eye.

"She said she wasn't feeling well," Forman interrupted, joining her. Something in Zeke's tone worried him. "Cut her a little slack."

"Feeling a mite protective, are we?" Zeke leaned back in his chair. "I suppose that's to be expected under the circumstances."

The air hummed with expectation. The look of terror on Angie's face had Forman reaching for her hand. Her fingers closed around his, and he felt glad he'd correctly read her need for comfort.

"What's going on, Zeke?" Jessie asked. "Do you know something about Angie?"

"Indeed I do. You may have noticed I spent a lot of time at the clinic this morning. I did some calculations, and, based on my recent personal experience about reproduction, feel I've reached the right conclusion." He turned to Angie. "How long are you going to keep quiet about your pregnancy, Cous?"

A tremor ran down Angie's arm. She nodded. "It's true. I'm pregnant."

Though her voice sounded strong, Forman detected microscopic variances in it. He set aside his conflicting emotions and gave her hand a reassuring squeeze. "Pregnancy isn't something you can hide for long. Aren't you happy about the news?"

"Sure, but I didn't want to be grilled. I hoped the island robes would disguise my rounding shape. I planned to take a vacation at the right time and return to the island later with an 'adopted' child. No one would be the wiser."

Not a chance Forman wouldn't notice the changes in her shape. Unless . . . that's why she'd been messing with his memory. To make sure he didn't put her on the spot. She wanted this pregnancy to be a secret, even from him. That hurt.

She glared at Zeke. "Thanks, Cous, for spilling the butter beans."

Forman didn't get what beans had to do with anything. "Why the subterfuge?"

Angie's chin went up. "I'm not married."

"So?"

"I didn't want to deal with being pressed about who, what, where, and when."

Jealousy flooded his processors. Angie had been sleeping with him and someone else at the same time? "Speaking of those w's, who's the father?"

"You don't want to know."

"Why not?"

Her luminous eyes blazed with emotion. "This was my decision. I wanted a child. Zeke's son needs a playmate. It's tradition. I was there for Zeke, and my mom grew up with his dad."

"Easy." Zeke and Jessie stood. "Let's take a moment, shall we? Angie's marital status and maternal status are her business. But Ang, having a child is a joyful occasion. You shouldn't hide the news from your family and friends. We love you."

Angie burst out crying.

Forman wrung his hands, paralyzed with indecision. His girlfriend was pregnant. Those words didn't compute. They clanked around in his head like the flat side of a wheel. He cared for Angie and wanted her to be happy. So why was she crying?

Jessie elbowed him out of the way and hugged Angie. Forman couldn't miss the murderous looks she shot at him. "It's all right, Angie," Jessie said. "I completely understand. These fellows mean well, but they don't get it."

Forman cocked his head to the side. What wasn't to get? The woman was pregnant and she'd concealed her condition. To keep her secret. "What—"

Zeke silenced him with a hand on his arm and a shake of his head.

Forman checked his stock supply of responses and came up empty. Frustration welled. He had no data in his emotion queue for this situation. None. The room whirled. He gripped the table. How could he be lightheaded? His mass didn't vary.

But Angie's would very soon. Her womb would fill with a living being. A child. Did that make him a surrogate father? Would she still want him in her life after her baby was born? Thoughts spun wildly through his processors. Good thing he'd been boning up on parenting for Zeke. Seemed like he might need frequent access to that data set.

"How can we help?" Zeke asked, filling the awkward void in the conversation.

Jessie stroked Angie's back. "She needs TLC. That's tender, loving care, and I aim to provide it. For starters, we need a pillow under her knees, tissues, and a cup of her favorite herbal tea. And personal space. You guys go take a long walk to the beach."

"If that's what you want," Zeke said. "We'll give you ladies some privacy."

"First, I'll make the tea and find you some tissues," Forman said, heading to the spacious kitchen. A few minutes later, Angie was nestled on the sofa, whispering her secrets to Jessie as he handed them the tea and tissues.

Forman hovered over Angie. He didn't want to leave. He wanted to be holding her, but his duty was to protect Zeke.

"You don't think I'm a wimp for crying, do you?" Angie asked him, her lower lip trembling.

Her continued distress compelled Forman to kneel at her side. He kissed the underside of her wrist. "No one thinks that. You're as invincible and bulletproof as Zeke. A tower of strength among mere mortals."

Her eyes flared in alarm.

Flerk. He'd hurt her feelings. He raised his palms in surrender. "Hey, I'm stating the obvious. You've never been a wimp. You're the most powerful, beautiful woman I know. Practically a super hero."

A smile tugged at her lips. "Good answer. Now be gone, the both of you."

Forman rose and headed to where Zeke stood propped against the wall.

"Before we go," Zeke said, "I insist on knowing who the father is."

"You know good and well who I've been sleeping with," Angie said. "Your fingerprints are all over Forman's modules. I know you were trying to figure out why I erased his memory. I did it to protect him. To protect us."

Zeke barred his arms across his chest. "Try again."

Whoa. Forman held onto the wall as his equilibrium took another blow. Angie's words seemed pure science fiction. He was the father? How was that remotely possible?

Angie's chin lifted. "Forman's the father of my child."

"Impossible."

"Nothing's impossible."

"Angie, dear," Zeke said, his voice dripping in sarcasm, "has it escaped your notice that Forman's an android?"

ABOUT THE AUTHOR

Formerly a contract scientist for the U.S. Army and a freelance reporter, Southern author Rigel Carson, the pen name of Maggie Toussaint, is a multi-published, award-winning author in suspense and mystery fiction. Her background in environmental science and toxicology, as well as years spent doing water research, provided the impetus for this new dystopian thriller series set in a futuristic Earth. Book 1 of this series, G-1, is a Kindle Scout winner.

Maggie lives in coastal Georgia, where secrets, heritage, and ancient oaks cast long shadows. Yoga, beachcombing, and music are a few of her favorite things.

Visit her online at:
http://www.maggietoussaint.com
http://www.RigelCarson.com
http://mudpiesandmagnolias.blogspot.com
http://www.facebook.com/MaggieToussaintAuthor
http://www.twitter.com/MaggieToussaint
http://www.twitter.com/RigelCarson
http://www.BookloversBench.com

BOOKS BY MAGGIE TOUSSAINT

Science Fiction, writing as Rigel Carson
G-1 (book 1 The Guardian of Earth series)
G-2 (book 2 The Guardian of Earth series)
G-3 (book 3 The Guardian of Earth series)

Mystery
In for a Penny   (book 1 Cleopatra Jones series)
On the Nickel   (book 2 Cleopatra Jones series)
Dime If I Know (book 3 Cleopatra Jones series)
Death, Island Style
Murder in the Buff
Gone and Done It (book 1 Dreamwalker series)
Bubba Done It   (book 2 Dreamwalker series)
Doggone It   (book 3 Dreamwalker series, Oct 2016)

Romantic Suspense
House of Lies
No Second Chance
Muddy Waters (book 1 Mossy Bog trilogy)
Hot Water   (book 2 Mossy Bog trilogy)
Rough Waters   (book 3 Mossy Bog trilogy)

Sweet Romance
Seeing Red

Short Stories and Novellas
"High Noon at Dollar Central" in Killer Nashville Anthology: Cold Blooded
"Really, Truly Dead" in Happy Homicides: Thirteen Cozy Valentine's Day Mysteries

Cookbook
KP Authors Cook Their Books (permafree)

Reviews are welcomed and encouraged!

www.ingramcontent.com/pod-product-compliance
Lightning Source LLC
Chambersburg PA
CBHW070857180626
46817CB00003B/810